LEAD US NOT INTO PENN STATION

Bruce Ducker

THE PERMANENT PRESS
Sag Harbor, New York 11963

Copyright © 1994 by Bruce Ducker

Library of Congress Cataloging-in-Publication Data

Ducker, Bruce.
  Lead Us not into Penn Station / by Bruce Ducker.
    p. cm.
  ISBN 1-877946-36-2 : $22.00
  1. Fathers and sons—United States— Fiction. 2. Young
men—United States—Fiction. I. Title.
PS3554.U267L4 1994   F IC T I oN
813'.54—dc20   DUCKER   93-32742
              LEA   CIP
              7/94

First edition: June 1994—1,700 copies

Manufactured in the United States of America

THE PERMANENT PRESS
Noyac Road
Sag Harbor, NY 11963

By the Same Author

RULE BY PROXY
FAILURE AT THE MISSION TRUST
BANKROLL
MARITAL ASSETS
LEAD US NOT INTO PENN STATION

- **1** -

Mr. Meadoff turns to his children, the long way around. His eyes are on the knife in his hand. He watches lest jam from its blade drip to the linoleum floor. He has wiped the blade on the bread before he turns, but still he watches. There will be no spill.

He turns because he needs to say something. Sensing his purpose from the look on his face or the way he turns, slow and without weight, as if submerged, the children settle to quiet. But he has no words. He is the message. A bottle washed to shore is no less a message for lack of a note.

He looks on his children. A moment passes while they wait for him to speak, and he turns again. The remaining quarter-circle. Continues his route, completes it, again faces the counter and resumes his chores. He makes each child a second sandwich. The children are marooned with their anticipation. They have been raised on cause and effect, so that chaos disquiets them. They look at each other, giggle. Joyce shrugs to show her perplexity. Rochelle, the middle child, rotates her index finger by her temple, to signal that their father is mad.

Laughter bubbles up, catches in their clicking throats, bubbles through Joyce's full mouth. Milk trickles out behind Joyce's taut lips, behind the fingertips she presses to her mouth. Now Danny and Rochelle shift their glee from their antic father to Joyce's predicament. Can it be developed, can it be brought to crisis? She may leak milk through her nose. She may spray chewed sandwich. It is all repulsive, all possible. Danny mugs like a dimwit, crosses his eyes, wags his head and Rochelle signals lunacy with both hands. Finger propellers cutting faster. Too late, Joyce has brought herself under control.

Their father feels the shimmer of their glee. He knows he is odd, turning the long way around—it would have been quicker to turn clockwise, to the right. Shuffling, not a military turn, but a shuffling. The slow planing of one foot smoothing ground then the other blading over, a masonry of a turn. Then at last when he faces them, faces where they sit for Saturday lunch eating butter and jelly sandwiches on balloon white Rainbow bread, he lifts his eyes as if it was he who had been summoned. It makes sense that they think him mad. Sensible children, Mr. Meadoff nods to himself, sensible children are a blessing.

Mr. Meadoff spreads butter first. Not too thick, evenly to the edges. Then the jam. He is a painter with a palette knife, and he spreads grape jam over a slick and perfect layer of Technicolor yellow. The grape is Technicolor too, the purple of some Amazonian moth. Is that a serious daydream for a man to have? That he is a painter making jelly sandwiches? Or are they the idlings of a man of no substance, a luftmensh?

He studies his task. Sugar gives his children energy. When his wife makes the sandwiches, she still keeps an eye to the jar. He can tell from the way Miriam measures everything out. She sees the family stores depleting, computes how much they have left, and considers when to note a replacement on her list. Not he. The years of watching how much grape jam goes on bread are behind him. He spreads with a luxuriousness that has been assured by the recent years of his business. Successful years, blessings and luck. He spreads an abundance of jam, with a confidence born of his company's after-tax earned income of 1951 and 1952 and 1953 and the first quarter of 1954. Those were years of substance. Years of a man of business, not a man of air.

True, since then it has not been so good, he thinks as he squares away three sandwiches on the wooden cutting board. Just as it seemed that the curve of Meadoff prosperity would climb like one of those aircraft carrier planes, the ones off Leyte in the newsreels, forever on a sunbent arc, just as it seemed that people would forever buy knit underwear from Paradise, the figures began to tail off.

He removes a bread knife from its magnetic wall holder and, his left hand steadying the first sandwich by opposite corners, steadying it professionally, the way a counter man might, he slices on the diagonal. The colors, the white of the bread, cut through to reveal glistening stripes of yellow and purple, support Mr. Meadoff's security. The sandwiches are geometry, geology, nourishment. They confirm his well-being. Never mind the last five fiscal quarters. Paradise Knitwear would come back.

Mr. Meadoff stacks the triangular sandwiches on a single plate and presents them to the three children. Joyce does not want seconds. Danny eats hers.

"Are you feeling all right, Joycey?" Wouldn't you know Joyce would lose her appetite as soon as his wife leaves. This is the worst time for her to fall ill. School is ending, the expanse of summer is only beginning. She assures him she is fine. Summer is the polio season. If she were to come down with something, these last days of June would be a hazardous time. He

[7

tells her not to get overheated. When his wife comes back from the white sales downtown he will pass this news along. Hazards lurk everywhere for his children. There is no relief.

Danny is telling his plans. Tomorrow he and his pals are going to Coney Island. Rochelle wants to go.

"You must ask your mother."

Mr. Meadoff knows her mother will say no.

He watches furtively while they finish their lunch. How many Saturdays, how many butter and jelly sandwiches can there be left? All of his life seems stitched together with time. The Hong Kong orders need to be shipped this week. The sixty-day letters of credit will expire Monday. They need to be rolled over to cover the shipments. The factors are owed monthly cash reports, but he doesn't want to deliver them until Hong Kong ships. And the bank papers: the renewable notes and revolving terms. Living with the factors is living in a quilt. You escape from one sewn square to another identical patch. The quilt is an endless recursion. The squares repeat, no pattern of the fabric the same as another and together they make a single pattern, one, stretched to the horizon.

What recurs is the trivial, the appearance of life. Orders are filled, notes are paid, new goods are produced, new notes signed. He pays the bank, the bank pays the factors, he needs to order more goods so he goes to the bank. What is stable and recurring in his life is the trivial. What is transient, uncatchable, is the center of life. These three, Danny feeding the last almond-colored corner of bread into his mouth, Rochelle arranging the crusts on her plate, Joyce spinning her glass and drawing letters on the table with traces of milk, it is they and nothing else that make life unbearably short. Mr. Meadoff pulls away his lidded glance and begins the dishes. When the children were younger, he would often slip into their rooms at night to watch them sleep, but that act has become too painful now. He turns away and lifts the unilever on the sink to rinse the few plates and single knife, stained with a color some chemist at General Foods has instructed the world is grape.

Years ago when his business was getting started, Mr. Meadoff often had nothing to do at the office. At noon he would walk to Union Square, this was before they moved uptown, and feed sparrows. No orders, no backlog, no problems. He would take the remains of his lunch, nothing more than crumbs—who had food to spare?—and spread them on the sidewalk in front of his park bench. Sparrows would appear out of the air. Dozens of them, where have they been? They eat pecks and drips, they eat like birds, and then they fly off.

Are my own children so insubstantial? Where do they go, what do they think about? Is there possibly time for them to learn of all the hazards that leap at their heels? Subway trains that can sever limbs, whole city blocks on their walk home that look like other blocks, electric outlets, electric wires, electric toasters, scissors, needles, dogs, heights, depths, water. There is water as close as Prospect Park—last week two boys drowned in it, swimming against the law. Two boys from Crown Heights, a nice neighborhood though not as nice as theirs. It is his task to teach them, yet what has he just done? Made six jelly sandwiches and washed up.

This is a good home, he knows. Miriam often says that very thing. They have made a good home for their children. Still, two boys drown in the lake, in the lullwater by the boathouse. From the hill where he took Joyce and Ro-ro sledding last winter, he might have seen the spot where it happened. Would there be a spot on the water? They make laws against swimming and you make a good home, and still.

Again he turns, this time to tell them, at last to speak to them, say something, anything, but they are gone. They are forever going. Their gaits, slow and fast, remain beyond the speed of his voice, and Mr. Meadoff knows his warnings will not catch them.

- 2 -

The train stops at Coney, pouring out immigrants in a new land and the boys are among the first off, first to trip over the gold that lines the streets, first to lay claim, to seize, to receive. Jammed to each other like tepee poles, they have been standing all the way from Newkirk Avenue, swaying together as the subway rolled down the Brighton line, past Kings Highway and Sheepshead Bay, a route to the sea, the direction itself different, alien.

They know the stops but not by heart. The train pops out of the tunnel and shoots overground, air smelling of fried meat and ocean and faint decay, sea air enlivening them swelling them like balloons before a parade, no one in the jostled car seeming to mind as they too swell with the anticipation of surf and cocoa oil and a whole June day for themselves.

The train stops at Coney, and the three of them, each carrying a bathing suit rolled in a white turkish towel, run out, Angie and Rick vaulting the turnstile with a hand on the token box, and Danny, shorter, uncertain, detouring through the spindle gate marked Exit, Angie crying "Geronimo" in exactly the way Aldo Ray did jumping from a plane, and all three sprinting away in the first heat of the day, the first summer Sunday of 1955, school not out yet but only books to be checked back and next year's room assignments to be made, and then nothing but an expanse of summer, an excess a surplus a plenty, better than a bathtub of lemonade or a roll of bleacher tickets thick as sausage links, an inexhaustible summer that stretches out like an ocean, this very ocean calling you to plunge into it.

Danny lags behind. Angie and Rick race each other to the Good Humor cart, the driver in his white hat with black patent-leather peak, white suit and a changebelt at his waist looking for the first crowds, race each other pushing off and laughing and finally, breathless, waiting for Danny as he knows they must. He carries their pooled three-sixty. Deal is, to last the day, carfare back, three-sixty for sodas to go with the sandwiches Danny has brought wrapped in wax paper, folded the way his mother does with the ends tucked in, and maybe for ice cream later if they don't spend it on rides. That's the deal, he tells them.

"Don't be a moron, Meadoff. What difference if we have ice cream before or after lunch." Rick recants, Rick an alcoholic ready to hit the first saloon after swearing the cure.

"Plans are plans," Danny says. He has been selected for his probity. Reaches a fist into his jeans and fetches the bills and coins wadded together and they count again. Rick pulls a mashed pack of Chesterfields from his pocket and offers smokes around. Danny singles one out. Angie shakes Rick off, produces a comb, and holding it at the corner by thumb and forefinger, turns it through a tangle of black, shining hair. Slides the comb back under the turned-up sleeve of his tee shirt, accepts the pack, pulls out the last, crippled cigarette, and leans into the flame that Rick has offered.

"Third on the match, dead in the foxhole," Rick warns. They share the totem. They are all veterans of war movies.

"Dead in the bunghole," says Angie and Rick laughs and punches him on the arm. Angie is over six feet, muscular, has a moustache that needs shaving every few days. His two friends regularly punch him to show appreciation, scorn, affection. Rick is not slight: he is almost Angie's height, but without definition, neither thin nor flabby but a little of each. He has sandy hair, a peninsula nose, a wide fulgent mouth. Best of all he has learned to bug his eyes. People have told him he resembles Harpo Marx, and he does a perfect leer to remind them.

Danny smiles. It is not Angie's wit. He cannot say why he smiles.

"We are short of bread," says Angie.

"It matters not," says Rick. "*No es importante, Inglés.* I spit on money." He spits to the side in what he believes to be Castilian. "*Tu.*"

They decide against food. Instead, they walk with the growing crowd towards the bathhouses. Cars jam the streets for the few parking lots close to the shore. Behind them, up Stillwell Avenue, are other lots, cheaper, but far from the action. The three friends walk past the freak shows, not yet opened. Plywood paintings advertise the lurid attractions: Margaret the Alligator Girl, Eddie Half-Man Half-Terrier, the Human Paperweight. They stop by a small, open park, the concrete painted with shuffleboard triangles. Several girls their age roller skate on the smooth finish. As they watch, a knot of younger boys, eighth grade maybe, chase the skaters off, begin a game of half-court basketball to the clanging iron backboard at the far end.

Down the block, scant yards away from the boardwalk and its air filling with the smells of zinc oxide ointment and cotton candy and exhaust, drivers lean on horns as if to hurry cars into the last remaining spaces of a parking lot. The noise is only celebration; the line of cars cannot move any faster. There will be a good crowd on the beach. Rick holds up his hand. It is the hand of Randolph Scott signalling his platoon and they stop.

"Danny, gimme a buck."

"No way, José. What do you need it for?"

"Just gimme. I get it right back."

Danny narrows his eyes, takes out their cache and separates a bill from the wad. Rick is gone at a sprint. They watch him with apprehension. What anarchy now? First ice cream in the morning and now this. What is the point of rules? Rick stops at the parking lot to talk to the attendant, who is just switching signs, laying out a large painted board that says, FULL. They watch helplessly as Rick hands over the dollar, one of three, prized and protected.

"Shit," says Danny. "Did you see what he did?"

Angie doesn't answer. His loyalties have been split by Rick's departure, and he is confused. Rick cannot do wrong, yet Rick has just diminished their day's outing and gone back on his promise. Before Angie has time to resolve the dilemma, Rick returns, a slab of plywood a yard square hoisted on his shoulder.

"Did you give that guy our dollar?" Angie asks. Danny is silent, beginning to realize what is happening.

"No, you dumb guinea. I invested the dollar. I put us in business."

Back to the basketball game. It is now three on three, shirts and skins, and the kids are good. The friends watch for a moment, watch a jump shot from the top of the keyhole slip through the netless rim and chunk against the pole. Angie whoops.

"Sorry, gentlemen," Rick announces walking on the court and showing the sign. "Game's over. Reserved for parking."

An angular and knobby boy, the one whose twenty-footer just fell, speaks up. "Fuck you," he says.

"Not me," Rick says, easy as can be. He one-hands the ball from the ground at his feet and gently bounces it off the forehead of the protestor.

"Not me," he says again even more friendly. "Fuck Mayor Wagner. Fuck the Parks Department. Me, I got no choice."

With that he tosses the ball inches beyond the reach of the boy. It bounds into the street.

"Assistants," he calls.

Danny has been holding their bagged lunch, his suit and towel. He hands everything to Angie, takes the sign from Rick and props it against a lamppost. Rick pantomimes a measurement of the court, writes without a pen on his palm, calls out to his pals.

"Twenty-three spaces. Downtown was right on the nose."

Now Danny is out in the street, waving cars over the curb and onto the cement court. Rick stands by the sign he has purchased, blue enamel paint on plywood, PARK HERE $1, collects bills as cars roll in. Angie, his green Police Athletic League baseball cap turned like a catcher's for authority, walks the lot, directs drivers to their spot and signals the engine-cut the way a carrier seaman does with paddles. In minutes seventeen cars pay and park. Danny counts out loud. As the eighteenth approaches Danny sees the basketball players at the end of Mermaid Avenue, walking and pointing towards him. They are followed by a large, phlegmatic cop. Danny gives a whistle, and the three friends are over the far fence, past Shannon's Tropical Fruits, past Your Name Here and Pizzeria by the Sliceria, through an alley and smack up against the wonders of Steeplechase, laughing, breathing hard. A cool profit.

Celebration. Six hot dogs with everything, three Nedick's. Angie downs a Mallomar on a stick. Over them grins the Steeplechase Funny Face, a monstrous head that is the trope of Coney Island fun but painted with an unconscious ferocity: forty-two teeth grinning, hair parted in the middle, jelly-red lips. They decide to put off the rides. Change, a swim before the crowds, then to spending their fortune.

Lepinskey's Bath House smells of steam, suntan lotion, urine. They share a single locker, jamming their dungarees, black sneakers, underwear, shirts rolled up into the tinny walls. Danny is entrusted with the elastic bracelet that holds the key, and he slips it on his wrist. The space presses in on them, and they rush the change without so much as a shove or a joke at each other's bodies. As they walk out into the sun, Danny tosses a brown paper bag into the wire trash bin. Six bologna on white with lettuce and Gulden's mustard, wax paper. Perfectly good food, his mother would say, gone to waste.

They hit the boardwalk. Each carries his towel around the neck, gripping the ends, in mimic of some team swagger. For Danny and Rick it is a conscious charade. Angie plays football at Erasmus, is in fact an athlete. They imitate his walk, his hold on the towel.

"So," Angie says. "We gonna pick up some girls or what?"

"Valerianus noble Roman," Rick tells him, "you couldn't pick up spit."

Angie spits. As he does, a pair of older girls, maybe eighteen, walk by and look in disgust.

"Suave," says Rick. "Very suave."

"Proving a point," Angie answers with an illogic they understand.

The beaches are only now filling up. The sand is disappearing under patches of colored cotton, and the sound of surf gives over to portable radios. It is still three hours from the Dodgers' opener, and a disc jockey is barking through the top twenty. They decide to see the sights. They ride the bumper cars, the Whip, the Revolving Bullet. Then the penny arcade. Test Your

Grip. All-star baseball, with line-ups from the Thirties and Forties and, as Rick points out angrily, only one Dodger on the whole National League team. Dolph Camilli at first. No wonder the American League, with Danny operating the lever to smack a steel ball the size of a plum pit around the hooded holes with players' names, no wonder the American League wins four zip.

At the back of the arcade are ancient peep show machines. For a nickel each, they look through the scopes, turn the crank and watch yellowing cards fall in sequence to show an animated thirty seconds. What the Fireman Saw, After the Bath, Puss in the Corner. Rick plays the Mechanical Gypsy for his horoscope. He looks around desperate to find his friends. Angie and Danny are bowling skee ball.

"Look at this," he says grabbing Danny's arm, ruining a shot. "Look at this. I knew it."

The card reads, "Aries. You're insights into people will make you a fortune while you are still young."

"For God's sake, Rick," says Danny. "It's not even grammatical. They use a contraction where they mean the possessive."

Rick stares him a dead-on stare, the Gleason fish-eye. "Meadoff, what is the matter with you? This machine sees the future. The Mechanical Gypsy is a seer, not third-period English."

Danny shrugs but is unconvinced. There is, he knows, a sanctity in grammar. Grammar is something you can believe in. Like geometry. Not true of all subjects. Angie has won several tickets at skee ball. They decide to go for a prize.

"Not here, though." Rick considers the odds. "Three of us, all highly skilled players . . . we go to Fascination."

And with that they run from the arcade down the boardwalk to Faber's Fascination.

16]

A doorless bay open to the passersby. Inside a space perhaps fifty feet deep and a third as wide sit chrome stools before two rows of long tables. This early—it is not yet ten on a Sunday morning—there are only six or seven other players. The game is to roll a ball into one of the holes at the end of the table. There, arranged as a square, with the center hole filled with a round rubber bumper, are twenty-four holes. Each is marked on the electric screen facing the player as a card, ten through ace. Straights, flushes, four-of-a-kind are winners, play till you win, a winner every time. For every game a ticket. Save your tickets, good for the prizes locked in the musty glass cases at the rear of the store.

Pay up and the game begins. The ball falls through and rolls back on plywood under the table. They drum nervously until its return, reaching up into the box.

Rick uses his Walter Winchell voice.

"Rappaport gets off to an early lead with aces back to back, filling those corner holes. He's a great favorite with the crowd, fans. There's young Dan Meadoff three clubs to a flush. Meadoff's a local boy up for his first year in the majors. Had a great season last year in Montreal but it's hard to tell whether he's ready for the big time yet. Valeriani can't seem to find the range, folks, this one is Rappaport, all the way only one more ace and he has it. It looks like Rappaport Rappaport Rappaport."

Rinnggg, a bell like the end of school and the gumball on top of Rick's machine flashes an orange light. The operator comes over, a butt smoked down so close it looks to make his lips blister, tosses a ticket on Rick's table, flicks a switch to start the game again. He grabs the gooseneck mike at the stool by the front and shills the crowd on the boardwalk.

"Every game a winner, folks, come in and give it a try. Three ways to win, vertical, horizontal and on the slant. See why they call it Faber's Fascination," pausing like a sibilant snake on the first syllable, Fasss-cination, and the boys pick it up.

"Fasss-cination," says Rick and he drops two queens and they're off again.

In a half hour, at ten cents a game, they've spent four-eighty for a stack of tickets. They stand in front of a counter surveying the possibilities. The hockey skates need three hundred and fifty, the genuine Gil Hodges first baseman's mitt six hundred and what they can get seems paltry.

"The clock," Rick says and they agree. In white ceramic, a bare-chested woman astride a bull. She is handsomely made, no less so for the clock implanted in her midsection.

"How we gonna split it up?" asks Angie. "We all won tickets."

"Choose," says Danny raising his right hand in a fist as if he had something to throw.

"Best of three," someone calls and they gesture once, twice and on the third extend fingers. In short order, Angie has won the clock.

"Perfect," says Rick. "It'll match your mother's china."

"What's that supposed to mean?" Angie says, but lets it go as the woman who handles the prizes, she too smoking down so she has to squint to see through the heat, packs the clock in its box and hands it across. Four tickets left over, and as consolation Rick and Danny each take a pack of Chesterfields, two coupons apiece.

A quick tour of the beach, eyeballing the flaccid figures in their one-piece suits. An isolated two-piecer, noted with approval, though the shorts have cuffs like a Girl Scout camp uniform and are separated from the tops by rolls of bluish, tubular flesh. No swim, they decide. The water is too crowded. Besides, they have much left to do.

Lunch. Potato knishes washed down with cream sodas for Angie and Danny and a chocolate Yoo-Hoo for Rick. Then to Whack-a-Crab for three paper cones, grease-stained, filled with crab and whiting fried in a universal batter.

Angie and Rick take the Parachute Ride.

"Meadoff, you faggot." Rick yells down as they lift off. "You shoulda come. I can see down their dresses," pointing to two pretty girls who stand by Danny.

Danny is stranded with embarrassment. Hoist the limp chute. By a braided rope the chute suspends an iron bench, where perch Angie and Rick kicking their legs as if they're being kidnapped, Rick announcing all the while, "It's the ride of the century, ladies and gents. Three ways to die, horizontal, vertical and on the slant—" and then, at the very top of the tower, release: chute and bench drop, the pop of air filling the silk, a free-fall guided only by wires. The riders' bravado falls also and Danny standing below hears their shrieks and is embarrassed again.

Back to Brooklyn pavement, full of stories from their journey, they are surprised that their friend, Meadoff the scholar, Meadoff the short, Meadoff the shy, has struck up a conversation. And the girls seem interested. What rides you been on? Where you going? The quaking steps, a divided staircase that shimmies as you walk up; the barrel; the horses that race around Steeplechase, the winner goes free. But it comes out that the girls will be seniors at James Madison, lofty, and bored by mere juniors, they wander off.

"What the hell did you say that for?" Rick demands. "I had them going."

"Yeah, sure," Danny says. "Going all the way to Canarsie. Besides, we will be juniors."

"Not the point. Tell him, Angelo."

"Not the point," says Angie happily. The day is glorious.

[19

Again the water. Too crowded. Not enough surf: foam shows its slip mere inches below the hem. They decide not to swim.

Rick sets the schedule. "It is time, *Inglés*, to blow up the bridge."

"The Cyclone," Danny says.

"It is time," Rick says flatly. "*Hay tiempo.*"

They wait. The roller coaster rumbles by and a few faint hearts slink from the line. Rick continues.

"When you go on this machine," he tells Angelo, "the earth will move. Beware of that, my little shaved head."

"The earth will move," says Danny, "and it will be good."

"And clean. It will be good and clean and surely the best place in the world."

Their turn comes.

The Cyclone whips them through the damp summer air. Rick and Angie sit in the front seat and Danny sits behind. They extract his pledge to puke to the side. Danny sits in tense resolve. It is only the first hill, where the cars are towed up to provide the momentum for the rest of the trip and you think your gizzards will go over the top levitated from your body, only that hill will be tough and for that he plans to keep his eyes closed. Though he cannot, he does not.

By four o'clock their money is gone. All but carfare. They change back to dungarees and tee shirts, open a last pack of Chesterfields and have a smoke walking to the elevated subway line.

"One more week," Angie says thoughtfully. "One more week, then no school. I gotta find me a job. Who's Vice-President of the United States?"

"Doesn't pay," says Danny. "And the only skirts you meet are middle-aged women from Pakistan."

20]

Danny has been chosen for a special course at Brooklyn College. Selected students will spend the summer studying Dante. His friends know but do not tease him.

"What will become of us," Rick says. "We could go to Florence. The fishing will be good in Florence. We could get tight on the wine of the country and take a swell bus ride to Florence."

"Can it, Rappaport. This is serious shit."

"Besides," Danny says. "There is no fishing in Florence. *No hay pescando.*"

"Ah, Santiago," Rick says. "You must believe the fish will come. If you do not believe there will be no fish. If I did not believe it I would not have seen it."

They board the subway. Only a few people are leaving the beach and they spread out on the seats.

"What you gonna do?" Angie asks Rick. "You got any ideas?" Danny looks around the car. It is almost empty. At the far end loose pages of the morning's *Daily News* blow in the tunnel's wind. Angie gets up and selects among available sheets.

"Ads for stock boys," Danny announces as he reads.

"You don't want that," Rick says. "Get something where you can make a bundle. My father's going to get me a job on Wall Street."

"No kidding." Angie is impressed. He is not sure what that means but Manhattan is consequential, adult.

"That's what you want. Something where you can see your future," Rick says. "You got to think strategically. Wall Street is a great future. See, Eisenhower is pro-business, so you want to get yourself in a position where that'll pay off. My father is pro-business, too."

Angie says he doesn't know whether his father is pro-business or not. Angie's father paints houses. "Why would you be anti-business?" he asks. "Why would you care?"

They retrieve random sports pages and piece them together. The Dodgers are in St. Louis for the weekend and have already dropped the opener.

"Dick Young is full of shit," Angie says, pointing to the column. They know the context. "Look at this. You put Robinson in the outfield, you lose at the plate. You'd rather have Gilliam hitting than Hermanski?"

No one disagrees. They are loyal to Hermanski. Junior Gilliam is untested. As a Negro he is presumed to be athletic, but he is yet untested.

The subway rattles towards the heart of Brooklyn. They pay no attention to the stops. When the train pulls into the station at Newkirk Avenue, Angie springs up.

"See you guys. Monday. Home room. Last week."

"Hey," Danny calls to him as he runs out the door. "Don't forget Europa." He grabs the box with the clock they have won and lobs it softly through the open train doors. Angie one-hands the catch.

The train pulls out. Rick regards his friend with curiosity.

"Who?"

"What?"

"Don't give me that. Don't forget who?"

"Oh, Europa. The clock."

"How do you know that's Europa. You used to date her?"

Danny shrugs. "Her name was on the box."

"I looked at the box, Meadoff. No name. It's just some broad with big gozangas."

"She was riding a bull, dummy. Europa was the wife of Zeus. They travelled incognito. He would disguise himself as a bull."

"Is that right?" Rick is silent. The stop is Danny's and he rises to go. Rick's is last, then a long walk down Nostrand.

"See you," Danny says.

"Yeah," says Rick, still pondering. "Sure."

The Meadoff home is a single-family house on the fringe of the Doctors' Section. It is grey-shingled with white trim and stands alone on its lot. For the area, one of Brooklyn's finest, the house is modest. Two stories, center hall plan, a garage that repeats in miniature a Dutch Colonial design. A pretty lot, perhaps eighty feet across. To the southeast corner stands a rare copper beech, and every year a tour from the Botanical Garden Club comes around to see it. Two sugar maples were planted to set off the symmetry of the portico, and still they mark the slate walk. But the Meadoffs are haphazard about vegetation and several volunteers have also sprouted on the front lawn, have taken root. Somewhere the lawn has lost its original pattern.

Danny mows the grass, one of his few household chores. Like every other homemaker in this plutocracy of three square blocks, Mrs. Meadoff hires out household tasks of peril or strength to Handy Andy Brown, the colored man who works the neighborhood.

Danny walks into the living room. His father is seated in a blue easy chair. Its button tufts collect grey stars of dust. All the other furniture in the living room has been slip-covered for the summer, but this is Mr. Meadoff's chair. In it he reads, in Talmudic cycles, Carl Sandburg's six-volume life of Lincoln. Tonight he sits with a folio-size newspaper tented before him, the Sandburg volume two, *The Prairie Years*, close by his elbow.

Mr. Meadoff folds the paper, looks up and asks.

"Good time at the beach?"

"Great."

"How was the water?"

"Perfect. What's in the paper?"

"Woodward thinks they ought to trade Newcombe."

"What does Woodward know?"

"Thinks they have too much fire power. Erskine, Podres, Lowes. Thinks they ought to get some young hitters."

"He's out of his mind," Danny says angrily. "They open the season twenty-two of twenty-four, those other three yenkels can't finish a game, they need Labine or Roebuck to finish for them, and he wants to trade away the one finisher in the group." Mr. Meadoff considers the strength of the argument. It pleases him.

"Thinks he's on his last legs. Too old."

"How old is he, Dad?"

"Newcombe? Maybe thirty, thirty-one."

"How old are you?"

"Forty-nine."

"I rest my case."

Stanley Woodward writes for the *Tribune*. Danny's father buys the *Trib*, with the *Times*, on Sundays. On weekdays his father reads the *Times* and the *News* going into the city, the *Post* and the *World-Telegram* coming home. His father has a long commute, longer than it need be because he takes the local. He brings all four papers home and Danny follows the Dodgers in each. The four gospels.

The *Trib*, Danny has decided, is a paper from some foreign country. It is written for people who live in Manhattan or Westchester, who follow crew or ice hockey and root for college teams. Its politics are Republican, its sports page an astonishment. Stanley Woodward is supposed to be a great writer. Danny suspects him of being a covert Yankee fan. A debate over the loyalty of Julius and Ethel Rosenberg might have two sides, but no one in Danny's acquaintance admits to ambivalence about the Yankees.

His sisters are playing Parcheesi on the floor in front of the dark television set. Waiting, he figures, until they can turn it on. A twelve-inch screen set into a walnut console with sliding doors. Mrs. Meadoff likes the doors to be kept closed, but tonight they are ajar and the dull grey screen shines like a moonstone.

Rochelle says nothing. She is presently at war with her brother, though he has forgotten why. Joyce looks up.

"See the freaks?"

"No. Didn't have time."

"Sylvester the Seal Boy. That's my favorite. No arms. Holds a pen in his teeth. I'm going with my friends next week. Soon as school's out."

"Over my dead body," Mrs. Meadoff walks in correcting. "All that *shmutz*. No Coney Island for fifth grade girls on their own. What do you think this is?"

His mother's positions are irresistible, unconquerable. Most disagreements end by her pronouncement of an absolute, a metaphysic. The mandala of Mrs. Meadoff.

"Daniel, after you put up your things help me set. And wash out that suit before you put it away. Salt water, bath houses, who knows what you're bringing in the house?"

That he never swam is not reason to provoke his mother's concern. He goes to his room, changes, washes out the bathing suit and takes it and the dry towel to the backyard where he clothespins them to the line. It is the day after the summer solstice. Earth at the sixth furlong pole, turning the corner and down the backstretch. He searches the sky to see if he can surprise the sun retiring early. Evidence for his sure knowledge. Just as the summer begins, it starts to end. He stands in the pink dusk sucking on this melancholy lozenge. He watches the silhouette of the house darken against the sky. It is easy to imagine the house as a three-masted ship, set in its course, fixed only within the convoy of neighboring houses. He puts his hand on its painted shingles and feels the tremble of the wind.

When he returns his mother wordlessly hands him five plates, and he arranges them around the enameled table in the kitchen. He prefers supper in the kitchen, where he and his father can linger afterwards while the dishes are done. When they eat in the dining room, the meal ends with his mother sending everyone to homework or chores.

This night his mother has made a brisket, with roasted new potatoes and carrots in the gravy. The secret to the gravy is the ginger snaps, his father will say at dinner or his mother if he forgets. Gervaise used to cook every meal, Gervaise, the honey-colored woman who has been around since the kitchen was remodeled. Early this year Mrs. Meadoff announced they were cutting back. Everyone would have to pitch in. Gervaise would come only twice a week, on Tuesdays and Thursdays.

"Dad," he asks as the family sits down, "are you pro-business?"

"Pro-business? I'm *in* business. Isn't that enough?"

"It's just that Rick's father is. He likes Eisenhower, too."

"Eisenhower. A general." His father likes to be asked. Danny can tell from the weariness in his voice. "A cossack from Kansas. This is a great country, Daniel. Here not only anyone can become president, anyone has."

His father uses his fork to mash the round, red potatoes and to hoist gravy over the flattened mass. You wouldn't think you could spoon gravy with a fork. It looks like a great way to eat, but when Danny does it, his mother tells him to stop. It's not good manners. His father also holds his fork as he holds a hammer, not balanced amid three fingers. Danny tries not to watch.

"That may be. But Mr. Rappaport really likes him. Mr. Rappaport is a Republican."

"Don't be silly, Daniel," his mother says. "He can't be."

"Why?" Danny knows what's coming and has prepared his forensic trap.

"Brooklyn people named Rappaport are Democrats."

"He's not, Ma."

"He's not what?"

"A Democrat."

"Daniel, what are we?"

"We're Democrats."

"How about everybody you know? How about Aunt Barbara and Uncle Sol?"

"Them too. But not Mr. Rappaport."

He looks imploringly to his father, who is considering the paradox.

"More and more," his father says and stows a forkful of potatoes. He uses a voice Danny likes, a voice you might hear on a radio show about world events.

"More and more, people want to forget who they are. Want to move away." His father has taken the crumpled paper napkin and wedged it under the far side of his plate, so the gravy pools in front of him. Danny watches but says nothing.

"So it can be," his father concludes. "Mr. Rappaport is pro-business. Mr. Rappaport is anti-union. Mr. Rappaport is a Republican."

"Next he'll be a Unitarian," his mother says.

"What does he do, this father of your friend Rappaport?" His mother doesn't like Rick. She has just said so. Mrs. Meadoff's important thoughts are interrogative.

"He's in investments," Danny says this proudly. Danny's discovery of his mother's antagonism salts his friendship with the exotic. "He works in Wall Street."

His mother snorts. It is not a complimentary snort, though she has those too.

"A tycoon," she says.

Danny is pleased with this reaction. His father does not show that he hears, keeps his head over the tilted plate.

"To be a Republican, that would be unusual. Maybe he's trying to prove something."

Danny is disappointed. His father has split the baby in half. His sisters stir with enjoyment: it is a partial repudiation. Both sides stand to lose.

Danny considers his next remark. "You really shouldn't do that, Poppa." Rochelle kicks her sister under the small table. They giggle.

Danny's father is not a large man. He has dark, nervous eyes. His hair, once jet, has begun to spot to grey. There is a skullcap of scalp showing through thinning hair on his pate, and two long parabolas creep up beside his widow's peak. His eyebrows remain black, vigorous, expressive. He raises them in surprise.

"Do what?"

"Prop your plate up like that. It's not good manners."

The girls observe closely. Danny and their father look at each other across the length of table, the same face separated only by thirty-four years. Mr. Meadoff recalls reading about a marriage initiation of ancient Phoenecia. The night before a wedding, the bridegroom is made to look into a copper bowl to see his visage. The curve of the bowl tricks him, shows him the reflection of a drawing, held up behind, of an old and sere man. He thinks on that refraction as he looks at his son.

"No," Mr. Meadoff says on deliberation. "Perhaps you're right."

After dinner Danny dries the dishes. His mother soaps them in one sink, rinses them off in the second, and then places them in the yellow Rubbermaid rack. The double sink was an innovation. Once they had remodeled the kitchen, his mother would bring in visiting relatives to see it. His sisters are too young to remember. Joyce doesn't go back before prosperity. Rochelle has decided not to.

Daniel takes the steaming Melmac dishes from the rack as his mother deposits them. He dries with a terry-cloth towel that says Lake Champlain on it, in script over a picture of a cheerful woman in a bathing suit. Behind her a man is water skiing and she waves from the dock as he sprays up a geyser of wake. It is Danny's favorite towel. His father sits at the metal table, drinking a cup of tea that has been allowed to cool to room temperature. It is his mother's remedy against the heat. Soup or tea. Let it cool, then drink it.

"Daniel," his mother says. "I want you to think about a job this summer."

"Happy to, Ma. Every day this summer I'll devote one hour to that very thought."

"Don't be a wisenheimer. I am serious."

"Let him be," his father says. "He's going to Brooklyn College for the summer. It's an honor."

"Fine for you to say. You want to make believe we don't need money, it just gets in our way. You want him not to know."

Danny looks to the sink. There is only the roasting pan to do.

"There is nothing wrong with Dante." His father says this to his mother's back. "Dante Alighieri."

"He should know," his mother says. "Maybe he'd do something. Not like you and Lindenauer." Lindenauer is his father's partner. They import knitted goods, mostly from the Phillipines, and sell them to department stores. Cotton underwear. When he can't avoid telling what his father does, Danny calls it knitted goods.

[29

"Tell him," his mother says. "He's old enough. Why should I have all the worry?"

"What's up, Poppa?"

"Nothing. Nothing is up. Your mother worries just because we have trouble with factors. We always have trouble with factors."

"I'm planning to get a job," Danny says. "I thought I'd look tomorrow."

"Good," says his mother. She takes the day's newspaper from the top of the refrigerator, stored with the brown paper bags. "Let's look."

"Miriam, leave the boy alone. Wait a week until school's out."

"School's out the schvartzes will have all the jobs. They don't go to school. Now is when you have to be thinking."

She opens to the want ads and reads.

"Here, 'Boy wanted.' " Danny gets a brillo pad and begins to scrub the roasting pan in the cooling, greasy water.

" 'Messenger boy. White Plains. Thirty-five hours a week.' Too far. 'Office boy, driver's license.' What kind of boy has a driver's license?"

"I don't want a boy job," Danny says. "I want something better." He puts the pan on the drying rack. The logic of the custom is lost in time, yet pots and pans are not wiped dry but are left to drain. Danny assumes the reason has something to do with metallurgy. He goes to the table where his mother has seated herself and watches her turn a page.

"All I know is you ought to be working." She gets up and walks to the sink, repositions the pan. The way the pan was set to drain was wrong. His father says nothing. Danny spins the paper around and begins to read.

"I'd like to do something different than a boy job."

"When you're a boy that's what you get. When you're a locomotive you get a locomotive job." Mrs. Meadoff undoes her apron, wipes her hands on it, folds its strings as if they were arms and she the arresting officer. Then she hangs it on the hook under the sink.

"What's important is that as soon as the summer starts you go to work. No more allowance. You want spending money, you earn it. This family is cutting back."

His father glances at another section of the paper. When Mrs. Meadoff leaves the kitchen, Danny searches the columns for something to discuss. His father is quiet. What are his thoughts? He is unreadable, like the evening sky.

His father speaks. "The second game of the twi-night double header is on the radio. Maybe we should turn it on. Later maybe walk up to Flatbush and get a quart of French vanilla and have ice cream. Get some for the ladies," his father says.

In the middle of the night, when nothing is certain but silence, Danny rises to go down the hall to the bathroom. Something draws his eyes through the slatted blinds that look down on the side yard. Perhaps it is the extended silhouette, the sense that there are extra and antic shadows on the lawn.

And there, blanched in the bulbflash of a white moon he sees a form, could be a man, standing behind the trunk of the copper beech. Standing, facing towards Flatbush and the north. A silent, frozen shape that was perhaps there. Or perhaps not, for when he comes back to his room, voided now of half sleep and the tricks of dream, there stands only the tree.

- 4 -

The Dodgers win both ends. Two days later, Danny meets his friends at Bernstein's to go over the victories. Bernstein allows them to sit at the counter and leaf through the prior day's papers before they're picked up for refund. Monday's *News* has the box scores. All the Dodgers are hitting.

"No matter," says Rick. "It is not the Redbirds from Santa Luisa I fear. I fear the Pirates of Pittsburgh. The Pirates of Pittsburgh where once there played a brother of the great Dimaggio."

"Rappaport," says Angie. "You are a nudnick. Pittsburgh won't be in the league by the All-Star game."

Rick has found a job. He starts the day school ends, at a dry cleaner's. Two stores on Flatbush and a third on New Utrecht, by the cemetery. He is to bag clothes as they come off the machines, write out prices, staple on tags. The presser runs the store, but the owner doesn't trust him. A shade, Rick tells them in confidence. A boogie. Rick is to make sure every item gets an inventory ticket. That way, the owner explained, nobody can cheat you. That way the cash in the drawer has to equal the amounts on the tickets.

"Is that paleontogic?" Rick asks. "Explaining as if I didn't get it. Do I look stupid? What you do, you take the presser in. He presses suits, I skip the tag, we pocket the cash."

Angie is impressed. "You gonna do that, Rick?"

"Nah," Rick says. "You could make some real money, but the presser won't cooperate. I explained it to my dad, though, and he said I had it figured right. That's business. But without the presser it won't go."

A Caddy, two-tone green, mint and forest, pulls up in front of the candy store. It spills over the parking slot saved for the delivery truck, chrome bulging beyond the yellow curb lines at both ends. Bernstein lays his cigar in the ashtray on the counter. The stub has been chewed into a fringe and is black with saliva.

Bernstein goes to the street and talks with the driver. The man wears rose-tinted glasses, wears a slate grey panama hat with a white band, wears a sports coat with the shirt collar out, saddle-stitched. The man sticks his chin up to speak through the half-cranked window.

"That's what I'm gonna drive," Rick says breathily. Then, in his announcer's voice, "The Cadillac Coupe de Ville. More than an automobile, the world's standard of excellence."

Danny studies the car. Its enormous grille wraps around in tiered sets of shark's teeth and two chrome tusks swell out from under the hooded headlights.

"The Coupe de Ville," Rick says. "A car you can beat off to."

Mr. Bernstein finishes his business with the driver, a short, stocky man the boys know from around, and comes back into the store.

"He your collector?" Rick asks him. "I didn't know Joey Ceravolo collects you."

"Don't stick your nose in," says Bernstein. "We got business together, is all. Don't talk about things you don't know."

"I'm gonna have me one of those," Rick says again, mostly because no one challenged him last time. "Zero to sixty in ten seconds, three-hundred-twenty horses."

"The Lincoln's got a bigger engine," says Danny. "You can get a Lincoln or a Ninety-eight with close to four hundred."

"Horses don't make it a Cadillac," Rick says. "That car's got class. Class has nothing to do with horses."

"What we want," says Angie, "is Sales." He folds the paper over and the two others lean in on him like Bill Ding blocks. " 'Sales' " he reads. " 'Extra money in your spare time. Big bucks.' "

"You got no spare time," says Rick. "Your time is running out."

" 'Sales. Easy money. Be your own boss. Car required.' "

"If you have your own a car, why do you need a job?"

"Here. 'Sell ice cream. Work outdoors. Must be eighteen. No license needed.' How about that?"

"Good thinking. Apply now, tell them you can wait three years. They should keep the popsicles frozen."

"Mr. Bernstein, I ask you," Angie says. "Can I pass for eighteen? Does the Pope shit in the woods?"

Bernstein comes over and takes their plates. Angie is absent-mindedly sprinkling salt on the counter, wetting his finger to pick up the grains, licking it off. Bernstein retrieves the salt cellar and aligns it with the napkin holder.

"That's forty-five cents for the egg creams and two dollars for the salt," he says.

Angie takes a dime from the counter change and goes into the booth to make a call. They watch. He closes the door. Minutes later he comes out, he's grinning.

"I got an interview. Tomorrow at ten. Opportunity is knocking."

"Tomorrow at ten, goombah, chemistry is knocking," Danny says.

"Ahh," says Angie. "She gonna flunk me? What do you think will do me more good, the valence tables or one-thirty-five an hour?"

Danny studies his friend. High, Mediterranean cheek-bones, deep eye sockets spotted by black marble eyes. Handsome for sure. Could they have read his good looks by phone?

They rise from the counter. To the stack of coins Danny adds a nickel for the *News*.

34]

"You come into money?" Rick asks him. "Maybe Tommy Manville died and turned out to be your uncle? We don't buy the newspapers here, we read them."

"I need the classified," Danny says. He will find a job. You don't want to get behind. Hit the ball out in front of you. You get behind, choices pile up—when one gets made, another is right after it. It is like drying dishes. Life is closer to drying dishes than to books. Characters in novels never have as much to decide as he does. One simply blows up the bridge. Another holds on to the fish. And Jake Barnes had to figure out where to take Lady Brett for a brandy. Nothing major.

Daily Mr. Meadoff travels underground to the City. It is a trip scratched into his retinal memory, scratched so deep that he visualizes it as he brushes his teeth, as the bristles make the train sound of his day beginning. Except for the need to get his body there, he wouldn't have to make the trip. He can make it in his mind. He has seen the movie before. Coming soon to a theatre near you.

He boards the subway at Cortelyou Road, blocks from his house, and rides to Times Square. Each station looks like the last. The simplicity of his ride adds to its monotony. He watches the eyes of his fellow riders. Are they better off? They left Cork, Minsk, Mississippi and who knows where to travel back and forth in this sunless world, the belly of this electric snake in a rock in the ground. They say they used trains to get the prisoners to the camps, and that no one complained because the rocking motion, the repetition of the sounds and the rocking motion are soothing.

From Times Square it is a short walk down Seventh Avenue. The offices of Paradise Knitwear are in the rear of the sixth floor of a ten-story office building in the gut of the garment center. 7,200 square feet, five windows. "What does an architect do after he has drawn this building?" Mr. Meadoff asks the puzzled receptionist this morning. See his priest? Go to the bridge of sighs and empty his pockets into the river?

He walks past her. His gait breaks in a rolling limp that has been with him since he was younger than his own son. He no longer thinks on it. His own office, in the far rear, boasts one of the windows. He keeps his blinds drawn; four feet from the sill is the window of Mortrose Fashions, ladies' belts and accessories, and he cannot bear to sit and watch its owner Morty Kaye toy with his nostrils.

The mail lies open on the metal desk when he walks in. He reads ten or twelve letters with a glance for each, writes notes on one or two, discards the rest. The last piece is a yellow legal sheet bearing two columns of numbers in a neat, pencilled hand. No salutation, no signature. With this sheet, he settles into the wooden tilting chair behind his desk.

The sheet contains the computation of credit he will be extended by his factor on last week's orders. The amount is decreed to him; he is free to accept it or close his business. The factors buy the Paradise receivables at a discount and make money by collecting the full bill from the retailer. If Paradise could wait, if it had the working capital, it would not need a factor. But retailing is a treacherous business: firms come in and out like ships in a harbor. Factors provide liquidity and, as important, insurance against failures. Once the account is sold, it becomes the factor's headache whether or not the store pays for the goods.

The sheet tells him what he feared. His percentages are falling. The more he sells the less his factors will cover him. But he must sell more because the interest on his bank debt is creeping up. His eye runs down the paper. The speed is misleading. He slogs through a slough of money, money that is not his. His steps are slowing and he is sinking deeper. Money buoys him up, it is the water of the swamp. Money slows him, the overgrowth. And money, money owed, is the muck into which he sinks. This is not the fate of a man of air. A man of air would not sink.

He walks through the outer office. The desks there match his. All the desks are grey metal, bought as an odd lot when he teamed up with Lindenauer and moved uptown. Was that a mistake? What does it matter now? Our choices line up and we pass by them once. Only our regrets lie in a circle. He realizes one of the young men has stopped work, looks expectantly at him.

"Did you say something to me, Mr. Meadoff?"

He is a pleasant young man, sallow and thin. His neck and cheeks are red from the irritation of shaving. He handles bills of lading from Manila. He has worked at Paradise five years. Meadoff cannot think of his name.

"Go figure," he says to the young man and walks back to his office. There will be a way out of this trap, he says to himself as he closes the door. He is conscious of thinking it and of not speaking. Sometimes the distinction between what he thinks and what he says is unclear. There will be a way I can spring out of this. I will sit down tomorrow and write out the possible solutions. I will use the accounting paper, lined and tinted green, and print the solution in columns.

- 5 -

Sunday morning and good intentions can sleep late. No one disturbs them, no one sends them underground to work. They lie in bed and luxuriate, they keep the shades drawn and for one last day avoid the desiccating sun.

Sunday morning arrives. Arises Mr. Meadoff, as always, before anyone can know. Six days a week he makes breakfast. On Sunday, it is purchased. Minutes before seven, for at seven the stores open, he will begin his walk up Dorchester Road to Flatbush. Bagels at Tishman's Bakery, cream cheese and nova at Gittleson's, and the papers at the newsstand run by the one-armed colored man. By the newsstand a second colored man hangs out, the one the kids call Hoot. Hoot plays a small saxophone and collects change. Mr. Meadoff will take his purchases in white sacks and his Sunday papers and leave a coin for the musician. He will talk to the one-armed man about the lead in the *Times* and the musician about a song and then walk home.

This Sunday Danny sets his alarm, and when his father unlatches the door Danny is waiting. They walk in the lingering cool of morning. His father asks about his friends, how they're doing in school, about their plans for college. The questions are not casual. Mr. Meadoff instructs through observations of others, the way a shy person might enquire of a doctor about the malady of a friend.

In a still moment Danny asks how is business. They are standing at Gittleson's chest-high counter, waiting as the lox is sliced thin on the rotary blade and wrapped.

"Why do you ask, Daniel? You have a sudden interest in knit underwear?"

"No," Danny says. "It's just I hear you and Mom talking about trouble with factors. And I just wondered."

"You know, Daniel, what factors are?"

Danny has pieced together an idea of his father's business from cuttings of conversation left untended. Tomorrow, his father would say, was the Chase letter of credit. Alexander's was going to ninety days. Factors were acting up. What did it mean for the factors to act up? Danny could only think of the Fuzzy Wuzzies in *Gunga Din*: when they acted up, Cary Grant and Victor McLaglen put them back down with hammer rifles. Were the factors going to storm their house dressed in loincloth? Words would pass, the children would sit silently and Mrs. Meadoff would shake her head or touch her forehead with the fleshy tips of her fingers—a sign, but of what? deferral? sympathy? fear?—and the unguarded moment would pass. Everyone would resume eating dinner.

"Factors," says Mr. Meadoff. From his tone it could be the last word he has decided to speak. He hands Danny the nova, wrapped in white paper and secured with white paper tape. The package bears markings of black crayon that only the cashier can read. They walk to the second counter for a small tub of cream cheese. The silent woman slabs it in with a wooden spatula, writing numbers on the lid, hands it across the counter. They are at the cashier before his father speaks again.

"Factors," he says. He pays with the exact change and they go out into the sun.

"In my business, Daniel, I have to get people to do two things for me. First, they got to make what I order. If I order and they produce and I change my mind, they are stuck with a hundred gross girls' size six apricot they don't want. Next, I got to get them to send it to me. If they produce and ship and I don't pay, maybe I die or I go broke or I go to Montana to ride the range with Hoppy, again they're out of luck."

They cross Flatbush to the newsstand. There is little traffic, but the sidewalks are filling up. With people headed to bakeries, for the papers, to the Greek Orthodox Church where bells have been ringing since he and his father left home. They take their papers from under pig iron weights and line up to pay. The

Times and the *Trib*. Until January the *Brooklyn Eagle* as well, but in January the *Eagle* folded. Brooklyn, a city of three million people, without its own newspaper, Mr. Meadoff said at dinner that night. The death of a newspaper is the death of a friend.

The man who runs the newsstand they call Sarge. Winter or summer he wears a faded Eisenhower jacket. Dark escutcheons mark the shoulders where patches were removed, and one empty sleeve is pinned to the front. That's all Danny knows about him, his name, and that he is Hoot's cousin.

The newsstand is a wooden shed, slatted tongue in groove and painted grey. It opens to the sidewalk by two wooden panels hinged at the top. Sarge unlatches them one-handed from inside, lifts them up, secures them with hooks screwed into the roof.

Leaning against the shed assembling his horn is Hoot. His open case at his feet shows two singles and a few coins—his seed.

"Hey Hoot."

"Hey kid. What's coming down?"

"You want to know this or not?" his father asks.

"Yeah, Dad."

"So. This is what I need people to do on faith. But the funny thing is, Daniel, people don't do much on faith. I tell them not to worry, but somehow, my assurance is not enough. They want to get paid. Now I don't have the money until I sell forty, fifty gross girls six apricot to Wanamakers. I won't have the money until I get paid."

His father puts a five-dollar bill in a triangular ashtray with "Camels" on its side. Sarge makes change.

"So what do I do? I go to banks. I go to factors. They pay the man in Manila to make, they pay another man in Manila to ship. I get, I sell to Wanamakers. I hound and hound and I get paid. I give the money to the factor, if I get it early I can keep enough money to buy Sunday breakfast, and we start again. This sound like a good business to you?''

''No,'' Danny says with a laugh.

''To me either. But it's what I got. That and Lindenauer.''

Hoot is playing ''June is Busting Out All Over.'' Danny loves to hear him. He plays the melody, then he plays something else, something inside the melody. Danny's English teacher used to tell them to read between the lines. That's the way Hoot plays. As Danny listens his father pockets the change from the one-armed man and hands Danny a load of papers.

Mr. Meadoff drops a quarter into Hoot's open case. '' 'Carousel','' he says to Daniel. Hoot keeps blowing. ''Majestic Theatre. 1945. Gordon McCrae. Cameron Mitchell.'' Hoot plays on.

''You have a sudden interest in the business? You're thinking of going into the business? I don't need the competition.''

''No, Poppa. I'm not.''

''That's good, because it's a lousy business.''

Danny cannot tell whether his father needs help. The only way he knows to find out is to ask, though he also knows that asking will be insufficient. ''I thought you were having some trouble. 'Cause if so, I ought to get a job for the summer.''

''And if not? What if not?''

''If not, what I'd like to do is take some courses.''

''*The Divine Comedy*. That's what you ought to do. I'd rather have you in class than pushing a rack down Seventh Avenue.''

They walk down the street. The Doctors' Section has roads named Albemarle and Beverly and Courtelou, cross streets named Rugby and Westminster and Argyle. The tulips of May have faded, but the aroma of the mock orange and forsythia is full, rows of poppies have started to bloom lavender and red, and the bursting pods of the linden trees give off a yeasty smell.

Danny's talk with his father has reassured him. His father has the wonderful skill of making bad news disappear, stirring it into some larger kettle so that it dissolves. After the papers have been read, he finds his mother in the kitchen. Happily he confides to her that things are not nearly so bad as they may seem.

"Daniel. You have to face up to life. You're as bad as he is. We're having troubles. Don't you see Gervaise isn't here every day? The factors have cut him down to a $25,000 maximum on any buyer. That means he's uncovered for the excess, he's not covered. Do you understand what I'm saying? He leans more and more on Lindenauer. Lindenauer will eat him alive. You need to get yourself a job. How else can I tell you?"

That afternoon, while his sisters and mother are at an air-conditioned movie with Robert Wagner and Terry Moore and his father watches the Dodgers drop one to the Cubs on the Dumont, he sorts through the classifieds and makes twenty-three calls. By the end of the day, he has a single possibility: an interview with John Everett Raycroft, whom the woman on the phone describes as the leading salesman in five boroughs for the Fuller Brush Company.

What the woman on the phone said was, "John Everett Raycroft will see you tomorrow morning, 10:30 at Dubroff's. Do you know Dubroff's?"

And Danny said, yes, he does. Dubroff's is a large restaurant off Kings Highway, not far from Rick's apartment. The Meadoffs go there sometimes for Sunday dinner.

Danny is early. He stops outside at the plate glass window and studies the pastramis, the tongues, the salamis depending there. He walks in and asks the woman in the flamingo pink dress and starched white cap for John Everett Raycroft, as he was told. Dubroff's has two tiers. A Thirties staircase trickles down: chrome banisters, suspended concrete slabs hung from rebar, curls down the room like the piano keyboard in Fantasia. Over there, the woman says, on the terrace. And indeed over there, sitting at the single table on the broad, pebbled landing, crouched behind a cup of coffee and a stack of pamphlets, is his man.

A little man, Danny sees as he walks up. Little body, coffee-cream puffy hands. Across the bent head, a few black hairs have been coaxed up from the side and cemented. They do not cover but relieve the monotony of the pate. Tread marks from a toy car. A gleaming lotion adheres these hairs, broadens them to a chemical width and gives the scalp, in the fluorescence from above, a high nacre. If this were a seashell and not the top of a man's head, it would be a thing of beauty.

"Mr. Raycroft?"

"Yes?" The little man is writing on a pamphlet and stops to looks up. Round face, pencil moustache in the style of William Powell.

"I'm Daniel Meadoff. Your ten-thirty interview."

Raycroft bounces from his chair—slides down, as if he were a child—and grabs Danny's hand.

"John Everett Raycroft," he says twice, with what actors call projection. "I haven't got all day. Campus fugit."

They seat themselves opposite each other. Mr. Raycroft flattens his hand on the stack of pamphlets. He may be about to take an oath.

"So you want to be a Fuller Brush salesman?"

"I'm not sure," Danny says. "I want to find out."

"Find out? Find out? What is there to find out? Working in this country's leading profession—are you aware that in the U S of A there are more salesmen than farmers?—working with a company founded in 1905. Did you know that? The world's largest brush company. Products that open doors better than a locksmith. I say I'm the Fuller Brush man and in five boroughs doors fly open. And with a hidden extra that I'm not even going to mention unless I like you. There is nothing to find out. You want us, all right. What's to find out is, do we want you?"

John Everett Raycroft takes a breath and squares off the booklets in front of him. "Now," he said, "tell me what you've sold before."

"Nothing."

"Wrong, my young friend. Affirmatively wrong. You sell every day. You sell yourself. To your teachers, to the bus driver, to those little girls to get into their panties." Here he leans forward and widens his eyes. "Every day. Everyone is in sales. Difference is, I get paid for it."

"How much?" Danny says.

"What?" Raycroft stops. "Oh, I get it. How much? I like that, Meadoff. Get to the point. I'll tell you how much. I get a senior sales commish. The top. Do you know who is the leading salesman for FB in five contiguous boroughs?"

"You are."

"Affirmative. So I get the top. I even get a little commish off your sales. Hardly pays for your coffee. You want some coffee? But I like to help young people. So it's worth it to me. Your commish will be twenty percent. I like you. I'm going to start you at twenty percent. Of everything collected. You hustle, you can make one-fifty, two hundred a week. These products sell themselves. All you have to do is make the introduction. Introduce the product to the lady of the house and don't let her say no."

44]

"One-fifty a week?"

"After you're trained. Now listen. I need a decision. The postman knocks twice. Opportunity knocks once. I've got lots of young men to do today. Are you in or out? Don't answer that. Let me tell you that hidden extra. Because I like you. I can see you got what it takes. "You go to college, am I right?" Danny nods. He's sure his age will keep this chance from him. Raycroft pays no mind. "College is expensive. But I am prepared to train you myself. Free of charge. You'll be going to the Harvard of sales. With Professor John Everett Raycroft, Ph.D. in the school of hard knocks."

"When do I get paid?" Danny asks.

"I like you, Meadoff. You got the right questions. You get paid when you get paid. Just like me. Just like Mr. Fuller. You make a sale you take a twenty-five percent down. Always get a down. You'll eat the sale if you don't. You take a twenty-five percent down, keep your commish. Give me the order and the rest of the money. I get it filled, give you the merchandise, you deliver and get the rest. Keep one-fifth and give me the balance. I meet you once a week. Right here, this table. Same time, same station. Now I ask you," jumping down from his chair and slapping the pile of booklets. "You in you out?"

Danny has been sold. At least it is not Boy Wanted.

"I guess I'm in."

"Great," says Raycroft, offering his hand. Danny stands, takes it. Shakes the little man's hand and stands grinning like a quiz show contestant. "When do we start?"

"When do we start?" says Raycroft, letting go of his hand and hoisting a black naugahyde case from under the table. "We have started, my young friend. We have started."

The little man leads Danny out of the restaurant, bobbing from the uneven load, pamphlets under one arm, satchel at the end of the other. The pace of the water bearer is his gyroscope, if he slows down he falls. He walks two feet ahead of Danny, talking all the time, straight ahead, about products, sales strategy, neighborhoods, tips.

"Swedes are cheap. Don't like the top of the line. But they're clean. Tell the missus the house is dirty because she doesn't use a refrigerator spray and you'll sell it. They stay home, too. Homebodies. Not like the Italians and the Greeks. They're at the beach. Swedes burn in the sun. Rainy day, the Mediterraneans, sunny day, sell the Swedes.

"Nobody home? Missus not home? Leave a brochure. It says, 'Call me if you need me.' They don't call you, go back, pick up the brochure, make a sale. Spooks you can sell too, if you know how."

They arrive at a battered Plymouth, the body tan, trim the color of Royal Crown Cola. John Everett Raycroft unlocks the trunk, the doors. In the back seat are more pamphlets, carton boxes, mops, toilet brushes, spray cans, toilet seats. Danny can't see what else. Raycroft is instructing: the Jews and the Irish are a tough sell. Tell the Irish the Jewish joke, vice versa.

Danny sees the day as endless chatter. He has tired of the job.

"Don't you have other interviews, Mr. Raycroft?"

"Who knows, Meadoff? Time is a wallet. Opportunity doesn't knock. It peeks in the window." He moves stuff, limitless stuff, boxed, spilling, naked, from the front seat to the back, from the back seat to the trunk. He finds a second sample case, sets it on the curb, packs it in handfuls.

"Samples," he is saying. "Now I'll tell you something. Rejections. People are suspicious, don't know what they want. You got to sell them. Pay no attention to what they say if the door's open. The door is open, you can make your sale. That's my motto. I'm the internal optimist."

The Plymouth belches and fires. Once in forward it slips gears—the dashboard announces Fluid Drive, a hybrid transmission—and they are launched into the sleepy streets of central Brooklyn on a Monday noon. Raycroft sits on a cushion set atop a folding spring seat. Still he stretches to peer over the dashboard. A purple glass knob is mounted on the steering wheel and he tugs it to make careening turns. The Plymouth dips and yaws like the square-rigged barque on its hood.

They drive north of Flatbush, towards Brownsville and East New York. The neighborhoods are unfamiliar to Danny. Here, the row houses are built of orange brick, the streets are a foreign width. Wait till he tells Rick and Angie. Raycroft is talking product.

"You'll get to know the line soon enough. Experience is the best teacher. You want to watch how I get their attention. I don't make the sale. I make a friend. Can't say no to a friend."

"I thought the products sell themselves."

Raycroft glances quizzically at him, falls silent for the first time. He pulls the car to the curb. When they were moving the air was fresh, city-fresh. At idle, unmuffled exhaust floats up through the floorboards. From the glove compartment Raycroft removes a worn, pocket-size notebook, opens it secretively, enters notes in a tiny calligraphic hand, closes it. Opens it again, separates the rings, removes a clean page and writes numbers on it. The numbers describe Danny's territory. Raycroft has listed the streets that are its boundaries.

"Start here. I'm giving you two maybe three thousand cherry families. Pure as rain. Two thousand families, maybe four people in each. Eight thousand toothbrushes. Two thousand brooms. Four thousand pounds of floor wax."

He snaps the book closed and they get out.

There is a summer's fog and once outside the car Danny can smell the lingering damp on the pavement. All the houses on the block are identical. Attached to each other with front-facing half-flights of stairs separated by brick walls. Almost every stoop carries a cement urn where geraniums blossom. One house is guarded not by the cast rhylos but by concrete lions resting on either side of a monogrammed aluminum door. That is the house John Everett Raycroft selects.

Raycroft pulls back the aluminum screen door. He positions himself against adversity, before the portico, squares himself, weight forward, opens his sample case so that its flap leans against the inner door, pushes the bell. It takes only seconds. The door opens a guarded inch. The darkness of a television parlor leaks into the street. An eye squints through and asks, "Yeah?"

"Good morning, Madam. The Fuller Brush Company has asked me to stop by. Drop off a free sample. Not here to sell today. A goodwill visit."

"Don't need anything."

"Just take these free gifts and I'll be on my way." Raycroft holds out his fist, palm down.

"What is it?"

"Goodwill gift. Free. No selling today."

The door hesitates, opens enough for a white arm to snake out, a moray of an arm, cautious but hungry. Raycroft drops something into it.

"Fizz top stoppers. Prevents the fizz from going out of the soda pop. Bet you wish you could do that with the real pop."

The white arm withdraws, the crack closes, the darkness pulls back into the house.

"Hold it," says Raycroft. "Don't forget gift number two." A plastic packet pops from his fingers, a card the magician has plucked, a white plastic packet the size of a stick of gum.

"What's that?" says the eye in the dark.

"Hand lotion, my dear. The best in the world. Make those little digits soft as a baby's cheek." Again the door hesitates. Moves to open, retracts, a maw of a tentative animal. Again the arm emerges, less carefully this time. Bam. Raycroft snares it by the wrist. Somehow he's torn the packet open, squeezing the lotion on, rubbing it in. "Feel that. Lanolin. Sheep's oil." Inside in the blue dark there's a giggle.

"Now," he says, "give me the other. Can't go around with one soft hand and one rough. Most good things in life take two hands." Danny cannot tell from his place astern who pulls whom but in a moment Raycroft is at the top of the steps holding his catch: a wide-faced woman with a shiny brow and mouse-colored hair. She is trying to pull back her arm but Raycroft has a firm grip on the wrist.

"Can't buy anything," she says urgently. She is pulling away but he has her. "Husband's home." Flesh at her elbow flags as Raycroft massages her flexed arm, opens the fist at the top, rubs lotion in.

"I won't sell you anything," he says. "I can't sell you anything today if you beg me. This is my day off. I'm going to leave some of our new products with you. Because I like you. You use them. I'll come back in a week, tell me if you want them."

Inside Danny can hear Vin Scully plugging Schaefer Beer. The game is starting. Fear not the Redlegs of Cincinnati, Rick told him on the phone that morning. If they see fear in your eyes they will know and will not dance the dance of death. It will be a bad thing.

The woman looks anxiously over her shoulder at the radium glow. Raycroft fills out a form. From the case he pulls several notions and jars. He offers her the pad and she signs.

"Now the three twenty-five," he says.

"What's that?"

"For the down. I need three twenty-five, darling, or the boss won't let me leave it. Don't worry. You use the stuff, you don't like any of it I take it back. I'll be here in a week."

The loudspeaker is announcing the Dodger line-up. They're taking the field. The sound makes the woman more agitated. Time is running out. She runs from the door, returns in seconds—the house cannot be more than forty feet deep—and hands Raycroft three squeezed bills and a coin. Raycroft has not finished. "You read this catalogue. I'll come back in a week and you can give me a real order. Next Monday. Or would Tuesday be better?"

"Yes," she says, hurrying him out from the doorway so the screen can shut. "Tuesday. Please."

The door closes. Raycroft wheels on the top step, holds out his hands and turns the palms up to the late June haze, the very haze Vin Scully just described for the audience as hanging over Brooklyn, turns his palms up and puts a foot forward, the trapeze artist returned to ground.

At the next house Danny stands three steps down. He studies the brick-work. Too irregular for stoop ball. Needs pointing, the masonry has begun to fall apart and bricks protrude. A ball would not take a true bounce. Danny stands and watches Raycroft fill an order sheet, start a second. Raycroft dances from one technique to another, changing pace, changing the attack. Never give them what they saw before. If they expect the curve, throw the high hard one. At the next house he startles the woman opening the door with a blast of foot spray—"Cool, huh?"—at the next he spills his case across the threshold, at a third he gets them both invited into the kitchen for a glass of Hi-C Grape Drink and vanilla wafers from a cellophane bag. At every house he sells. Two dollars, six dollars, at one house a phenomenal forty-one. Danny computes commish on each transaction.

Danny is excited. He forgets the game, though through the reluctantly open doors he follows its progress. Finally, with the Dodgers coasting 6-2 in the eighth and Podres rearing back and throwing hard like, Vin Scully says, the great workhorse he is, Raycroft hands Danny the case.

He mimics Raycroft's moves. He palms two lotions, one stopper. Plants himself on the top step, rings the bell. The door opens wide. A woman who looks like Loretta Young appears.

"The Fuller Brush Company has asked me to deliver a free gift for you, Madam. No obligation." He holds his hand out. Only then he realizes, there is a screen door that opens out. He backs down two steps. Raycroft backs down behind him. The woman watches.

"What is it?" she asks.

"Let me show it to you." He is beyond reach. She pushes the screen open and he hands her a stopper.

"Are you working your way through college?"

"Yes," he says. "Yes I am."

"That's wonderful. Here," she gives the sample back to him. "I'm sure they charge you for these."

The screen swings shut and she turns.

"Wouldn't you like some hand lotion," Danny calls. "Makes rough hands smooth as silk."

"Do you think I need it?" she asks with a coy look.

Danny is stumped. She moves her fingers in a wave goodbye and slowly closes the door.

Danny turns to find Raycroft, whom he's forgotten. "A little work," Raycroft says thoughtfully. "A little work and you'll be cooking with Crisco."

- 6 -

The run for home. Danny off the bus, lugging the kit of his new profession. The gravity of his trade is counterpoised by the lift of profit, of possibility, of the commish. On two more tries he sold nothing, but Raycroft said he had the knack. Said only a matter of time.

It was dinnertime when Raycroft freed him from that cross-border land, its streets secretly charted in a five-ring notebook stashed in the glove compartment of a wheezing '49 Plymouth— Raycroft the missionary—freed him so that a commonplace city bus could deliver him only blocks from home. Lost and delivered. What will his father think? He has secured the number one job in the U S of A. If you can sell, John Everett Raycroft told him, the world is your oyster. But is that good? Concerning oysters, Danny is of two minds.

He rounds the corner of Westminister and Dorchester Road and looks for the grin of his house. Danny sees faces everywhere. By the subway stop for the dentist stands a tree trunk that resembles C. Aubrey Smith. A radiator in his basement has two faces on its side, Laurel and Hardy—one long and solemn, the second short and jolly, with the pipe of the steam valve in its mouth. The masks of comedy and tragedy. And a smiling face glowers in the porch of his own house, a screen porch that wraps under gable and two windows. A fixed smile, but not a warm one. Sometimes mocking, the leer of a bully who's played a joke on you and sometimes, especially in the winter with the screens down and the porch light off, hollow, grimacing, mournful.

This summer evening he cannot see the face. Angie and Rick sit on the front steps, and their dimension dissolves any illusion. They call his name, run at him. Angie waves Danny's bat and glove.

"Where you been, wage slave? Workers arise." Rick takes the sample case from him. "What's in the case? Don't tell me. You're a doctor." He jangles the case up and down and bottle stoppers, napkin rings, tin thimbles jangle together. "Christ, will my mother be proud. A gynecologist."

Angie puts the fielder's glove on Danny's head like a cap. Rick hands him back his case, bounces a shape that used to be a baseball but is now covered with black electrical tape and has the contours of one of Pluto's moons. Bounces it against the pavement.

"We thought, Catch-a-fly-you're-up or something," says Angie.

Rick finishes. "So I wait for goombah here to get off from work and what do we find. You're gone. You are fickle, *Inglés.* You forget your friends from the country, your friends who will kill for you when it is time. It is not good. *No es bueno.*"

Danny waits. Then he tells them. About Dubroff's, the Plymouth, the lady who bought the mops. The chance to make maybe a hundred and a half, two hundred a week.

"That's a lot of jujubes," says Rick.

It turns out Rick is unemployed. The job at the cleaner's had limited horizons. He has quit. He may hitchhike to the Catskills. You can make a fortune waiting on tables and dancing the cha-cha. But it may be you need working papers, and he does not yet cha-cha. Better, his father may get him a job on Wall Street. Nothing big, but a start. His father is very heavy into Boeing. It looks like a sure thing. The broker owes his father a favor, because now the broker is heavy into Boeing too.

Angie likes his job O.K. Selling ice cream on the beach. You load up these boxes. Metal and insulated. You throw in some dry ice, put in the ice cream bars and cups and popsicles, some more ice, and sling it over your shoulder. Angie lugs two boxes at a time. That way you don't have to come in so often.

Rick listens. He asks questions. He is forming a judgment and the other two give him respectful silence. When do you work? Where is the boss? Can you smoke? Then he pronounces.

"It's a close call. Meadoff is more his own boss. That of course is the goal. That's an entrepreneur. But so far he's sold bupkus, nada, vernicht. Valeriani's got to work week-ends. No choice. And he's out where they can see him. But he's in the open air, all the women are in bathing suits. And ice cream. What would you rather sell, what gives more pleasure, ice cream or toilet brushes? Give the world pleasure, it'll kiss your ass. The decision goes to Valerio. On points in the tenth. Unless..."

He has them. A competition of which they were unaware is about to be decided. There is a chance for an upset, a judge's ruling.

"Unless Meadoff takes advantage of the nookie factor. If Meadoff gets laid on the job, he wins."

Danny is embarrassed.

"Come off it, Rappaport. I'm selling brushes."

"There he is, fans. It's a hot, steamy afternoon in Greenpoint. Our demure housewife is all alone, listening to Helen Trent. Can a young girl from a small mining town in Pennsylvania find happiness as the wife of a titled English lord. The doorbell rings. She puts down the meat loaf before her, wipes her hands on her apron, expectantly opens the door. What does she find? Our man, full of grace. Try this broom he says. *Por favor*, my little rabbit. Feel its smooth handle, see how satisfying it is."

"Yeah," says Angie, breathy, encouraging.

"Whale shit," says Danny.

They are sitting on the Meadoffs' lawn, cross-legged, idly pulling grass from its roots.

54]

"That's the unknown factor here, sports fans. The nookie factor. Valerio Valeriani's got no chance. He's out in the open. All he gets is some bare eyeball. But Meadoff toils in the dark, cool corridors of Brooklyn's bedrooms. Death in the afternoon. Can he pull it off, or will he just have to pull it?"

At this they squeal with laughter. Danny leaps on his friend and double-backed they roll over the earth. Rick on top. Angie shoulders him off, sits astride Rick's chest. Danny, the victor, kneels on Rick's arms, feeds him grass. Rick is yelling. The noise brings Mr. Meadoff from the house. Angie sees him first, gets up, pulls Danny off easily, gently by the back of the shirt.

"What is the fighting about?"

"Only round one, Mr. M," Rick says. "Just getting warmed up. Louis vee Schmelling."

Mr. Meadoff nods, unconvinced. "Louis knocked out Schmelling in the first round. I thought you boys were going to play catch. Daniel, you've been gone all day." Rick releases Danny.

"Poppa. Wait till I tell you. I got a great job."

Mr. Meadoff raises his brows. It is an ambiguous gesture. Surprise, yes. But approval? Congratulations? Danny can't tell.

"A job?"

"Selling Fuller Brushes. Door to door."

"And Dante," Mr. Meadoff says. "What happened to Dante?"

"He didn't get the job," Danny says. "They don't like Italians." His friends laugh at his wit, but Danny sees his father is displeased. "He'll still be there, Dad. I'll get to him later. But by then I'll be an entrepreneur."

Again a shrug. A shrug for a world that spins beyond his control. For the illogical and antic. Rochelle's moods, the problem of evil, the B that Danny got in gym, Jackie Robinson's arthritis. You could study night and day and still not figure it out. My eldest child and only son is an example. You want the melting pot to work, but maybe not so well. Maybe he should be a little less melted. With a friend named Angelo and a job knocking on people's doors selling them brushes. Maybe not so melted. Once he gets himself good and melted, whose son is he?

Into the street by the Meadoff house. They run its dimensions, know its geology. Not idle knowledge. Where the tar is thickest, on hot summer days the ball will bounce low. With a man on base, play up to the break in the curb that marks the double: cut off the run.

Danny plays deep, Angie short. Bat poised, Rick underhands the ball into the air and swats. Over the outfielder's head, a homer—the barrier that expands with respect. Doubles are hits beyond the cement break, triples the fielding team metes out. A matter of judgment.

The ball they use finds employment in only this game. Misshapen and heavy with electrical tape, it can be poled out over the figurative fence by Angie alone and then only with a running start. The glove, too, a fielder's mitt signed by Nellie Fox on the heel where it says Rawlings. Seasons of neatsfoot oil and nights of caress have softened it to a chocolate brown. Its strap, never undone, fastens to a brass button. Underneath the button you can see the aureole of gold that was the leather's original color. Between thumb and fingers is webbing where the ball, if only it can be induced to land there, sets up easily, offers itself up so the fielder can pluck it out, wheel to first and make the peg. Mr. Meadoff had chosen the glove for Danny's twelfth birthday. Telling Danny, doomed to be short like his parents, that he was like Nellie Fox, the tenacious second baseman. By flawless defense, Nellie Fox made size his advantage. His father, laden with the joy and relief that his son had made it unamputated, uncatastrophied to twelve, had gone through all the Rawlings mitts at Davega's to find it.

What his father could not have realized, of course, did not know until he saw it in his son's eyes, was that it was exactly the wrong choice. For one thing, Nellie Fox was in the American League. Worse, he played for the White Sox. Less than anonymous. One's glove might as well be endorsed by a swimmer, a Patagonian.

Danny never puts on the glove without the taste of that bittersweet day like bad mayonnaise. Adults want to feed you one emotion at a time. But Danny is beginning to suspect that purity is not their natural state, that always feelings are found in alloy. On that birthday he fixed a smile on his face. Only later, alone, he sat with hot tears in his eyes convincing himself that the Nellie Fox glove would not jinx him.

Rick announces while he plays. He bats. Two singles dribble past Angie then a third pop-fly out. Angie strings together two doubles and a homer, finally flies out. Danny has the advantage of batting against Rick's infield. The ancient bat, nicked from years of play, from hitting pebbles and pieces of asphalt when there were no playmates to field, fits Danny's build. He chokes up on its bottleneck grip and punches singles to the left and right of Rick. Angie moves up to cover and Danny lifts a looper over his head. But Angie gets a hand on it and the judges pronounce a ground-rule double. Two on, trailing two to one to zip, Danny takes a mighty swing and undercuts the ball, only a piece of it, for what Rick describes, in professionally undulating tones, as "an easy last out to short center, as the fans file out from stately Ebbets Field to their cars and their loved ones beyond."

-7-

Danny awakens to a workday. He has set his alarm, has determined to breakfast with his father, so together they will ride off to make a living. At dinner he argued his opportunity to the gathered family, mostly in Raycroft's words, and afterwards he studied the catalogue and wrote his name and telephone number in a hundred pamphlets, as Raycroft had suggested.

"The pamphlet sells when you're not ringing bells," Raycroft said, and he said it, too.

Rochelle pronounced the job pedestrian. "You knock on doors asking people to buy things. It's so demeaning." Rochelle is the ticket taker at Loew's Fox downtown. Minimum wage and half-off at the snack bar. She brings home boxes of Nonpareils, and at night closed in her room brushes all sugar paste from the chocolate. She chews the chocolate by the handful, first picking off the little white balls of paste, rolling them in a shower across the linoleum floor, collecting them on a sheet of folded typing paper and offering them to Joyce. Rochelle eats only the chocolate.

Joyce saw Danny's job as a great adventure. Mysterious apartments, asking a cavalcade of women he didn't know if he could come into their houses, to talk cleaning, scouring, brushing. The way she described it, like a radio show, she sounded like Rick. After dinner Joyce brought her brother the sample case and made him explain the lotions and the sprays and how the needle threader worked. She would pull some gadget from the littered floor of the case, some obvious gadget like the magnetic pin cushion or the eyeglass wipes and say, Okay Mr. Salesman. Show me this.

As father and son leave the house, Mrs. Meadoff calls after them. Remember what I told you.

"What, Ma?"

"Not you. Your father."

They go down the steps together. The morning is warm, full of life. It could be they live in a terrarium. Mr. Meadoff carries a cheap leather portfolio that Danny made for him years ago at Camp Nehoc. Danny stitched together leather flaps with rawhide and on the lower right corner he burned in his father's initials with an electric tool you couldn't use without a counsellor. Danny carries his sample case.

"What did she tell you?" Danny asks.

"Just business," his father answers. Then after a pause, "I'm to say to Lindenauer to go ahead without me. He wants to put up his house, he can do it without me. That's what your mother says remember."

"Mr. Lindenauer is building a house?"

"What?" His father is looking beyond the traffic. When he walks outdoors with his father, Danny notices the limp. Maybe he doesn't limp inside the house. "Oh no," his father says, almost amused. "Nothing. Just business."

"I think I'm going to like business."

"Good. You make a fortune and I'll retire. Someone in this family should make a lot of money."

His father's limp makes Danny taller.

"I've been thinking about investing in stocks, Dad. I think Boeing looks good. Mr. Rappaport is heavily into Boeing."

"He is?" The remark seems to please his father. Danny is gratified. "Heavily, is he? Well good luck to you, Daniel. But before you invest a lot of money, remember to make it."

They come to the subway steps. Danny visualizes his father's office. He was there last on a school holiday. He took his friends up after a triple feature in Times Square. He was surprised. He had been there before, but he remembered it being grander. It was not an office like they have in the movies, the ones that start with an aerial shot of Manhattan, say Van Heflin's office in *Patterns*. Paradise Knitwear was five tiny rooms filled with grey desks and stacks of paper. From the grimy window his father had a view of another window and a concrete wall. It was the kind of place Cagney would break out of.

"I know, Dad. But I'm thinking long-term."

His father looks at him with smiling eyes. Danny thinks for a moment his father is going to say something, but instead he turns and joins the crowd descending the stairs.

Mr. Meadoff stands at the very front of the front car. Lights and the mouths of tunnels go by in newsreel grain. The passing of another train leaves a streak on his retina, a smear that fades even before the plangent screech disappears down the track.

Here is where the Inquisition should have been conducted. Here is where the monk Torquemada and Mengele and Stalin should have done their work. No one would have heard. Or if they did, noticed.

Act as if your body leaves a trail of light. Somewhere he remembers that Talmudic instruction. If my body left a trail of light, a tracing, you could find your way from Brooklyn to Paradise Knitwear. There would be a trail of light like the Milky Way. Except you couldn't see it from the air. You would have to pick up the trail of Meadoff underground.

"Coffee?" asks Bernstein. "No egg creme?"

"Too early," says Danny. "Besides, I'm off to work. Did I tell you? I'm selling Fuller brushes."

"Not to me you're not."

They talk over yesterday's game. Danny reads from the box score in the Mirror. The Dodgers are way out in front.

"So what good is it?" Bernstein asks. "For all their efforts. Who will they play in the Series?"

"Looks like the Yankees."

"And when the Dodgers play the Yankees, who wins? It's like the Israelites against the Pharaoh. Not a question of long odds. Some things are not meant to be."

"The Israelites got away from the Pharaoh."

"Is that the case? You read that maybe in the *Trib*?" asks Bernstein. "Tell me, Meadoff. You are a smart boy. So they got away. Does this look like the Promised Land?"

Danny doesn't answer. He is sure Bernstein is kidding. Life turns and each day is newer than the last. It doesn't look bad to him. That's what Danny tells him, this last, tells him, then lifts the plastic cover from the cake stand and pulls out a jelly doughnut.

"Says you," Bernstein counters. "Why am I behind a counter? Do you think if I called Mr. Harriman and said to him, 'Avrum, I'm exercising my free will. I've decided to have your life a while, you come down here and sell Coronet Magazine,' Do you think he'd agree? Things are decided. He has his fate and I have mine."

Danny eats around the doughnut so the surrounding walls are all but gone and there remains only a womb of raspberry jelly.

"Not so," says Danny. "If the World Series is decided, why do so many people bet on it? Why don't they know, too?" He slips the red bud into his mouth and lets it dissolve.

"Look." Bernstein speaks with the aggravation of certainty. "For years the Yankees beat the Dodgers. They have Mr. Di-Maggio, and he comes in and beats the Dodgers. Finally Mr. DiMaggio is finished. He has troubles. His heel hurts. He dates the blond lady who announces she goes around without underwear. Mr. DiMaggio starts acting like a movie star too, giving his mother who raised him, I'm sure, Catholic ulcers, take my word. So what happens?"

"What happens?" Danny asks.

"The Yankees come up with another. Another Sampson. This Jewish kid."

"The Jewish kid?"

"The Jewish kid from Oklahoma. Mendel. Mickey Mendel. So the Dodgers have to wait up until he meets his Delilah."

Danny finishes his coffee, pays a quarter, puts the *Mirror* back on top of the pile and leaves. Down the street by the subway kiosk Hoot is warming up.

"Hi, Hoot."

"Hey Kid. You blowin' horn?" Hoot points at the large black case Danny carries. He tells him about the job.

"Sweet," Hoot says. Danny is not sure what he means. "Sweet," he says and Danny understands he approves. "Bread jus' fall into your box. You can't be bruised."

Danny tells him about the territory, the products. Hoot nods enthusiastically in a rhythm, up, four-fours.

"Look out," Hoot says. "Startled doe, ten o'clock." Danny sees a handsome black woman in a red dress go by, smiling, down the subway stairs.

"So what do you think, Hoot? This a good job?"

"What do I think? I think you fight for your life, till death do you part, then you got it made."

Hoot licks his reed, comes in two beats this side of the bridge of "Body and Soul." Music disappears into the fragrant morning air. The air you can take in handfuls. Inside the terrarium life stirs. Danny checks his watch. Eight-thirty. Time to go to work. He waves goodbye. Hoot's eyes have closed.

For his first day Danny chooses a part of Brooklyn he knows. On Ocean Parkway stand six- and seven-story apartment houses,

62]

the tan of oatmeal, with mythic names like Argosy and Poseidon and Versailles. Behind the boulevard two-story row houses domino up. The brick of each house is whitewashed except at the corners where the raw red crisscrossing gives the buildings the appearance of being stitched together. Like his father's portfolio. A tidy section that houses tidy and not unprosperous tenants. Look for people who like to sweep up, said Raycroft. He enters the foyer of the first apartment house. The lobby door is closed, locked. Choosing a middle floor he pushes the bell for 3A. No answer. At 3B a voice crackles through the speaker.

"Mrs. Galena? It's your Fuller Brush man."

"Who?"

"Your Fuller Brush man."

"Fuck off."

No one home at 3C. 3D says she'll call the super. Danny leaves. Supers are unpredictable. They speak fragmented English, they haul cans up and down basement steps, ash cans that weigh as much as a body, and they are never without a pipe wrench. Besides there are hundreds of apartment houses on Ocean Parkway.

In the second house, a bit of luck. The lobby door is propped open to let in some air. Again he starts with 3A, this time in person. A polite refusal. Same at 3B and 3C. But at 3D he uses what Raycroft calls a sales aid and it works.

"Hello, Mrs. Koeningsberg. I'm the Fuller Brush man. Just wanted to drop off the catalogue you ordered, see if there's anything I can help you with."

"You know my name? And what catalogue? Who ordered?"

"Mrs. Koeningsberg. Would I come halfway across the city this morning and up three flights for exercise? You must have forgotten. Look, long as I'm here, take a couple of samples. I'm

[63

only supposed to give them out with a sale, but you take them. Lighten my case.''

Danny has maneuvered into the living room. The prints on the walls are of anthropomorphic cats with enlarged, sparkling eyes. They might be mutants. He lets go a volley of words, fearing she might stop him if he takes a breath, fearing she'll ask for the real John Everett Raycroft. Neither happens. He writes up an order for a nylon bristle hairbrush (women's/coral) and a can of air freshener. He asks for the down. She pays in full.

The day goes quickly. Danny begins to relax. Some of the words that come out are his own, and to his delight they do equally well as Raycroft's. He makes an occasional sale, but he is not yet emboldened to spray an unsuspecting foot or massage a wriggling and reluctant hand.

In his zeal he skips lunch. When he needs a bathroom, he cannot bring himself to ask a housewife as Raycroft does. Instead, he goes into a candy store, buys a dish of ice cream, uses theirs. Three scoops of vanilla are bought that day from the down—his money, really. At the end of the day he has booked seventy-five dollars in sales, has collected almost thirty. If he gets paid in full, close to twenty of that will be his.

"It isn't earned yet," Raycroft cautions, "Don't mount your chickens until they're hatched.''

Raycroft is pleased, paternal.

"Another thing. Net out your samples and catalogues. This is Business One, Meadoff. I get charged, you get charged. Net them out. Otherwise, you can give away all your profit.''

It is true. Danny finds it salubrious to hand away samples, forces them on women who want to see him gone, his shy tribute for having rung their bell. The week wears on and Danny walks his territory with more assurance. Down apartment house halls, white and gold fleur-de-lis patterns, Louis Cinque country scenes, antebellum plantations. Down scrubbed blocks of Mediterranean town houses. Every day offers a ganglia of arbitrary paths. Shall he skip this house, this block entirely? Shall he attack 5L with the spilled case or a tale of fatigue and frustration? When you multiply the choices to be made by Daniel Meadoff in a single day, one presence only now pushing down on the earth, add the choices made by the woman in 5L and the woman in 5M, add their husbands and greengrocers and in-laws and the people who sell them rib steaks and who Hollandarize their clothes, the quotient is dazzling. The infinite multiplied by the infinite. Posed is what his geometry teacher would call a problem that cannot compute. The very problem dizzies him with vertigo: the question peers over some cosmic edge. Here he stands, suddenly aware of a capacity, minute but measurable, of displacement. Danny Meadoff has dived into the sea of commerce and the shoreline has imperceptibly risen. It is a paradox; it proves the contrary: displacement in a limitless space means the space is, too, measurable. Measurement becomes a mark of consciousness, of humanness. It is the first paradox Danny has had a hand in—he is proud of the thought, as proud as if it were a lanyard.

Raycroft appreciates his pupil's results, rewards them. His tiny hand dives into a coat pocket like a forest animal, surfaces full of plastic bookmarks on which Fuller Brush is written in gold script. No charge, he tells Danny. To show a job well done. Like a medal, Raycroft says. Instead, Fuller Brush gives bookmarks.

Lindenauer pays an unannounced visit to Paradise Knitwear. He is an owner fifty-fifty with Mr. Meadoff, but he offices somewhere else. Lindenauer is wealthy. Paradise is one of several ventures in the clothing industry. A men's belt manufacturer in New London, New Hampshire, two hosiery factories in the Carolinas, a line of high fashion blouses under the registered mark Debbie Dewdrop. His office answers "Lindenauer Investments." Mr. Meadoff has seen him up and down Seventh Avenue. He roams the garment center like a raptor, ranging vast distances each day in search of enough scurrying life for his meal.

Ten years ago, Mr. Meadoff wanted to expand. In business by himself, he wanted his own private-label operation, but he needed capital. Lindenauer had heard he was a hard worker, he needed money. Lindenauer came to him. Lindenauer would put up the money. Meadoff would run the business. Any debt, they'd sign fifty-fifty. At the closing, Mr. Meadoff realized Lindenauer was providing a source of borrowed funds. But by then Mr. Meadoff had no option. In return for the Lindenauer guaranty of bank loans, without which doubtless the loans would not have occurred, Lindenauer got half of the stock of Paradise Knitwear.

Since then Lindenauer had encouraged him to expand. They pushed up credit when times were good, and they had done well. Three years running they were able to take out of the company more money than Meadoff had aspired to. But starting last year, the retailers seemed to lose their appetites. Large manufacturing commitments arrived in the Paradise warehouse and had to be sacrificed to pay off the factors. There was little left over. Then the factors began cutting back, making it harder for Paradise to sell the same volume in the next round. Mr. Meadoff found that each month his personal debt, the amount of money he had committed to lend to the business, would grow. True, Lindenauer matched him dollar for dollar, but Lindenauer's pockets were deeper. Mr. Meadoff knew enough to avoid a bidding war with Lindenauer. That was a war he couldn't win.

Too, since the business had begun to slip, Lindenauer's behavior had worsened. He had always been rude, presumptuous. He had a way of putting you to work for him. Little things. Hand me that pencil. Tell your secretary no calls till we're through. I've scheduled you for the bank tomorrow. Little charges, nothing big. Like daily interest. But lately, with Paradise Knitwear fighting against the torque of lower capacity and the need for maintaining volume, Lindenauer had turned from haughty to insulting.

Today on his surprise visit he walks through the front door and says nothing. Moves by Mr. Meadoff talking to the bills clerk, goes back to Mr. Meadoff's office. Mr. Meadoff finishes his conversation, follows him in. Lindenauer sits in his seat, reads what is on his desk.

"Who is going to buy this?" he asks Meadoff, jabbing his thumb at a list of manufactured goods. "Come September you are going to be standing on Fortieth and Seventh, giving this away."

"Filene's bought them. Forty-five days. They want again as much."

"They going to pay their bills? You know what they're saying up and down the street about Filene's? Can't pay their bills."

Mr. Meadoff doesn't respond. From his desk drawer he pulls the yellow sheet showing that the factor has picked up 100% of that receivable. Lindenauer studies it silently, breaks open a silver tube and slips out the cigar, puts the cigar in his mouth unlit.

Lindenauer rolls the cigar in his mouth, wetting its tapered end. "What we need, my friend, is more money in this business. I can see it coming. You better be ready. 'Cause I ain't no charity."

Mr. Meadoff rises from his chair. It is grey metal with a green cushion and back rest. He can see through the blinds.

[67

Across the airshaft Morty Kaye of Mortrose Fashions is talking on the phone. Does he have a Lindenauer too? Mr. Meadoff wonders.

When he sits down again, Lindenauer is watching him. Lindenauer sits alert, expectant and holding the unlit cigar by its end, straight up. Perhaps he is about to give a downbeat.

"You know what Lincoln said about capital?" Meadoff asks him. "He said labor is the superior of capital and deserves much the higher consideration. You know why? Because without labor there would be no capital. But not vice versa."

Lindenauer purses his lips. He might be about to play the saxophone, to spit. Instead he puts the cigar in his mouth, stands, and walks out. One of the secretaries comes over and closes the door that Lindenauer has left ajar.

Mr. Meadoff pulls the cord to raise the wooden blinds on his window. Morty Kaye of Mortrose Fashions sits back in his chair, talking on the telephone and slowly twirling the eraser end of a yellow pencil in his ear.

How many trees, says Meadoff aloud, how many trees would my grandfather be able to call by name? How many can I? Ash, beech, birch, catalpa, there must be a D. Elm, eucalyptus, fig, ginkgo. Would I know them? I would not. I would not know them if I met them, if they said to me, Hello Meadoff I am Eucalyptus. I have lived on this earth since before you. I thrive in Tasmania and oil from my bark stimulates wild thought.

I could not say, Of course. I knew that. I saw you coming. I recognized you.

-8-

He studies them. To spy on them is easy, for they are alien to scrutiny. They are parents, they are the watchers, not the watched. How much of the world do they understand? Only when his mother has seated everyone at the table will she rise to carry in the meal. Does she tire of this? Gathers food at the A & P. Lugs it into the house through the attached garage. Cooks it, serves it, clears the plates. Scrapes the leavings, stores the excess, and starts again. What is she thinking when she stands over the kitchen sink, the new stainless steel sink, and peels away the pebbled skin of carrots for the evening's stew?

Danny sits with his father at the enamel kitchen table as the dishes are cleared. Overhead an electric clock set into a red plastic teapot whirs. It could have been a prize at Fascination.

"Here's a problem, Dad. What are the odds of a baseball game repeating itself? You know, where every pitch is the same, ball or strike, and every hit goes to the same spot."

"Couldn't happen," says Joyce. She stands at the dining room buffet putting flatware in the drawer. The sound she makes, a muffled clinking, is a familiar one.

"I'm not saying it could happen. I'm saying it tells you something about the world."

Mr. Meadoff nods slowly. His nod gives the question its gravity. He has been asked for a textual interpretation.

"Everything in the same order? Stolen bases, pitchers from the bull pen?"

"The same."

"Whether the player bats right or left?"

"No," Danny answers. "Just the game. Not the players. Just the action of the game."

After another minute his father says, "I don't know."

"See," says Joyce from around the corner. "I knew it couldn't happen." She enters the kitchen in triumph.

Mr. Meadoff sips from the glass of cooling tea in front of him with a corrugated, surf sound. He unscrews the top of the salt shaker, palms it, puts his two fists before him, presents them to Joyce.

"Pick a hand."

She picks the left.

"What's the chance that you're right?"

"I'm always right," she says.

"What's the chance?"

"Fifty-fifty," Joyce says.

"Right. And what's the chance you'll be right the next time?"

"Fifty-fifty."

"And the chance you'll be right both times?"

"Fifty-fifty," she says smugly.

"Wrong," Danny says. "Twenty-five percent. Your chance on the first times your chance on the second."

"So," his father says, as if that was the conclusion. "So if we knew how many possibilities the first pitch of a baseball game had, we could compute its chances to be a ball or a strike."

"Or a hit," said Joyce.

"Or a hit, grounder to second, pop to right, double, foul ball caught by the third baseman. You need a list. But it could be done. Now you would have the first number. You'd be on your way. Then you have to do the same thing for the second pitch. Maybe it has as many chances. Maybe if the first pitch is a hit and the man is on base, you have a different list."

"Balk," says Danny.

Joyce gets it. "Pitch-out, sacrifice bunt, throw to first to hold the runner," she says.

"But still a number. Now you take the chances for the first number and multiply it by the chances for the second number and you're on your way."

"So you could figure it out?" says Joyce.

"I suppose," says Mr. Meadoff. "I suppose if you had enough paper and time."

Rochelle walks through the kitchen. "That's a perfect job for you, Danny," she says. "That'd be perfect for you and your stupid friends." She passes through and goes up the stairs. Mr. Meadoff looks after her. His eyelids close tentatively. They do not stay closed. Rochelle's passing breaks the mood, and that angers Danny. The full moment of the conversation has subsided. His father had understood. For a brief moment, he, his father and Joyce had tied into a cosmic ride.

"You really could figure it out?" says Joyce. "That's weird. It'd be a big number, though."

Their father turns back to them.

"Yes," he says, but now he is weary when he speaks. "It'd be a big number."

Afterwards, Danny lies on his bed, holding a model of a B-17 Martin Marauder. He considers its construction. Sanding the pre-cut parts to fit, cutting out the template patterns, gluing the plane piece by piece with that wonderful stuff that came in a tube and leaked through the bottom so you'd have to peel the dried glue off like a second skin. And the smell, like a medicine you knew had to be strong. Then you'd sand, start with the coarsest and go to the finest paper, and paint using what they called dope from two-inch bottles. A brush the size of a pen's nib. He'd kept the extra bottles—he had almost enough to camouflage their house in an emergency. Last, the decals. Magically stuck to clear plastic sheets. You cut them apart, pry them off, then carefully, for you only get one shot, fix them to the models. White star on blue background for the U.S., red, blue and yellow targets for the Royal Air Force.

[71

His father has not spoken that much for a long time. Most nights after dinner his father retreats to the desk on the landing and adds columns of numbers. Tonight Danny had him going. The next question was, what are the odds that two people will live the same life. If you can compute a baseball game, shouldn't you do that too?

He noses down the bomber at a severe attitude. It enters a steep bank, sixty degrees, to avoid attack, to give the rear turret gunner a better angle. Plagued by enemy fighters, as the great fish was plagued by sharks. He considers calling Rick when the door to his room opens and Rick walks in. Rick has been showing up often lately, usually for dinner or breakfast. Danny hasn't been to his apartment in months. Just as well. Mrs. Rappaport puts Danny off. She is at you all the time, acting as if you want to have her around.

Downstairs, Danny's sisters are baking cookies and Rick comes in tonguing a gob of new batter on his finger. He points it at Danny, offering a lick. Danny declines.

He tells Rick of his day selling. Rick, jobless, is depressed. He is considering the Catskills. Rick's cousin works as a waiter at Kutcher's and clears a thousand a month in tips.

"It's not only the money," Rick says. "It's the women. What happens is, they come up on Monday and hang around until the weekend without their old man. Nothing to do but play canasta and pick out a bus boy."

"Can I be of service, Madam?" Danny says archly and the two howl in laughter. Rick flops onto the second bed and covers his face with a pillow.

The Meadoff house has four bedrooms on its second story. When they were small, Danny's sisters shared this room, but last year when she turned thirteen Rochelle insisted on her own space. The spare room was converted, to Joyce's dismay for she liked having her sister near. At the time the process puzzled Danny: how do you weigh one daughter's wish to be alone with the other's to stay together? But problems of parenting did not concern him long. They all seemed self-induced. Danny moved into the room with two beds. It faces the east and south prospects of the house, and its windows look down on the long side lawn and the large copper beech. A tree of the imagination.

Rick lies on the spare bed and mumbles into the pillow. Danny cannot understand. He reaches over and tears the pillow off his friend's face. "I said," Rick repeats, "I got something to show you."

Rick's shirt is hanging out of his dungarees. He lifts its tail and pulls a folded magazine from his back pocket. "Wait," Rick says of nothing, for Danny is waiting.

"What?" says Danny. Rick is looking at him with an unmistakable expression

"Wait." Rick sits beside him and slowly turns pages. Phosphorescent photographs of beautiful, naked women. In the center, the pages unfold to a poster. "I can't believe this," Danny says. They have finished leafing through, front to back. "Do it again."

They start at the table of contents. They arrive again at the fold-out. Rick holds it a full arm's length away.

"If I were two feet tall," he says reverently, "she'd be life-size."

"Where'd you get this?"

"My father bought it for me."

"No way. No chance."

"Swear."

Danny is dumbstruck. The news is more shocking than the magazine itself. Rick's father tells the boys an occasional dirty joke, but this gift goes far beyond. He feels a careening surge of envy, a heavy surge that may double his body weight like the pull when an elevator starts.

"My father doesn't know this exists," Danny tells him. Rick gives a smug and knowing nod.

"My father always says he's not only my father, he's my pal. It's brand new. Published in Chicago."

"Wow," says Danny. "Chicago must be something." They continue to turn pages. Golden bodies balloon up from the pages. For the second time that evening Danny is transported. Like the contemplation of probabilities, the magazine propels him aloft, out of the world of Rubbermaid dishracks, of aunts and sisters, away from the aroma of Toll House cookies coming up the stairwell.

"My parents didn't notice?" Danny asks watching to be sure the woman on the page doesn't move.

"Under my shirt. Just said, Hi Meadoffs and kept going. Besides, they never saw me. I think they were having a fight."

"My parents?"

"Yeah."

"They don't fight. About money?"

"Yeah," Rick says.

"They do that these days. Fight about money. We're not supposed to know."

Rick is quiet. Danny waits but nothing comes. Rick always tops him. When Danny mentions his mother's pot roast or his father's pipes, Rick always has a better story. Good or bad, high or low. His mother's pot roast has wine in the gravy. His father's cigars smell worse than anyone's.

"You ever notice," Rick asks, instead. "You ever notice how adults ask questions they know the answers to?"

"What do you mean?"

"They ask, how's school? What are your plans for college? They don't want to hear troubles. 'Well, to tell you the truth, Mrs. Valeriani, I'm bombing out. All my chemistry experiments turn into jizzem and my gym instructor won't pass me unless I kiss him on the mouth.' 'Oh. That's-a nice, Reek. I'm glad you happy.' "

The smell of chocolate and heated dough seeps under the door, thick and furry. Rick grabs the magazine from his friend. "Let's go eat," he says.

"I don't know." Danny feels closed in, overcrowded. He looks up at his shelves. Airplanes peer down from their stands, amongst his favorite books. He knows the location of every book he owns. Could close his eyes and read their titles in order, blindfolded could guess the book from the feel of its cover and spine. Tries it sometimes when he's bored.

"You go," he says. "I'm not hungry." His friend leaves, tromps down the stairs, and he remains in tentative exile.

- 9 -

The train continues past his stop. It is no mistake. Mr. Meadoff knows that it is happening. For all the years of Paradise Knitwear and the years before that he has disembarked at Times Square. This morning he surrenders to the rocking, to the rhythm, and stays in his seat. He finds as they pass through midtown that the crowds leave, that he has the train to himself.

He rides north, the street numbers grow beyond familiarity. Where does it end? He has seen the names of destinations on the front of the trains: Van Cortlandt Park, Woodlawn, Pelham Bay. The bay would be nice. A stroll by the water's edge. Woodlawn, he believes, is a cemetery. It all depends on what line he has boarded, and he does not know for sure. Still, he can stay on, he will know when the train stops moving.

If a fish disappears from the sea, would not the level of the ocean drop? Not much, perhaps, but enough. Just enough to displace the mass of the fish. And a person? If a person disappears?

The train comes to rest in a station and a conductor walks through. "Last stop," he calls to Mr. Meadoff, who nods and departs. On the subway platform, in blue tile, the sign says "Fort Tyron Park" and under that "The Cloisters."

Mr. Meadoff walks out into the day. In office buildings that he left behind him men are looking at their desks. Factors are telling them how much they owe, how much they have to pay. Mortie Kaye next door, even Lindenauer. But not him. He is following the signs to The Cloisters, and he does not have any idea what he will find. It sounds peaceful. Monks, parchment, soft gentile prayers of forgiveness. It sounds made to order.

The walk is longer than he had thought. It is a warm day and he sheds his coat and carries it over his arm. He walks on a path lined with trees full in their summer leaf, and the walk is pleasant. He rounds a curve and there, to his amazement, is a building from somewhere else. He cannot tell why it looks exotic, but it does. Red tiled roof, small arched windows, and a square tower, a tower that must have overlooked vineyards, farms set into the sides of hills. A tower that might house great, tumbling bells. He did not expect this.

He pays his admission fee. The attendant asks if he would like a brochure and, unsure whether there is a charge, he declines. An Oriental couple enters with him. They have a brochure and ask him something in a language that could be English, but he cannot understand. He tries several times to make out their question, but they are growing embarrassed and he excuses himself. Most of the people seem to be going in and out of the various buildings. The day is too glorious for him to be indoors, he determines, and he walks the paths among the gardens. One entire courtyard is filled with rose bushes and he walks among them. Someone has left yesterday's *Daily Mirror* and its pages are beginning to blow among the bushes and their slim stakes. He collects the pages, refolds them around the paper.

Beyond the large building with the tower a long green lawn slopes down to the wrought iron gate. Beyond, he looks over and sees the cliffs of what must be New Jersey. It does not look like the place that houses his mother's nursing home. It looks like a foreign land, a land of space and promise. Although it is only midmorning, he decides to lie down. The grass is deep green, cut short as a carpet. He stretches himself out. The newspaper is still in his hand, he had neglected to throw it in a trash basket. He takes the cover sheet, stiff with the sun, and places it over his face. Underneath the paper he smiles. He hears the buzzing of some insect nearby, perhaps inches away, but he simply smiles.

It is not long before he is roused. He lowers the paper and looks up. The guard is speaking to him. "You can't sleep here, this is not a flophouse." The guard has a gold tooth in his grey face.

"I'm getting up," he says.

"You can't sleep here," the guard says again and places the toe of his black shoe under the thigh of Mr. Meadoff.

"I'm getting," says Mr. Meadoff. "You don't have to nudge me."

"And don't be littering with that paper," the guard says. "It was all over the rose garden."

"I paid my admission," says Mr. Meadoff. "I am not sleeping." He says this with a surprising force. Then he looks up.

Several people are watching, including the Oriental couple. He thinks to explain, then goes out the gate.

When he reaches his office he realizes he is only an hour and a half later than his usual arrival. "Sleep late, Mr. Meadoff?" someone says, and other than that the day seems like every other.

First, deliveries: the completed transaction, the short arc that closes the commercial circle and traps money at the very center. Money pools where the point of the compass punches a hole. All sales stick and the balances are paid. During these first weeks, Raycroft summons Danny regularly to the table overseeing the chrome sweep of Dubroff's. Once Raycroft has determined Danny won't run off with the funds, the meetings fall off. Only Mondays. Unload the orders, pick up deliveries, hand over the cash.

Raycroft eggs him on. Be more aggressive. Push the cleaning line. How could you take yesterday off? They'll buy when the old man's home just to get rid of you. S.O.S., Meadoff. Sell on Sundays.

It is a Friday. An inevitable heat has rolled into Brooklyn, heavy as a moving truck, parked the length of the curb. Danny works Shore Parkway, a pretty section with large apartment houses bordering on a park, each with a wary doorman who must be eluded. From the sidewalk he gazes over the highway at the Narrows, where barges and freighters are stuck to the horizon. The day smells of heat, gasoline, sea air. He has developed his own strategies for gaining entry. He helps tenants with packages, greets strangers warmly. Today entry is not his problem. Today he cannot seem to make a sale.

Raycroft has given him advice for these times too.

"When all else fails, stutter. 'M-M-Madam, I'm with the Fu-Fu-Fu-Fuller Brush Company.' People don't like to be cruel. They'll buy. See what you learn from me," he says, poking Danny's arm. "I should charge tuition."

Whatever embarrassment Danny first suffered has evaporated. He tries Raycroft's pose, reads a credible role, makes no sales. On the top floor of one house a woman asks Danny if he would like a cup of coffee. He sits in her kitchen of checkered curtains and Aunt Jemima pot holders and blows across the steaming cup. She buys twenty dollars and pays in cash. She is blond, not old, neither fat nor thin but unyieldingly unattractive. Danny tries to determine why. Set too high on her face are lifeless eyes. Their pink lids blink constantly in the reflected fluorescent. Is she in fear? She looks like a tropical fish, he decides, not a person. An albino gourami.

It is pleasant to sit in this woman's cool and orderly kitchen and talk with her. She asks about his work, whether he likes it, where it takes him. When he writes up the order, she tells him her name. Frances Gunnerson, she says. Mrs. Frances Gunnerson.

Few other sales. Danny walks listlessly through his rounds, decides to give himself the rest of the day off. Saturday his father will be home. Angie is selling ice cream out in Rockaway Beach and Rick has hitch-hiked up to the mountains. He'll sleep late and watch the game with his father.

He finds no one else to listen to his pitch. He considers the Raycroft stammer, but has no enthusiasm to try it again. Odd. He went through a time when he favored handicaps. Sat at the dinner table for a week with a facial tic no one noticed. Last January he found a single black leather glove and wore it without explanation to classes, avoiding the use of his left hand entirely.

[79

That evening he calls Rick's house to see if they know when Rick will be home. His mother answers. He is wary. She can turn aggressive, seductive, maternal in the same minute. Today her voice is low and gravelly.

"Any word from Rick, Mrs. Rappaport?"

"Any word, Danny darling? Any word? Yes. The word is Shit. He's right here, Marco Polo the world traveller. Hitch-hiking, I don't have enough grey hair. Rick," she calls, "it's that handsome friend of yours." Back to the mouthpiece. "You know what I think, Daniel? I think he went up there to get laid. But he couldn't find any action so he came home. Here, I'll put him on."

Rick gets on. No luck, zero, zip, nada. No jobs. Try later in the season.

Danny lies in bed that night, considers the ocean that is his week-end. Sleep into the morning, get up and read some favorite chapter. Maybe in *The Count of Monte Cristo* or *Two Years Before the Mast*. His versions have full-page illustrations—they are abridged, children's editions—and the parts he likes explain the pictures. Maybe a little radio. Radio used to be terrific. The joy of being sick from school. His mother was terrified of po-lio—if it can happen to the President of the United States it can happen to anyone—and her fear turned a sniffle into a day's convalescence. Daytime radio was a parade of afflictions. Home just for the day, you weren't able to follow one story through its inconclusive months. But it was equally satisfying to hear all the stories briefly. Disappearances, divorces, inheritances. Ra-dio lives had nothing to do with his, the Meadoffs, the family of an importer of knit underwear. The commercials especially were peopled by foreigners. Women who greeted each other over backyard fences and talked cheerfully about washday dis-coveries, women who dropped into each other's kitchens con-spiring like Bolsheviks to improve their coffee and their home permanents. It all took place somewhere else. Missouri or Oregon or Babylon.

That night Danny wakes to the silence of the large house. He lies still and listens for the noise of the avenue, blocks away, but there is no sound. He rises and walks to the window looking down on the side yard. The tree stands mute and the shadows are undisturbed. For some reason, he is not assured by what he does not see. Yet he goes back to bed, pulls the cotton sheet to his chin, and easily finds sleep.

Danny's morning does not go as planned. It is eight-thirty when Rick bursts in, imitating Art Carney bellowing for Gleason.

"Hey, Ralphie boy. Wait'll you get a load of this. It's the best idea I had since canoe racing in the sewers. Come on, up and out."

Covers are pulled off, clothes thrown at him, Danny staggers to his feet and begins to dress.

"Tell me if this isn't a stroke of brilliance," Rick asks. "What do you have that I don't?"

"Good looks, brains, a twelve-inch cock."

"Serious. Be serious. A job. That's what. Now you have a territory you can't cover in a million years. All of Brooklyn."

"Not all," says Danny. "A piece. Raycroft just hired another kid."

"A big piece. Same thing. So what's the only bad thing about your job. Good money, on your own, an entrepreneur. Think. What are you missing?"

Danny shrugs.

"Your pals," Rick announces. "Your friends. You never get to see them. So, here's the deal. We work for you. Angie and

I. Your boss doesn't have to know. The three of us hit a territory, blanket it, one for all and all for one. We meet at lunch, compare notes, see who gets the most sales. You report all our sales as your sales. We triple your output.''

"Angie's got a job. At Riis Park.''

"That's why you're dressing, Ralphie boy. Sometimes I think you take stupid pills. We're going out there and get Angie and get him on board so we can S.O.S.''

"S.O.S.''

"Sell on Sunday. Get your Fuller Brushes here. Tomorrow the three Musketeers hit Bensonhurst.''

Danny dresses, puts on a bathing suit and pulls chinos over it. They eat breakfast, Rick for the second time that day, and set out.

"Why are we doing this?'' Danny asks as the bus crosses the bridge to Breezy Point. "Why don't we just call him?''

"Because I tried, he's already gone. Besides, you wanna convince Angie, you gotta get him face to face.''

Eleven o'clock by the time they reach the boardwalk. The papers have promised a scorcher for this first day of July. People strewn everywhere, an amphibious assault. Some down on the beach, the first casualties. Others on foot, packing in: the infantry. They carry umbrellas, beer, coolers, rafts, salamis, battery radios tuned to William B. Williams and the Make-Believe Ballroom. Cameras, baguettes, pink spaldeens, diapers, netted Provolone cheeses, plastic shovels, webbed chaise lounges, umbrellas. The food stands hawk hot dogs, egg roll, knishes, french fries, ice cream twenty-eight flavors, flavor of the month Cherry Marshmallow.

"Herring?'' Rick says to the counterman. The counterman is dressed in white. He wears a white soldier's cap, white with lime green trim and on the front of his uniform is written Howard Johnson's in script. He has one gold tooth, an upper canine, and he keeps his tongue on it to shield it from the heat of the grill. With the ease of a gleaming spatula he turns a row of plump kosher dogs. They spit grease and glow red, but they turn.

"Whaddaya mean?"

"You got twenty-eight flavors ice cream, you got herring?"

"Beat it, kid."

They ask around to find Angie. Are told he's working Bay Twelve, far end of the Park. The beach miles long and two city-blocks wide. Jetties divide it, constructions of logs each thicker than a man, pile-driven into the sand as a tide break. Kelp has gathered on the jetties, studded with strings of mussels and glued together by oil flushed from the holds of tankers, and the roped logs shine black and green in the sun. Rick and Danny stash their sneakers, chinos and shirts under the boardwalk and trudge ankle-deep across the hot sand toward Bay Twelve.

On the horizon they spot their pal. He is the modern water bearer. Each of his shoulders is creased by a wide, webbed strap from which depends a black tin box the size of a two-suiter. Angie stands astride a beach pebbled with bodies, at its very crest where the tide has subsided and the sands that slope down to the water are dark. Sunlight comes off the ocean liked a skipped stone. Angie doesn't see Rick and Danny. He is looking only for waving hands. As they approach they hear him shout,

"Heyice cream. Heyice cream here."

The call strikes them as funny, and they begin to laugh. As they catch their breath, Angie lets go again.

"Getcha ice cream here."

Finally he fixes on them and slogs through sands that cover his high-top Keds.

"Great. Great. Out for a swim?"

"No, brother," Rick intones somberly. "We have come to save your soul. Save you from this awful fate."

"This isn't so bad. Picks up after lunch. Hot day, I'll sell." He stops to hand a child an orange creamsicle. The kid takes a step, drops two nickels of his change into the sand. Angie goes to his knees, sifts through, comes up with the coins and the kid is on his way again.

Rick explains the scheme. Angie is unconvinced.

"Hey, listen. I'd rather be here. Whenever I want I can sneak a smoke, have a Dixie cup, take a dip."

"Valerio, you *are* a dip. What about one for all and all for one. What about going to Pamplona and running with the bulls?"

Angie does brisk business as they talk. People come up to him, and pick their way through the cardboard, wooden spoons in flimsy paper, dry ice in his cases.

"Lemme try this," Rick says. "I can do this." Angie slings a strap from his shoulder and hands the case to Rick. Rick sticks his arm through, staggers under the weight, does an elaborate pratfall onto the sand. Two pretty girls on a nearby blanket laugh. He gets to his feet and calls in Angie's exaggerated voice.

"Heyyice cream."

Rick makes his first sale, is off again, carrying one of the boxes. "Heyyice cream. Getchyo red hot yice cream. Fun in the sun. All proceeds to the Jacob Riis Scholarship Fund. Heyyice cream."

Rick sells out his supply and hurries back to his friends. "I'm on my way. That Coup De Ville, maybe with a monogram. How much did I make, Paisan?" He hands Angie a pocketfull of bills and coins.

"Maybe a buck. Figure a buck a box."

"What? You nuts? I bust my ass selling ice cream for that? Come on Valerio. Mops cost six ninety-five, am I right, Meadoff?"

"Minimum."

"Minimum. You get a twenty percent commish. That settles it. Let's eat the ice cream, drink the wine. Head for Pamplona. There'll be a swell fiesta in Pamplona."

Angie stares at them for a moment, drops his case, strips off shirt and chinos to a bikini suit underneath and runs with a yell into the water. They follow him, cannot keep up. He swims beyond them. They let him go. The lifeguard perched in the pyramid chair on Bay Twelve whistles him back. Too far, they hear the megaphoned voice.

They come out. The air dries their bodies, leaving salt on the skin. Angie is committed.

"Now to tell my boss."

The administration and catering offices are in the far side of the single structure that also serves as a bathhouse. It is a building of a curious architectural awareness so distant, the building must have a design, but it is hard to link to function or history. Narrow, flat, in crescent shape. Its brick walls were long ago painted white, but the brick color is now reemerging in blotches as the salted air works off the paint. Its roof is a green, overlapping tile. Two octagonal towers that might be minarets sit at either end, each with a small blocked window facing blindly to the sea.

Angie walks the boys through a maze of offices, refrigerators, store rooms. He carries the empty tin boxes by the straps. They enter a tiny office where a large, rounded shape is punching keys on a Freidan adding machine.

"Mr. Kalijian, it's no good."

"What's not?"

Mr. Kalijian is a dark man, powerful. Clumps of grey hair spring at the vee in his shirt like pfitzers. The hair threatens to overtake the shirt, to bury it in growth. "The job. I can't sell any ice cream. I'm not cut out for it." "You outa you fucking mind?" "Nope. It's just, nobody's buying." "Nobody's buying? I don't believe my fucking ears. There gonna be a hunnit thousan' people out there today. It's the hottest day of the year. They're gonna kill for ice cream. It's the fucking Fourth of July week-end."

Mr. Kalijian has risen from his chair and walked around the desk. He stands on curls of adding paper coming out of the machine, and in one hand he shakes loose pages like a tambourine. The movement of his legs and arms riffle in paper.

"Yeah, well . . . look. I'm paid through yesterday. I'll check in my bank and they can inventory me there." Angie has a friendly way of speaking. You would never think it was bad news.

"I'm warning you, kid. This will go on your fucking record. You walk now you'll never hear the end of it. It'll keep you outa college."

"Medical school," says Rick. "He's on his way to Johns Hopkins."

"It'll keep you outa medical school," Mr. Kalijian corrects himself, happy for the advice. He is yelling now. "I'll fucking see to it. You can't do this to me. You can't do this to Howard Johnson's."

"Mr Kalijian," Rick says softly. "We appreciate the spirit in which you're taking this."

But for the three of them and the driver, the bus heading back across Jamaica Bay to Brooklyn is empty. Danny tells Angie and

Rick about Frances Gunnerson. They don't get it. He can see that. On the surface there is nothing to tell. She bought some brooms, she sat with him at a glass breakfast table. This table, you could see through, like a fish tank, to the wrought iron frame below and the yellow and green seat covers in a tropical pattern and her sad pink satin slippers, new-looking but frazzled, as if she wears them all the time. He tells them this but it's hard to explain the significance, even to your friends. They like events: where you went, what you got on a theme paper, what was the final score.

They listen. Rick makes remarks, but Danny's story slices through those. Rick can be hard to talk to. When you tell a story to Rick it always gets down to whether you won or lost. The darkest egg cream, how many pretty girls at your subway stop. Once at the RKO Ditmas he had them all count the licorice pieces in their Good & Plenty boxes. The easiest thing, Danny decides, is to ignore him.

Angie listens. Every now and then he nods. Especially when Danny tells about how her eyes look. Red and wet. They always look as if she just stopped crying.

"Maybe she has conjunctivitis," Angie says. His voice is pliant with concern. "There's a lot of that going around."

Sunday Danny tells his mother he's going out for breakfast.

"Out? On a Sunday, maybe you're Bernard Baruch? You need a solid meal to start the day, Daniel. You hear what I'm saying to you?"

He takes the oath of a good breakfast and leaves.

He is early at Bernstein's. Hoot is in the street setting up. A reed sticks to his tongue and he flashes it at Danny like an insect. Hoot is almost six feet, but he slumps as if he's sick. Do colored people get flushed or pale? Danny wonders. If not how can their mothers tell when they're sick? In his house flushed or pale gets you through triage, gets you the next lab test: a wrist across the forehead. A warm brow fails, and you are home for the day. Pass and you're healthy. In his family a dead child, cool to the wrist, could still have perfect attendance. Receive a certificate at final assembly signed by the principal.

Hoot is in a short-sleeved shirt, light blue with dolphins on the pocket, long tan pants. Even in summer, he wears a grey knit vest with wooden buttons and a leather cap. His face is sharp, and the bones in his skull could be made of tin. The glove-soft brown of his skin is mellow, calming, and when his face is at rest he looks kindly. But most of the time kindness is chased by the red of his eyes and the anger of his mouth. Throughout the day he buys a can or two of Kirsch's No-cal Black Cherry Soda from Bernstein, drinks a long swig, then replaces what's gone from a bagged bottle he keeps in his alto case. He speaks only to the newsstand man, Sarge, and to a select group of kids. Danny is pleased to be one of them.

"Hey Hoot."

"Hey Kid."

"How you feeling today?"

"Out. Missed my man last night. Missed my medicine."

"Oh," says Danny. "Sorry to hear you're sick." Hoot is fingering the keys of his horn, running up and down achromatic scales, looking for something.

Danny tells Hoot about taking in his pals.

"So?" Danny says at the end.

"What you mean, 'so'?"

"So do you think it's a good idea?"

"Hey man, how would I know? How you gonna know till you try it?"

"Yeah, but what do you think?"

"Shit, man. Look around you. You see my band? You see all them cats? This is my band, you dig? That way, someone hits a bad note, I don't have to guess who."

Danny goes in and sits at Bernstein's counter until his friends arrive.

"God," says Rick. Bernstein is in the back room. Rick takes a pack of Chesterfields from the rack, strings it open, offers it around. Danny and Angie pass. He lights up.

"God. Did you see Faye Emerson on TV last night. If that dress was any lower and any higher, it'd be a belt."

Bernstein emerges. They order coffee and pick doughnuts from the round plastic cake salver.

"Quick," Rick calls. "Three best bodies on the silver screen."

"Ava Gardner, Terry Moore, Jane Russell," says Danny.

"Jane Russell no," Rick says. "Old, she looks like Mafia. She could be Angie's uncle."

"You said bodies."

"Valerio."

"Monroe—you gotta have Monroe—Sophia Loren, Anna Magnani."

"Not bad," Rick says. "Weighted towards the Mediterranean but not bad. The correct answer is," he says with suspense, "La Monroe, Ava and Debbie Reynolds."

"Best outfield playing today," says Angie.

"Easy," says Rick. "Musial, Williams and Mantle in center."

"Mantle," they both cry. Angie puts his hand on Rick's head and squeezes.

"Not a Dodger in the group," says Danny. "Rappaport, you're ashamed of your country of origin. What field?"

"Ebbets," Angie says.

"Then you need Furillo. I give you Musial for left, Snider in center and Furillo to play the scoreboard. No one better."

"Close," says Angie, "but no cigar. The correct answer is Snider in center, Furillo in right, and Robinson in left."

Danny beats on the counter with his palm. Angie's solution is ingenious. Rick protests.

"Robinson's an infielder, for Chrissakes."

"Where did he play last night?"

"Left. But he's over the hill. He played his best at second. Nineteen forty-seven to fifty."

"I didn't say where they played their best. I just said playing today."

Rick is trapped by the premise. Danny pounds again in applause.

"An all-Brooklyn team. Valerio," Rick says, "you're amazing. I'm surprised you didn't come up with three Italians. Dimaggio, Furillo and Al Gionfriddo. An all-spaghetti team."

Angie is pleased. He has bested Rick. He reaches over and palms Rick's head like a melon, pounds his one hand with the fist of the other.

Danny spreads out on the neighboring booth. He divides his samples into three, his pamphlets and catalogues. He shows them the day's area. They are to start together, watch him make a few calls. Once trained, they'll work down the blocks behind Utica, walking parallel, meet at noon.

No horsing around: he could get fired if Raycroft finds out.

Rick and Angie stand on the sidewalk for the first call, but Rick cannot keep still. He needles the woman for turning them down. Soon he has everyone laughing. She takes a bottle of chrome cleaner for one ninety-five.

"O.K.," he announces. "I'm ready."

"You don't want to see another few?"

"Are you kidding? What's to see?"

They split up. Danny has a poor morning. When they meet for lunch no one has sold much. But the afternoon is better, and the idea looks promising. They have agreed to pool the profits, work the same hours. His father would be pleased. Enterprise modified with cooperation. Neither capitalism nor socialism. Common sense, his father would say.

- 10 -

Danny knocks each day out. Drives the days, spraying them to the outfield in looping arcs, catch-a-fly-you're-up. The papers say that Walter O'Malley is threatening to pull the Dodgers out of Brooklyn unless someone builds him a new stadium. Speculate he may, thirty-two thousand seats aren't enough. It is, the boys decide, a bluff. Unthinkable. Let him try moving the White House to Asbury Park. You could re-route that upstate river through the Bronx, Rick argues and they are convinced, you could still call it the Niagara, but you won't get anyone to go see it.

Put aside the threat of catastrophe; Danny is disturbed that the owner of his team is a heathen. That doesn't happen to the Yankees. The Yankees' owner has regular at-bats in Earl Wilson's column, chatting with Thomas E. Dewey or having drinks at the Stork. O'Malley is a heathen, a mug. It brings no comfort that their Dodgers sit comfortably on top of the league. Bernstein is right. The fall will bring the inevitable confrontation, the inevitable denouement. Is it better to avoid adversity than confront it and be vanquished?

" 'If I had never met the fish,' " Rick instructs them, " 'I would not have lost him to the sharks. But he was a great fish.' "

The Dodgers are not Danny's only concern. In his new role he supervises his friends. Raycroft thrills to the inflated numbers he brings in, showers him with samples then charges his account. But Rick is quickly bored with the routine and Danny wonders how long he will last.

And there is the dinner table. A chill ripples through whenever the price of anything is discussed. All the players tense, like a young team in a big game. His sisters wear glasses to read, and Mr. Meadoff announces at dinner they should get their prescriptions checked before school starts. Rochelle complains, "School just ended. You shouldn't talk about when it starts. It's a jinx." Joyce agrees. His mother nods over a cold roast chicken. It is unclear what she agrees with.

"And we'll send the bills to Lindenauer."

"Miriam, please," his father says. "These are their eyes. We are talking about our children's eyes." The chicken is served, and Mr. Meadoff does not eat anything.

Danny watches the signs. When he goes to the ball park he often tries to decode the signals the third base coach flashes to the hitter. Concealed in a filibuster of nulls, of empty moves, is the word: belt tug, cap off, ear pull, cap on, right shoulder, top button. Now Mrs. Meadoff responds with a shrug, a lip curled inward, eyes rolled to seek help in the cracks of the ceiling plaster. Is the debate ended? Postponed? His father signals back. Danny tries to steal the signs. The talk settles back to Rochelle's needs for summer camp, Joyce's reading schedule.

Family grievances are not shaken out or dry-cleaned. They suspend in the gel of the air. They cling to the draperies and blinds, they wrinkle the summer slip covers on the matched sofa and chairs in the living room, they slow the hinges of the screen door. His mother inflects by placement of a soup plate. His father replies with the clink of spoon on china. There are secrets in the sounds as his father drinks his soup, messages in the silences between the sounds.

And it is the silences Danny must listen to, the puffs of air that slip from the mouth's corner, the ordinary spaces of eating, sipping, sleeping.

.

Delivery days substitute cash for surprises. Danny saves Frances Gunnerson's order for last.

She lives in a sunny apartment off Shore Parkway. It has a view of Owl's Head Rock, the Narrows filled with ocean traffic, New Jersey beyond. If you lean off the balcony, she shows him, you can see the Statue of Liberty.

She is happy to see him, she says, and when she smiles she is almost pretty. Her face has no shading. It is all a single white, a single consistency like the trim you would cut from a ham, but when she smiles you see the pale pink of gums, large gums that show as much as the teeth do. It is an appealing color, that lively pink, say, for a bathtub, but you do not expect to find it in someone's mouth.

She stands at the counter making coffee.

"Or would you rather have milk? Or a Pepsi?"

"Coffee's fine," Danny says. Coffee advances his age. He seats himself at the see-through table as she fills a small aluminum percolator.

Frances joins him and stacks the boxes he has brought on the table in front of her. This could be a birthday party, she says cheerfully. One guest and the birthday girl has bought herself all the presents. She opens each box, examines its contents, reads labels to him. He tries to match her enthusiasm for the E-Z wax shoe polish and the Silver Sparkle stove cleaner.

She wants to know whether she should order more and he agrees to leave the New Product insert.

"I had no idea," she says, studying a bottle of window spray, "you had so many items. I mean, you have much more than brushes, don't you."

"Yes," Danny admits. He wants her to understand the company is not his. It is not he who has thought up the four-point plan to make the housewife's burden easier. Somewhere in Hartford he envisions workers stuffing boxes, cutting bristle, executives dreaming up snappy names.

She wears a loose flowered robe with ribbon lapels, sashed at the waist. Beneath, for the robe is too large for her and tied so that it billows when she sits, beneath she wears a white slip, blanched and white, only a tone more vital than her skin.

"You know," she says and rises with her emptied cup, "I believe I'll have a glass of wine. Would you like to join me? I guess you're a little young for wine."

"Oh no," Danny says. "I have wine all the time. But not now, thanks. I'm on the job." He has heard Jack Webb decline a drink with that very line. Mrs. Gunnerson moves to the refrigerator. All the appliances are a pale green—avocado, she told him when she was ordering the stove cleaner.

"You have brothers and sisters, Danny?"

He says yes and names them. "And you, Mrs. Gunnerson?" He hesitates, not sure whether he has asked about her siblings. "Do you have children?"

She has taken a long, graceful bottle from the refrigerator. It runs with sweat. She wipes the moisture with a fresh dishtowel, puts the towel in a corner hamper, unscrews the top of the bottle and pours into a tulip glass. His mother would hang that towel inside the door under the sink. It is, after all, perfectly clean. He admires Mrs. Gunnerson. The wine has a bright, plastic color. Strawberry. She puts the glass on the table, at her place but more in the middle, as if it might be for someone else, and walks back to the counter.

He guesses the question he has asked was the wrong one. She recaps the bottle, places it slowly in the refrigerator, comes and sits down.

"It's a rosé," she says.

"Sounds French."

"Yes."

"Wine is one of France's chief exports," he tells her. The subject came up in the seventh grade.

"I'm sure that's so," she says. "Are you taking French in school?"

"No, Spanish. My friends and I take Spanish so we can speak it to each other. Like a code." He is sorry for his exaggeration but cannot get it back.

"Someday you must learn French. A good part of the world's great literature is in French. Baudelaire, Mallarmé, Flaubert. Have you ever heard of Madame Bovary?"

"I think so," he says. "I think they're reading her in senior year."

Mrs. Gunnerson slides the wine glass from the center of the table towards her. Moisture from the air beads on the bulb of the glass. She fetches a cloth napkin and places it under the glass. Then she takes her finger and runs lines from lip to stem. The beads coalesce, run down the stem, blot on the napkin. The napkin is printed with nautical flags.

"It's only three-thirty," she says. "I don't usually do this, but today is like a celebration, isn't it?"

"Oh yes," Danny says. "A birthday party."

Finally she takes a sip. A long one. She sets the glass back on the soggy napkin.

"Now," she speaks in a teacher's voice, "tell me about your sisters."

He looks at her. She seems to have changed expression. The crease where brow meets nose has filled in, as if someone ran a thumb over a crack in moist clay, and there is a sleight tremble in her sable eyes before they tune him in. Like the test pattern. When the Meadoffs got their first television set, Danny would awaken to see the test pattern come on. Before six there would be static, snow they called it, chaos. Promptly on the hour the test pattern would appear. Then for the first minute or two it would wander a millimeter right or left. Danny wondered why but there was no one to ask. Her eyes have the same impalpable uncertainty.

If he is to sell anything today he should go. Deliveries have taken almost seven hours. He reflects for a moment and decides to stay.

He finds himself talking to Mrs. Gunnerson about Joyce, about what a great kid she is but no one sees it because she's no trouble. Rochelle is moody and they're on him about his friends and his future, so they spend mercifully little time on Joyce. Mrs. Gunnerson gives out little noises to show she follows.

"We used to go to this cornball place in the Finger Lakes. For vacation. Since the business difficulties—my father is having business difficulties—we haven't gone. My mother thought it was a better class of people than the Catskills, but I guess it was pretty much the same. When everyone there is looking for a better class of people, that tends to make it the same class. The guests pack themselves with food—it's American plan. Three meals a day. Snacks in between. Snacks mean herring, cold cuts, potato salad. And waiter, just a little slice of the honey cake.

"Anyway, one night we're up late, Casino Night, and Joyce and I are sitting on the front porch and I'm showing her the Big Dipper. Well she couldn't see it. I pointed out every star and she saw the stars O.K., but she couldn't see the picture. We try for maybe half an hour, and finally she says, oh yeah, I see it. But I could tell she didn't. She just wanted me to be happy.

"Then about half a year later, we're back in Brooklyn. Winter. It must be two in the morning. I'm dead asleep. She comes into my room and pounds on me. I thought the house was on fire. 'Danny, Danny, come on, come on.' So I get up and we go out on the lawn, and it's freezing cold. And she points up. 'There,' she says. 'There it is. The Big Dipper.'

"She was so excited. Course, it's been there all along, but she got so excited."

The All-Star Game passes, summer slipping through cracks, water spilled on a boardwalk, water into sand. At home Mr. Meadoff appears less often. He leaves early, misses dinners. He is sinking from sight.

One night in Mr. Meadoff's presence Joyce and Rochelle begin the debate about Nehoc. This year as an economy their mother has announced they are attending camp only for August. Rochelle complains: all the friendships will have been made. Joyce doesn't want to go at all.

"Nehoc's not even Indian," she argues without focus. "It's just the owner's name spelled backwards."

Mrs. Meadoff declares she will send no child who is not appreciative. She gets no gratitude, only relieved silence. Mr. Meadoff says nothing. He listens to the talk and rocks gently in his chair.

[97

Late that night Danny raises himself from the bed. Something pulls him to the window, a sense of kinship or peril. He does not know the time, cannot see the dial on the clock radio. Years ago he and Rick scraped the luminous paint off the hands for some experiment. He wanders softly to the window's sill. There, not fifty feet away through slats of ash wood, in the flat moon of July, a figure stands under the copper beech. This night there is reflected light, although still the figure seems to stand in a pool of blackness, and this night Danny has been awake and. knows he is not dreaming. His father stands under the ribbed shadows of branches, stands in silence and looks out, over the rooftops, where there is nothing to see.

- 11 -

His pals begin to lose interest. There are no assignations and few sales. Each morning they arrive later for their rendezvous at Bernstein's. Danny sits at the counter, spinning the chrome stool. He checks the cleavage in yesterday's *Post*, reads the sports pages, shoots the breeze with Hoot, who drinks his morning coffee thickened to soup with cream. This morning in Earl Wilson's column Danny reads about an asbestos heir who is marrying for the eighth time.

"Why do people marry?" he asks Hoot.

"Loneliness. They needs to be with someone when they loneliness sets in." Hoot smokes Pall Malls. He holds one berry-red between his first two knuckles. Its ash stacks up in an imperfect column.

Danny remains puzzled. It is clearly not carnal. He knows too many bloodless people who are married. Perhaps it is like needing two hands for some jobs. One to hold the nail and one to wield the hammer. Hoot's answer does not help. Danny cannot see a connection.

Hoot leaves, goes out to play. When his friends arrive, Danny asks them the same question. "Why do you suppose people get married?"

"That's nothing," says Angie. "A chocolate soda with vanilla ice cream is a black cow. But a vanilla soda with chocolate ice cream has no name. Why do you suppose that is?"

Rick is reading the *Mirror*. The racing forms.

"Ever been to the track?" Rick asks. No one has.

"Let's go," he says.

They can't go today. Today they have deliveries. Pick up from Raycroft at noon, split the goods three ways. Deliveries go faster with the three of them.

"Tomorrow then," says Rick. "Let's go tomorrow. What's the good of being an entrepreneur if you can't take a day off and go to the track?"

The idea rings with adventure, freedom. They forget the territory and instead group around Rick and his open *Mirror*. Bernstein comes over, explains stakes races, weight allowance, what the records mean. You can't do anything without the morning line. Tomorrow's line, he tells them, won't be out until that afternoon. The *Morning Telegraph* will be on the street at four, the *Mirror* early edition at ten-thirty. You get the morning line you figure to bracket your money.

"We'll hit it then," says Rick. "Here at four and figure the morning line."

Bernstein is proud of his work. "You're sounding authentic. Like real players."

"That's us." says Rick. "We'll be players."

They push him. How are the odds? Is it smart to play the double, to cross the board, to hedge? Do you have a better chance with the numbers?

[99

"Nobody makes a living off numbers. That's for *patzers* and the colored. You boys are smart. You study the form charts, you'll learn fast. There are people make a decent living at the track."

Rick shakes the paper to see if a tip will fall out.

"Just what my father says," he tells them. "You got to play smart. Play with the odds. Make them work for you. All business is is odds. Once you understand that, you got the world by the tail."

"You get the world by the tail," Danny says, "it'll dump on your hand."

"The trouble with you Meadoff is a literal mind."

They leave the store. Around the corner at the light, Rick gathers them around and crowds them close. He lifts up his shirt with one hand and catches his loot with the other. A pack of Chesterfields falls to the sidewalk. There are two candy bars, a pack of gum and more cigarettes.

"Rick, you nuts?" Angie says. "You're knocking off Bernstein?"

"What difference? You know how much he makes on a vanilla coke? You know how much soda water costs? We're just getting even on our money."

Angie is put off. "Still, it's Bernstein."

"Don't be a bloody steer, Valerio. You remember? Pamplona? They put the steers in with the bulls to quiet them down so they don't use their horns against each other."

"That's not the point, Rappaport."

"It is the point. *Claro que sí.* I give you my two friends. One is a literalist and one is a fascist. Do not be a bloody fascist. I obscenity the facists. Have an Almond Joy."

Angie receives a candy bar and Danny a pack of Raleigh cork tips.

"Now," says Rick. "Let us go out to the streets of Brooklyn. Perhaps we will meet a woman without age who will buy our brushes."

The boys board the subway and get off arbitrarily in the heart of a new territory. Only an hour left to the morning, they spend it rambling through squat apartment houses in the Stuyvesant area and to their amusement do well. Women they find at home are pliant in the heat. It is too hot to resist. The day promises hotter. The summer has been kind so far, the warmth terrestrial, tolerable. Today the sun shines as if it is closing in on them, perhaps the days of the planet are numbered, and the city streets respond and soften. If the world is to end in conflagration and the rock of earth to melt, Brooklyn's streets could go first.

When they meet for lunch and deliveries, Rick announces a surprise. His mother is coming. She has offered to drive them around. Danny and Angie are genuinely pleased, but Rick apologizes.

"That's being an only child for you." Rick makes the point before anyone else does. They sit on a low brick wall waiting for Mrs. Rappaport. Angie carries a small rubber ball that he squeezes to strengthen his forearms, and to kill time they toss this against the house behind them.

"Being the only child, you guys don't know," Rick goes on. "When I was a kid everyone tells you, look out, you'll get spoiled. Your aunts, your teachers, the goddam nurse at school when you get stitches in your foot. Like it's their business. I don't know what they expect you to do about it. You supposed to buy a brother?

"You want to know what I thought? I thought it was like fruit. I thought that's what they were talking about. When my parents were out I would go into their room and stand in front her dressing mirror—it had three panels. I'd strip down and try to see if my ass had dark soft spots. That's where I thought they'd be. When pears spoil they go soft on the bottom, where they sit in the bowl.''

The boys look at each other. Angie shakes his head with respect.

''You wanna hear something?'' Angie says. His voice is somber and confidential. They lean to hear him, a tepee for whispers. ''I thought, in the Lord's Prayer, they were warning us. Lead us not into Penn Station. What did I know?

''The first time I had to change trains at Penn Station? We were going to a Knicks game, and my brothers said we had to change at Penn Station. Christ, was I scared.''

They sit shaking their heads with increasing solemnity. Finally, with a cry Rick pushes Angie over and Danny jumps on. When Mrs. Rappaport finds them they are a tangled pile.

''You boys going queer?'' she asks from behind a receding push-button window.

Angie, on top of the pile, untangles the other two and smoothes back his hair.

''Hello Mrs. Rappaport'' he says.

''Sylvia'' she coos. ''Sylvia you call me, now that you're filling out your BVD's.''

Danny and Angie hurry into the back seat, Rick gets into the front, and they are off.

The car is a Buick Century. The '55 model. Four hundred and sixty-one horses, Rick tells them, hardtop. Two tones to give the appearance of a convertible, with no post between the side windows. Designed also to suggest something nautical; along the hood are squarish portholes. Mrs. Rappaport has had the car shined to a pearly glisten. Its body is creamy white, and its top and upholstery are St. Louis Cardinal red. Danny and Angie are swept back into the simulated leather seats as Sylvia

Rappaport guns down Fort Hamilton Parkway, acceleration bullying them back, the car saying, listen punks, sit back and listen.

They pick up from Raycroft, load the Century, and begin deliveries. They stop block to block, leave the car armed with sponges, spray cans, brooms. Mrs. Rappaport sits peacefully behind the wheel to wait for their return. In the heat her eyes droop half shut, and she lifts her head as if she is taking the sun. She is already deeply tanned; her posture suggests a deck-chair passenger of a Caribbean cruise. Head back, arm resting on the Cardinal-red door pull, a bare and freckled arm ending in dragon nails. Her lids are shellacked a neon purple, and she has drawn a soft line out from her eye corners in the same color. She catches Danny staring at her and cocks her head.

Startled, he says the opposite of what he is thinking.

"That's a very becoming eye shade, Mrs. Rappaport."

"Why, Daniel," she says. "Are you flirting with me?"

Rick joins them at the next intersection and the car lurches ahead. Mrs. Rappaport speaks up.

"It's a good thing you rescued me, Angie. I think Mr. Meadoff was making his move. He told me he thought my eyes were pretty."

Angie, sitting next to Danny in the rear, pokes his thigh. Rick looks straight ahead.

"I think he's interested, your friend Meadoff the masher. You hear me, Ricky-Ticky-Tavi? Your friend Mr. Meadoff. He doesn't think I'm an old bag."

Rick stirs, is silent. A light changes.

"Nobody said you were an old bag, Ma."

"They didn't, huh?" Mrs. Rappaport's voice has gone jagged. Its glassine varnish has shattered. The boys are still. Rick flicks on the radio, spins by the voice of the Dodgers to hear what's doing. Just music. The team is travelling. The Rappaport car is tied up in traffic. A double-parked bakery truck is unloading. Horns begin. The cabin cruiser that is the Buick Century is becalmed and they breathe the air of each other's exhale. Mrs. Rappaport asks her question again, but there is no answer.

She looks sharply over her shoulder—adrenaline shoots blood into Danny's cheeks. Is she looking to him for an answer? No— and in a fluid, startling move, spins the wheel to the right, gasses the car so it yaws in a climbing turn, a chandelle, and carves out of traffic into the opposite direction. A second squeal of tires as the car rights itself on course. Heads turn, but Mrs. Rappaport fighter pilot disappears before the oncoming traffic can sound their curses.

"They didn't, huh?" she says again and sulks.

They make their last deliveries in silence. Danny walks to the driver's side. "Well thanks," he says.

"Get in, Daniel. I'll drive you home."

"No, that's O.K. I have to go to the dentist. He's right around here. Tell Angie and Rick for me, would you? Thanks again, Mrs. Rappaport." He backs away.

"Sylvia," she says. For a moment, he is confused, wonders if there is someone behind him.

"Oh, yeah. Sylvia," he says. He heads down to Fourth Avenue where he can secretly catch a bus, happy, as he drops his coins into the windowed box, to pay the price of manumission.

Mr. Meadoff arrives home from Manhattan and changes for dinner. Every workday of his life. Before he kisses the cheek of his wife, before he inquires of his children about their day and their news, he goes upstairs and performs one of the few private rituals remaining to him.

He first removes his shoes. Without sitting to untie them. He pries one against the toe of the other and uses the stocking foot to shed the second. That single act fills him with a relief, a buoyancy, as if these shoes magnetized him to the earth's iron center. Does anyone feel greater relief? he wonders. Do Bill Mauldin's soldiers or a Georgia chain gang or the people who buy the weighted boots sold on the inside back cover of barber-shop magazines to help your physique?

Then the socks, liberating his feet to the air. The ablution of freedom. There are jobs in which you don't wear shoes. Beach bum. Lifeguard. On his first trip to Manila, he splurged: he was pulled around the entire morning by a rickshaw driver who tirelessly ran the streets of Manila without shoes. If you were single it would be the ideal job. Then he sheds the rest of his work clothes. He drapes the trousers over the wooden hanger while still in his suit jacket. This evening he is wearing the grey tropical worsted. His wife selected it, said its flecked pattern wouldn't show spots. He dislikes the suit. It shows nothing. He removes his tie, and as he often does, considers it. What does this say about me, that I wear this piece of cloth around my neck, that I neither chose nor understand. I wear it every day. What does it signal to other wearers? Are we some tribe signalling to each other? Who is Spartacus? His speculation comes up empty. It is not purposeful. In the morning, when he brushes his teeth, he invariably hears the tune "Turkey in the Straw" in the riffing of the bristles. It has no significance.

He removes his tie and hangs it on the pegged rack Rochelle made at day camp. A wonderment, a tiredness twinges at the back of his neck: that his daughter was once eight years old fitting pegs into this rack at Broad Channel Day Camp and is now fifteen years old and while he is upstairs, while the sweat of the day is cooling from the damp lumbar of his shirt pressed against him and his body rests in the quiet, she lives her life downstairs without him. It is an extension of day camp. He is absent and he is relying on the presence of surrogates to raise his children. It used to be at least he knew the surrogates. They were teachers, neighborhood kids. Now who knows who they are? They could be anybody. And what will his children know about him? That he hung his ties on a rack they made for him.

Now he removes the shirt and feels the weight of his water in its cloth. Removes the sleeveless undershirt and stands in the air stripped to his shorts. The dampness of the day leaves his skin slowly, for the air is humid and absorbs little. He stands there drying out, freed for a moment, freed only to return. But for the moment freed.

He walks towards his closet. On the way he passes his wife's vanity table. It came with the bedroom set, all four pieces done in a burl veneer so thin it curls up from the underwood at the seams. He watches himself in the table's mirror, crossing left to right; returning to inspect himself, again leaving the scene. There is a director's power in the gesture; if the mirror were a camera he would be passing by it. Or choosing to address it. In either case, the ability to move in and out of the world is for the moment his. When the actor is offstage, is past the camera, he disappears.

The body he sees holds no message for him. How curious. How odd that it has stopped speaking to me. What does it mean if our very person stops speaking? He inspects smallish shoulders, thin but taut biceps, overdeveloped forearms. The skin is a color of indoors. Still, the arms have kept their power. He played a great deal of handball as a young man, even with the bad leg. Handball and pitching ice from a delivery truck gave him large forearms. To the figure who looks back at him, the critical figure in square boxer shorts, a thin, aging figure, he gives a shrug.

Now he slips on a short-sleeved cotton shirt and a pair of wash pants. He puts his feet, emancipated only minutes ago, into a pair of crude leather slippers. And now, before more time slips away from him, he descends the stairs to his family.

- **12** -

Aqueduct. A long, two-tiered grandstand that packs them in for weekends and big stakes races, but today yawns down on near empty concrete. Out in the sun, track level, the regulars fill the field. They stand flank by the fencing chatting up their ponies, letting them know how important this race is. My last ten bucks, haven't had a winner in a week, do this for me and I'll send a dozen roses your way. We'll both eat, sweetheart, oats for you, T-bones for me. The field is filled with regulars and shills, crumbums hawking mimeographed tout sheets for a buck, players who can tell you every winner for three years back.

The boys can't get in. Must be eighteen, the sign by the turnstile says, and the orange and blue uniformed guard enforces it. "Must be eighteen or accompanied," he reads to them and refuses to look at Angie's credentials. Angie carries identification forged for him by his oldest brother, an expired Massachusetts fishing license that establishes its carrier to be thirty-one.

They find an uncle. Or he finds them, bounced from the turnstile and he picks them up on the short hop.

"Must be eighteen or accompanied," he tells them and Rick says, "So we hear."

"Two bucks and you're accompanied," he offers and for the price of a sucker bet they are through the gate.

"Sid," he tells them. "Call me Sid. You boys gonna need some help."

Sid says hi to the ticket-takers and the program seller and waves to the Pinkerton at the men's room. He shows them the windows, how to get your money down. Sid looks to be in his seventies, frail with a neck Angie's hand could wrap around. It's the middle of July, but Sid wears a grey windbreaker zipped to his Adam's apple.

"You follow the horses, Sid?"

"I follow horses that follow horses."

They stand by the entry for the parade of the first race. Sid shows them the yellow and purple silk of Wheatley Stables, the cherry and black of Ogden Phipps. He gives quick signs to a few jocks who pay him no mind. He points out how there's special taping for splints, and when Rick says he's going to back a big red colt Sid says to save your money because he's been painted for bucked shins.

They stand through a race or two without a bet. Sid chatters advice at them. Dead weight is harder to carry than live. Look for good blood lines. When you see the right horse make sure he's in the right race.

The boys bet cautiously. Sid touts them in the third and they get a ticket but the horse finishes in the pack. Two races later Danny bets with him and collects five and a dime on a show. Sid takes a dollar of it.

"It's the custom," he tells Danny.

"These are tough times. Flats in the afternoon, trotters at night. How's a man going to make enough money to bet day and night?"

In a late race the boys pool ten bucks on a long shot. Sid runs the bet for them and disappears. They never get the ticket but the horse finishes last. Sid is gone.

In the ninth, a claiming race for two-year-olds, appears a sign, a natural choice. Destiny's Brush is going off at twelve to five.

"You don't pick a horse for its name," argues Danny.

"Are you kidding?" asks Rick. "Here's a horse running second choice in the money, and we are three prosperous Fuller Brush salesmen at no dollars, and you want to pass this up."

Danny looks around for Sid. Just when you need a friend. Twenty dollars, the bankroll, goes on the nose of Destiny's Brush. Benjamin Franklin to win.

Destiny's Brush is off well, in the pack and saving ground. He moves up and for an instant it looks like he's in close quarters. "Let him through," yells Rick and sure enough the horse ahead turns wide and he's through. He's lying fourth in the backstretch.

Destiny's Brush cooks on the outside around the turn with everyone in view. Into the stretch his jock goes to the stick. The horse lays back his ears and gets to running. He passes the third horse and the second and Angie is standing on the footrail and Danny and Rick are calling to their horse, calling his name. He's moving on the leader and he closes on him, at his throat latch and he looks to have him.

And the jock stands up. At the eighth pole coming on and undeniable, the jock stands up in the stirrups and Destiny's Brush breaks stride and stumbles across in a crowd.

"My entire two days' earnings," complains Angie on the train going home. "We got stuck on that last race for two days' earnings."

"We'll take it," says Angie earnestly "from the first sales we make. Pool the money at lunch."

"Or," says Rick with Harpo's leer, "easier. Back it out of the winnings from the first race tomorrow."

At dinner that night the talk is of politics. Maybe they will give Stevenson another chance. Mr. Meadoff loves Stevenson, and speaks in these matters for the family. On global and cosmic questions his father prevails. Do we recognize Red China? Was it disease or meteors that killed off the dinosaurs? How are we to rectify the treatment of the Negro race in much of the country? Anything that might be on the front page of the *Times* his father has the say. The other issues—where the kids go to school, what the family eats, what they spend—are left to his mother.

When his father talks politics, Danny listens. You learn other things. It's like an advertisement that he once answered had promised about stamps: Become a collector and discover the world. Danny discovered where Cameroon was, but he could have found French Equatorial Africa on his own. He learned not to believe advertisements, but when they could get his father talking, the ad could have been written for the Meadoff dinner table.

There are several possibilities. Symington from Missouri has the appeal of tap water. Kefauver isn't bad. Tough on crime. Popular from his television appearances, popular enough to take on Eisenhower. But a Southerner. Mr. Meadoff cautions them: is it possible for any Southerner to address the country's single communal failure? The South was the situs of the Scotsboro trial, of the brutal murder of that young boy in Mississippi for saying hello to a white woman. In the South, his father told them after travelling to Memphis to testify about the failure of a cotton shipment, in the South the lawyers in the courtroom remove their suit jackets on hot days. The South seems to be casual about human rights and Puritan values. The son of immigrants, Mr. Meadoff is ferociously loyal to both. Despite what Senator Kefauver might want to do, his place of birth conspires against him.

And what about Stevenson? Brilliant, liberal, witty, divorced, the Illinois governor regularly quotes Lincoln. Mr. Meadoff is devoted to him.

"So the question Mr. Lippmann asks," his father speaks through a mouthful of rye bread as Danny looks away, "is this: will the party pick someone other than Adlai and merely disappoint him, or will they pick him and let the voters in November break his heart?"

"Why?" asks Rochelle.

"Why what?" Mrs. Meadoff says. She directs questions to their proper destination, a switchboard operator.

"Why will the voters break his heart?"

The question silently passes to Mr. Meadoff. He is carving meat from the leg of a boiled chicken. He slices from the bone with knife and fork, picks up the bite with two fingers and puts it into his mouth.

"Because," says Mr. Meadoff, "in November, Adlai will lose."

"How does this man Mr. Lippmann know what will happen in November?"

Mr. Meadoff chews and swallows before he answers.

"Because, Ro-Ro, because Walter Lippmann knows. Because the American people don't want someone better than them. They want someone *like* them. They want Ike."

"Who is *he* like?" Rochelle asks. Danny smiles. It is a good point. The genial blue-eyed general resembles no one in their family, their neighborhood. Danny does not know a single person who plays golf.

Mrs. Meadoff deflects the question by re-answering the earlier one.

"He knows he'll lose because of the divorce," she says. The word comes out leaking air, a punctured bladder. Mrs. Meadoff countenances no moral ambiguity.

"But so what, Mom," Danny says. "How does being divorced hurt Governor Stevenson when he has to decide what to do about the Channel Islands or foreign trade?'' The point is not Danny's. It has been made by Kempton and Lerner in the *Post*, Sulzberger in the *Times*. Also by Mr. Meadoff. Four of the most impressive minds in the area are to a man behind Stevenson. Danny has won debates with chums citing little else.

His mother fears no adversary.

''Because, Mr. Fuller Brush. Because America wants its president to stay home. Not to be a single bachelor honkey-tonking all night, dancing all night at El Morocco.''

''Oh, Ma. Governor Stevenson doesn't go to night clubs. He stays home and reads books.'' Danny counters fancy with fancy. How this private and remote man spends his free evenings is nowhere reported.

''Besides, if he doesn't have a family,'' Danny says, ''maybe he'll be a better president. Maybe he won't have so much to worry about and can concentrate on the budget and NATO.''

His mother is undeterred. ''The American people,'' she says, her shoulders rising with the burden of her representation, ''the American people want a family man. A man with a wife, with children who know how to behave. Grandchildren. That's more important than Princeton College.''

''Princeton University,'' Danny says. His mother has fingered a weakness in the Stevenson armor. Here is a candidate from the Protestant rich. Still, Roosevelt went to Groton, Harvard. It can happen.

''And don't think I didn't hear that dig,'' his mother says. ''A family is not something you worry about. A family is what you have. Who else are you going to have to live in your house?''

The debate has ended. Mr. Meadoff is pleased. Governor Stevenson would be gratified by his son's support. It is a good sign.

Joyce clears the dishes and Mrs. Meadoff serves dessert. Butterscotch pudding in parfait glasses, their sides incongruously decorated with luggage tags from the world capitals. Danny gets Bangkok. The original set included a pitcher but it shattered last summer, when Angie fouled off a sinking curve. With the pudding Mrs. Meadoff brings to the table a new product. A bright red can that sprays whipped cream with a rude blat. The topping turns out not to be whipped cream at all, rather something that looks similar, an airy substance tasting of milk and chalk. It is a great hit.

- 13 -

How long has he known Rick? Rick is his oldest friend. They found each other standing on the Church Avenue platform. Waiting for a train. Recognized each other from class, grammar school, a grade so long ago you had one teacher all day. Danny watched, did not speak.

"Want to play Hat?" Rick asked.

"What's that?"

"You know. Hat. Watch me."

A train pulled into the station. Rick marched by the cars on inspection. He found an open window where a man sat in a grey fedora, his back to the boys. Rick pointed him out.

"Is that it?" asked Danny. "You have to find someone wearing a hat?"

"That's a start," said Rick.

The train lurched, began to roll. Quick as a fly, Rick grabbed the hat. The train pulled away with the face of the cursing man, an angry thumb out the window.

They have been friends since.

At home Danny omits mention of his trip to the track. He is independent and his money is his to do what he wants, but still. He will tell Mrs. Gunnerson instead. She has telephoned and left word that she wants to place an order. Rochelle took the message. The seriousness with which his family treats his work assures him.

The day after the races he calls on her Shore Road apartment. The morning is metal grey, the hot spell intermitted now by a sky without sun, drizzle promised for the afternoon. Rick said if it rains they should take in a movie, it's a sign from God to take the day off, but Angie, who needs the money, said no, he was going to make up what they dropped on the ponies. Danny likes the phrase. It has a hip ring to it. Playing the ponies.

Mrs. Gunnerson buzzes to unlatch the lobby door without asking who it is. She is standing at the open doorway when he reaches the end of the corridor. The apartment building is called the Napoli, and the hall wallpaper shows scenes of people at street cafes, couples in gondolas. The halls are cheerful, not from natural light but from the many overhead chandeliers each sprouting a dozen bulbs. Danny realizes it is luxury to spend money on the hallways. In Rick's house, a respectable apartment, good families, the landlord barely lights the corridors. They are dark as the roadway under the El.

Danny comments on the wallpaper, its scenes in repeating patterns, drawings made to look like embroidery, drawings of the Alps, of shepherds and mountain climbers.

"I went to Italy once," Frances Gunnerson says. "I think it was the happiest week of my life. I've done my apartment to remind me of the hills of Tuscany." She regularly speaks words into air, words Danny believes she would say even if no one were there.

Mrs. Gunnerson holds to her throat the catalogue Danny has left her. Danny follows her to the kitchen. He takes out his order book. "Now," he says.

"I've been thinking about what I need. But I want your opinion. What would you recommend from the Fuller line?"

She is wearing a new garment, this too a housecoat. It is pale pink with small flowers in its pattern, and against its washed color the pink of her gums shows vital. Loose fitted but floor length, with padded shoulders and a waist with pleats. It wraps around her like a double breasted suit and looks several sizes too large.

Perhaps she's been ill, Danny thinks. That is why she never dresses. She's been sick. Sunlight and the street air might burn up her flesh, collapse her. She is an invalid, perhaps like the aunt on Our Gal Sunday. Three-fifteen on WOR, brought to you by Rinso-White. That woman has a heart. She was bedridden when Danny was in the fourth grade and again when he checked in on her last year.

"What good," Mrs. Gunnerson is saying and the mewling sound brings him back from the radio. "What good is it to have a friend who's a Fuller Brush man if you can't ask him for advice?"

She speaks softly with hardly any cast to her voice. Danny listens carefully, unsure whether he has been asked a question.

"Oh, yes," he says.

They speak only above a whisper. It is the sound of subterranean animals discussing owls and hawks. It is the sound of a conversation between rabbits.

He tells her of the products. He has studied the catalogue as Raycroft instructed. While he speaks, she puckers her brow. He begins to lose heart. Does she see through him? He sprays household deodorant from his sample case about the kitchen and describes the piney smell. He spreads a thick unguent on the refrigerator, wipes it clean with the back side of the cloth and asks her to compare the enamel lustre. Despite her earnestness he is losing heart.

Yet when he is done she places a substantial order. Danny writes it up and fills out a receipt and Mrs. Gunnerson pays him in full. She pours herself another cup of coffee and he tells her about his visit to the track. Behind her on the counter is a stack of papers a foot high, balanced, a cairn of magazines, boxes, newspapers in tenuous balance. As Danny speaks he watches to see whether it will tumble.

"Do you think you could call me Frances?" she asks. "I mean, we're not that far apart in age and it wouldn't make me feel so . . . ."

Here she waves her hand in a vague figure. Danny steps in. He fears she may have lost interest in finishing the sentence.

"Sure," Danny says. The way she asks him, as a favor, isn't the same as Mrs. Rappaport's.

"What does your husband do, Frances?"

"He's in imports."

"No kidding. So is my father. Knit goods, mainly. Maybe they know each other."

"I doubt it," she says. "Mr. Gunnerson imports coffee and tea. He travels around buying, and then his firm imports and sells coffee to distributors."

"Maybe they don't then," Danny says and immediately feels foolish. "Still," he says rising. He feels light-headed. The possibility that Mrs. Gunnerson's husband knows his father. What could it mean? He needs to get to work. He squeezes by her chair and steadies the pile of papers. On the top is a neat stack of unopened mail.

"This stuff," he says and hands her an envelope. "It's not opened. Don't you want to see what it says?"

As he speaks the stack slides. Beneath the mail is a week-old *Look* magazine whose glossy cover provides no purchase. It slides and the mail tumbles to the floor. Revealed is an open-lidded box holding a half-eaten coffee cake, a ring of keys and a fresh tube of toothpaste.

"No," she says casually. "No, I'll get around to it."

A week, maybe two weeks of mail. The rest of the apartment shines. The glass spray Danny has sold her is unneeded, for the window panes and the top of the breakfast table glisten. He leaves confused.

"You dummy. Make your move."

Rick bugs his eyes, leans forward. "Why do think she brings up her husband being away all the time?" Danny wishes he had said nothing. It is hard to explain Frances Gunnerson.

"It's not like that," Danny says. "She really wants someone to talk with. A friend."

"She wants a friend, she can buy a dog. Make your move, Meadoff. What she wants is clear, my little rabbit. *Claro que sí.*"

Rick has summoned them this evening to Angie's house. Why not his own place Danny doesn't know. The Valerianis live in a brown row house on Fourth Avenue. On the wall in Angie's room are old clippings about his brothers from the *Eagle* and the *News*. In one photo Phil, the oldest, sinks a hook shot against Bishop Laughlin, in another stops a halfback over piled and padded bodies and over the headline "Valeriani Turns Back Perpetual Help." Angie has his own press, though none of it has been tacked to the wall. The sportswriters think Angie is the one with the real talent. He started at end in his sophomore year, and scouts from Syracuse and Holy Cross have already approached him.

Rick produces the *Daily Telegraph*. He has found, he tells them, a sure thing. You got to look for a horse coming down in a claims race, unknown on the circuit. Means he needs a win or two. And this one is going off at four to one.

Danny argues against it. They agreed to the ponies once a week. If they start going to the track every day they'll end the summer in the red. But that's the beauty of this, Rick argues. This is a sure thing and at four to one, we make yesterday back and more. There is magic in four to one. There is magic and miracles in plenty from nothing. They gather around and consider weight, past finishes, lineage.

Angie's father walks through the living room. The boys put down the form charts and greet him. He is a large man with a long, sad face, draped with jowls, lengthened with jowls and lobes. His voice grates as if he smokes though he doesn't, and he wears the specked white clothes of a house painter. The room smells of turpentine, tomato sauce, coriander. Angie gets up and hugs his father, who kisses him noisily on the cheek.

The three boys move out the front door for a cigarette and sit on the stoop. They are undecided about the track tomorrow. Angie wants to go but intends to be loyal to Danny.

"Doesn't all that kissing get you down?" Rick asks him.

"What do you mean?"

"Your father treating you like a little kid. Kissing and everything."

"My father kisses all his kids. He kisses his brothers," Angie says. "They're fifty. Over."

Rick contemplates a chip of concrete on the top of the front steps. They are sitting each on a different level, he at the first step. He scratches the chip on the cement, then flings it so it strikes the hub cap of a car parked at the curb.

"It would get me down, is all. It's symbolic."

"Symbolic of what?"

"How your father keeps you in the house."

"I *am* in the house, for Chrissake."

Rick changes the subject. He tells them of a woman on his route who has invited him to come back and make his presentation when she is not entertaining her group for mah jong.

"Tell me," he says, "if you don't think that's a sign." He cannot get anything going.

Danny is quiet. He is thinking of Angie's father. Danny looks through the concrete balusters on the stoop. Piled by the steps that go down to the outside basement door are throw canvases, mixing sticks, gallon cans of paint. Angie's father has the expression of a cartoon hound, and white paint dots his stubble and the hair of his temples, where the hair protrudes from under the cap. When he paints peach his hair is flecked in peach. Every day in a different apartment doing the same thing. Someone has moved, someone else is moving in. A new coat. Danny remembers the discussions between his mother and their apartment super before they lived in this house. It hasn't had a freshen up in five years, she would say whenever she saw him, it needs it. She would hector and convince and eventually get her way. And when she did, the landlord would call in Mr. Valeriani, and he and his son Phil, the one in the news photo hitting for two against Bishop Laughlin, would paint the walls with long-handled rollers. Semigloss on the woodwork. He would unscrew all the outlet plates first and detach the telephone box and take off the hardware from the doors. Once the job was done, he would reconnect it all, chiv the windows so they wouldn't stick, and come home to this house.

He would come home and greet his wife and call her Mama. She would not turn around from the stove. Then he would embrace his other two sons and kiss them loudly on the cheek. And they would sit down to dinner in the kitchen.

Why did it make Danny sad?

Rick hoists his cigarette butt between thumb and middle finger, aims, shoots it into the street in a spray of spark. He stands to leave, Danny stays. Rick is saying something about Frances Gunnerson, to bait Danny, but Danny has missed it. Danny stays because the evening seems to have the whole summer in it, is the summer, and who would want to walk out on summer?

"Tomorrow," Rick says. "Three-fifteen post time. A four-to-one shot that Rick Rappaport describes in today's paper as a Can't Miss. Three ways to win, a winner every time. Horizontal, vertical and on the slant. See you then, fans."

Rick walks down the block to catch his bus. Danny hears his bark as he crosses the first shadowed street.

"Aaand, they're off!"

-**14**-

Mr. Meadoff enters his son's room, pushes the light, looks around. He has not come in here in months. Not that he is barred. It is merely that no occasion has arisen. This is where Danny does his growing, sleeping at night and growing. His children are the reciprocal of plants—plants inhale their breath, grow in the sunlight. His children live off the sweet oxygen of new leaves, sprout in the moon's eye.

He wanders around the walls, touching his distance like a blind man. Studying the baseball photos. There a scorecard signed by a utility infielder. For Danny's seventh birthday, a

Wednesday, the two of them at Ebbets Field. Danny wanted to be the first ones at the stadium, so they arrived before lunch. On their way in they passed the players' entrance, on Bedford. Danny recognized a man sitting morosely in his convertible and the man signed the scorecard, but it turned out he couldn't hit the curve and was sent down in the middle of the season. A woman was driving the car, a pretty woman with brown, curly hair and lips red as some tropical fruit. She was very pretty. She wore a saucer hat of white straw and Mr. Meadoff looked at her and realized she was watching him watch Danny and they smiled at each other. "Maybe we should get your autograph too," he said to her and she said with a laugh, "Oh, no. I'm not anybody." The ballplayer hadn't liked that but she had, you could tell. He was angry and he hadn't had an at-bat in weeks. She looked like a movie star.

Mr. Meadoff walks to the spare bed and sits on its corner. It is covered with handouts and order forms, neatly stacked. Danny will make a good businessman. He'll keep an orderly desk. Not like mine. He thinks of his crowded room at work, visualizes the disarray. Chaos to a stranger. To me, order. I can close my eyes and name every piece of paper. Read it back, if you want. That's not chaos. Look at this crap, Lindenauer had said. Look at this debris. A man's work should not be thought of as debris.

His eye sweeps over the bookshelves. Plane and boat models separate authors and sets. A P-48 props up the end of Mark Twain and a Flying Fortress sits poised by the collection of Albert Payson Terhune. The wallpaper is a pattern of overlapping plaids in tans and browns. Masculine, his wife had called it. On the floor is a hooked rug they had bought on a trip to the Finger Lakes. Where they used to live, the old apartment, Danny's wallpaper had fighter planes on it. He had picked it out and Danny had loved it. All sorts of airplanes and Danny knew them by name and manufacturer. Then one day, Danny was no more than a kid, he and a friend took crayons to it. They drew tracer bullets and smoke from the guns, and when pilots scored hits they drew bushy explosions in red and flame orange. The walls became an enormous, wrap-around dog fight. Cinerama. After they shot down what they could reach they stood on chairs, but there was still a squadron of untested, unmarked craft at the highest altitude, ringing the room.

It had upset Miriam. She was angry at Danny, angry at him. Not that you could blame her. He had suggested the wallpaper in the first place. Wallpaper was expensive, and even if they steamed it off themselves, it would have cost to have new paper hung. Instead, they moved. Danny and his friend shot down most of the air force, and faced with the burden of rearmament, the Meadoffs moved.

Of course business was better then. Right after the war people wanted everything. You couldn't get goods fast enough. Reconstruction put capital into the Philippines, and they went over and made their connections. They were ready. They tied up the sources, froze out the competition. Those were good times. Didn't have to travel. People would come to them. Now it's tougher. Everyone has a source. He suspects some of his customers, the big retailers, are going direct. They don't tell him, but he's sure they do. They beat him up on price, then they beat him up on terms, then they order somewhere else. Has to be their own sources.

So his partner is pushing him into new products. It makes him uneasy. For one thing the business is a plaything to Lindenauer. Lindenauer doesn't need Paradise Knitwear. He has a dozen investments like it. And Lindenauer is pushing him to put more money at risk in products he doesn't understand. These are chances he shouldn't be taking. So what is he supposed to do?

Sell out? There are no buyers. He is riding the back of a tiger. Better not to get off when the tiger is hungry.

Where is Danny tonight? Either at Rick's or at Angie's. He should stop worrying about his son. They're nice boys. Miriam thinks Danny should have a better class of friends. More like him, interested in books and stamps and studies. Not baseball all the time. The fact is, and Mr. Meadoff smiles, Danny likes baseball. On the top shelf Danny has stored two stamp albums.

What will become of his children? With Joyce it's too early, the troubles come later. Even too early to worry, though this does not stop him. Rochelle is so into herself. Miriam says these years they're into themselves. He'd like to think so. Like to think it an aberration, an imbalance that Nature will aright. High pressure areas flow into lows and equalize, stabilize. That is what Miriam would have him believe, and he would like to believe it. It is nothing more than a blot of bad weather that will swirl around the mid-Atlantic states as they say on TV, and then blow out to sea. Let it envelop someone else's daughter.

Danny shouldn't be thinking about business. Let him find something where he's independent. An architect, perhaps. Architects don't need a partner. Someone wants a building, he hires you and you draw it. You find a builder, you supervise him. At the end you get paid and you have something to show for it. A bridge, a building. Something you can drive your children to and point at. Not just a pile of papers on a desk, in a room where you can't even see the sky. An architect doesn't need capital. If you don't need capital, you don't need factors, and you don't need Lindenauer.

A pile of papers on a desk can be blown away. A wind blows, no more papers, and who is left? A man of air.

This new venture, women's knit jerseys. They've agreed to start small. They don't know the factory, and the units are more expensive. But the first order went well and with Lindenauer's encouragement they are rolling the dice again. Plunging. They are more heavily into the factor than Mr. Meadoff would want, more than he has in the bank by three or four times. We'll work something out, Lindenauer said. Don't let this chance pass us by because we didn't grab for the ring. Tomorrow he goes to see Lindenauer. What will they work out? He should think of something. If he doesn't, Lindenauer will.

His gaze hits on the prow of a grey destroyer, set back in a high shelf. He gets up, walks over and carefully pulls it down. It was built the same year of the wallpaper dogfight. That November. Danny got scarlet fever. It was, the doctor told them, a bad case. They worried through the many bedridden days: now he has forgotten—does scarlet fever leave children deaf? Is it something worse? How could he forget? Afterwards in the long recuperation, he would come to Danny's room with the dinner tray and they would talk or read or do puzzles. He would bring something home every night. He had done that with Ro-ro's mumps and Joyce's broken leg. Connecting the dots, pushing the wooden tabs to get the numbers in order, a little box where you rolled the tiny steel balls around until they lit in each hole. But the little bee-bees didn't stay put. One bump, one mistake and they popped out.

One night he brought home the model destroyer and they assembled it together. He helped Danny with the sanding and the templates and showed him how the turrets fit. They had to use tweezers on the ack-ack guns. Danny wanted to do the finishing himself. He had gotten it painted and the signal flags hung. But the decals were fragile and one had ripped. The last number came in half, so the identifying number had, instead of an eight, an abbreviated "c". Destroyer RDL-14c. Danny had cried in fury and he had come in and comforted his son and made up a story about what the little c meant, how all the other ships when they saw that broken eight knew to stand alert. He sat on this very bed with his arm around Danny telling him how the head of the O.S.S., General Bill Donovan, had thought up the code, his arm around his son and in his other hand, bobbing in an easy sea, the destroyer RDL-14c.

Danny sits on the Valerianis' stoop and talks with Angie after Rick has gone. It is a damp night, the asphalt sweating from the afternoon showers, and everywhere the smell of water—from the hydrant the kids opened that morning, from the air, from the great bay down the avenue, the scent of water mixes with the hard scent of concrete. They talk of the curve ball. *Life* magazine has published photographs taken seconds apart. Bobby Feller threw a ball while a camera took shots. The pictures prove the curve exists, bury the argument that it is an optical illusion.

"That's what they told me last year in the Borough finals," says Angie. "I stood up there and took an optical illusion in my ear."

Danny takes the train back. As he walks up the subway steps into the neon light he hears a lyric horn, a line you've never heard except maybe falling asleep and now it tumbles down the stairwell of the IRT. He follows the music to the surface. Hoot is way off, a long line that starts where he stands and goes off like a freed kite, lifts itself aloft without wires, without street lights. Danny recognizes the changes. Hoot gathers it in, ends with four bars of original melody. Lover Man.

"Hiya, Hoot."

The man opens his eyes, peers out. His eyes are small and glassy. Danny isn't sure he is recognized.

"It's me. Danny."

"Yeah," says Hoot.

"That was terrific. God, that was terrific. I didn't know you played at night. I've never seen you here."

"Cause you never looked, man."

He closes his eyes, licks the reed, plays another chorus. This time up tempo.

"You play here every night?"

"This my gig," says Hoot. They stand facing each other for a moment. Danny is waiting for Hoot to play again, but Hoot is through. He starts to dismantle his horn. Danny helps: takes the coins and the few bills out of the case, wraps them in the handkerchief Hoot points him to, ties the corners into a knot.

Hoot smiles, palms the packet to feel its weight, looks at Danny. Then he does a curious thing. Casually, without looking, he tosses the bundle into the street. Danny doesn't hesitate. He leaps out and grabs it. A taxi honks.

"Hey," Danny says handing it back. "What you doing? Don't you want this?"

Hoot is laughing softly. "You see, man? White folks can't live without money."

Danny laughs too.

"Money's important," he says.

"No, man. Only when you need it."

They nod goodnight. Hoot snaps his case closed and walks off.

Danny walks down Flatbush to his corner. It is marked by the barber's pole. Fathead Marrone cuts hair, phones in small bets on baseball and the trotters. Not the flats, though. Someone else covers the flats. Brooklyn is a fiefdom, a thousand fiefdoms. Danny resists haircuts, has since he was a kid. Fathead Marrone knuckles your head and uses a three-inch straight razor to shave your neck.

Danny turns the corner. The walk home is easy and familiar. He is thinking about nothing, about Hoot and the curve ball Angie took in the head. Across the street is a tiny park—a pocket park the City calls it in a sign they put up—maybe fifty by a hundred feet. People use it to eat their lunch or just sit in the shade on a hot day. Facing the park is a slatted bench, and on the bench, sitting motionless as a mound is a man. If Danny didn't know better he would have said it was his father. But his father would not leave home blocks away to come down to Flatbush and Courtelyou to sit on a bench in the middle of the night. He can sit at home. As Danny watches the shoulders of the figure raise and lower in a rhythm, two-beat, and the man leans over. Leans over, pulls up his legs, and placing his head on his folded hands, lies down on the bench.

Danny swallows the word in his throat. It cannot be he. Danny walks the remaining streets slowly. A man who sits on a bench is one thing but a man who lies down on a bench, on a public bench is quite another. A man lies down in a field, in a trench, on the floor of the ocean. It cannot be he.

The Meadoff house is dark but for the yellow porch light his mother intends for him. He sees the face in the house facade. Tonight the smile holds no ridicule or menace. It is a fool's face, grinning, risible, harmless. He unlocks the door, clicks off the light to darken the joker's smile, and without looking for his father goes up the stairs to bed.

- 15 -

It is only a question of time. Mr. Meadoff emerges from the IRT station at Forty-first and Seventh. His suit jacket drapes dead as a corpse over one arm and he sweats lightly in the morning heat. Warm water and salt. Even the rubbery pages of the newspaper hold heat. They would make good kindling if I knew someone who needed a fire. Who needs a fire in July?

It is only a question of time before the heat melts us down. Are we going to survive it? Does the garbage survive the garbage collector? The crush is geologic, unavoidable. Heat and the press of the city will liquify us, press us back to material of the earth. They thought they really had something. Miraculous, they thought. An island of rock, where they can build a city that lasts forever. Where they can build skyscrapers and the foundations won't sink. But the people do.

Already we ride underground. We ride underground, we work out of the sunlight, and in time our spirit dies and we turn to liquid. Our flesh turns to a crossword solution: magma. Plastic for the earth to turn over and reuse. These people I'm walking with, stopping for this light, we're landfill. That place in New Jersey they have my mother in. That's not a nursing home. Who's nursing? And who calls it home? It is a processing plant.

He smiles at his joke and the light changes. Why is it called a plant? Vegetation. The underbrush of time is reclaiming her. Animal yields to vegetable, vegetable to mineral. First the human in us disappears. Once we marked time by joy. By ecstasies. Then the joys even out. We keep track of light and dark. We get fed, we get watered. We mark time by the ordinary pain of living. Somewhere along the way the human parts fall off, insight and language, the joys beget troubles and the troubles don't leave room for anything else.

I am walking crosstown in step with a thousand people I don't know. Is that a human act? Does that remind you of Lincoln? or of cattle? It happens to all of them. They lose touch. One day sex is sex, the next day it's politics. One day you have a family, a source of pride, the next day they are another business problem, cash outflow competing with variable curves of income and will.

Lindenauer's office is only blocks from his. It is in a modern building, part of the renovation of midtown. Meadoff feels the difference before he enters the lobby doors. The brass of the revolving doors gleams skin perfect, unscratched. He whooshes through—even the slice of air he brings with him is refreshed as it enters—and into a high-ceiling marble room with mural art and guards in livery.

He is kept waiting an uncharacteristically short time. Only ten or twelve minutes. The woman asks him if he'd like coffee or a soft drink. Lindenauer is the new businessman. He goes in for this gentility. Keep you waiting but they serve you ginger ale in a glass for the heartburn you get while you're waiting. "I had my breakfast at home," Meadoff tells her. The magazines, too, offend him. They say, How do you like our manners. We spend a bundle on subscriptions to these fancy magazines because we are going to rub your nose in them. It won't be long. We knew you were coming and we knew we would have something more important to do, so we ordered you the best.

"Mr. Lindenauer can see you now," he is told and he pushes up from the couch that is too low and walks in. Usually the secretary beats him to the door, opens it for him, says his name, but today he doesn't wait.

"Meadoff," Lindenauer says like it's a lucky guess and waves to a chair. He doesn't look up from his desk. More a table, a long flat board with consoles built into it for telephone and intercom. This man belongs in the movies, not in the garment district, Meadoff thinks. Lindenauer is still waving after Meadoff has seated himself.

"Paradise Knitwear, Paradise Knitwear," Lindenauer says.

"You're trying to remember or trying to forget?"

Lindenauer ignores the joke, but at last he raises his head. Meadoff thinks, not for the first time, how odd Lindenauer looks in these surroundings. Egg tempera paintings lit with individual frame lights, extreme Bauhaus furnishings, the large plate glass windows at the building's corner, expensive space, one view uptown to an orderly, glamorous city and the second west to the Hudson. Lindenauer sits in a leather Knoll chair, his feet barely touching the ground, and crouches over the table top. But it is not he who is unfamiliar. Meadoff realizes it is not Lindenauer who feels uncomfortable rolling his chair backwards to reach the cigar humidor on the credenza then with a balletic touch of his toes back to confront his visitor.

"Meadoff, there's nothing to say. We agreed to get into knit jerseys we got to do it right. This first order went well, we got to replace it."

Lindenauer is prepared. Mr. Meadoff knows where the conversation is heading. This new line might be a bonanza. There is only one way to find out, but to find out they will get more heavily into the factors than ever. Meadoff has to step up and raise his share. If that means a lien on the house, that's what it means. Not a large one. Not so much that one successful season in knit jerseys wouldn't be worth it.

"Of course, we could always call it equity," Lindenauer says. "I could put my share in as equity and when you get the money, you could match me. We'd be back at fifty-fifty." Lindenauer's stare says, I know your answer.

On the table in front of Mr. Meadoff is a crystal paperweight the size of a sandwich. He picks it up and hefts its weight. It is an odd thing for this porcine man to have, this man whose arms are tufted with black, bristly hair. Meadoff himself is short and Lindenauer is probably his height. But Lindenauer conceals it, stays seated, scoots his chair from credenza to phone to desk. Meadoff has rarely caught him on foot. His limbs do not seem useful. He wears shiny, soft-leather shoes in a little size and his hands are delicate and groomed.

The paperweight has stopped Meadoff's eye. It is polished crystal. Inside the glass, frozen inside the glass and out of the air, is a beautiful flower. Purple and black and pale yellow, it is an intricate tunnel. It folds in on itself, seems to grow from hidden passageways out to the blossom. Meadoff doesn't know the name of the flower. Could it be an orchid? He is not sure he has ever seen an orchid.

"You like that?" Lindenauer says. "You know why you like that?" Lindenauer leans forward and leers at him. "Because it reminds you of pussy."

Meadoff slides the glass paperweight to the table. He launches it with his thumb and it glides several inches on the polished wood.

"We could do this as equity," Lindenauer says again.

"We have an agreement," Meadoff says. "I get to carry my weight." If he lets Lindenauer buy stock for providing the money, the ratio changes from fifty-fifty. Once it changes, Meadoff fears he will never recover. "I'll carry my weight."

Lindenauer is holding an unlit cigar in the fingers of both hands. Like a flute. He looks at it carefully, as if it might suggest the outcome of this talk. He rolls it in his fingers and studies it.

"If you can," he says. Then with a kick he swings his chair around so that he is looking out both views. The meeting is over. Meadoff pushes back from the table, rises, and walks out.

He emerges into the street and finds it is raining. Light rain, rain that does not cool the air. Who ever heard of such a thing? If you put water on fire it should douse the fire. Where does the rain come from? Does it hold somewhere then slowly migrate over like a dirigible? Was this rain stored in the Poconos or in Pennsylvania? The dampness will ruin the press of his suit.

Saturday morning the rains blow out and are chased by a fresh blue sky, a coolness that hints that the concrete heat of summer is not forever. The freshness of the day encourages the Meadoffs. They decide at breakfast to make a pilgrimage to see Mr. Meadoff's mother.

Bubbeh Meadoff is in a rest home. Her son found it and pays monthly for her care. The sum seemed small when orders were coming in. She has been there since shortly after her husband died, three years ago, taking everyone by surprise. Pete, who spelled his name Pyet, had been expected to go on forever.

As Pete was young, his wife was old. Danny could not remember a time when she was not aged, invalided, smelly. Her accent was so thick Danny could only guess at what she said. Pete had made a point to learn colloquial English. When he spoke to his wife, he used their secret tongue. He spoke it only with her and at the Garden, at the hockey games. Pete was a regular when the Rangers played at home. There Danny and his grandfather sat with the Forty-ninth Street goal judge who was, like Pete, from Kiev. The judge saved seats for them, and he and Pete would sit amid the roar and speed and chatter in Russian.

When Pete died, Mr. Meadoff had no choice but to put Bubbeh in a home. Over time, their visits dropped off. Sometimes Mr. Meadoff went alone. It was a hard journey, without surprise, each trip Bubbeh slipping a little further away. Holding the hand of one over the ledge, holding tight while the hand shrinks, slips from your grasp. The kids found excuses not to go, but when the day turned out pleasant and, like this one, empty, the family would pile into the DeSoto and motor off to Englewood Cliffs across the river.

Two rivers, actually. From Brooklyn they drove through the Battery Tunnel under the East River, up the Drive to the Lincoln Tunnel and under the Hudson.

The DeSoto has seats upholstered in cloth, flannel soft. The knobs that crank the windows are fake tortoise shell and from where Danny sits reflect in their concave globes the rear passengers and the light from the far window. No matter how you turn them. Danny points this out to Joyce. He sits with his elbow on the arm rest, his chin on his fist, and stares out. Joyce and Ro play a game in a large, soft-covered book with coarse pages.

"If we traded it in, what would we get?" his father is saying.

"Something sensible," says his mother. "An Oldsmobile or a Chrysler."

"First you're scrimping, then you're splurging on a Chrysler."

"We could afford a Chrysler. That suits you more. A DeSoto doesn't suit you."

Danny agrees with his mother but no one asks. DeSoto doesn't advertise. Every other car, except perhaps the Hudson which no one takes seriously, every other American car stands for something. It broadcasts who you are. Danny follows those messages. When he told Rick they had a DeSoto, Rick asked why.

"I don't need a car to suit me," his father says. "I need a car to move me around. This moves me fine."

Out the window buildings speed by. From the Gowanus Parkway, a four-lane elevated highway fringing the northwest arc of the pie plate that is Brooklyn, Danny looks into second story windows not ten feet away. Inside, people pay no attention. No one bothers with blinds or drapes. Occasionally from an open window, flimsy white glass curtains, sucked out by the whoosh of passing traffic, wave as the Meadoffs speed by. Within the flats, grey men and women sit in their underwear, their pajamas, reading the paper, drinking coffee, arguing. The highway climbs a half-story. Danny looks out and sees an entire city at roof top, a black tar field sprouting telephone poles, pigeon coops, an occasional church spire. Many people who live along the Gowanus keep pigeons. Some are on their roofs, fussing with cages and flying their flocks. In the sky pigeons wheel in moving, apparently random clouds. It is not random: instead they are loosed to pick off a straggler or to raid a smaller flock. It is a silent war.

In the first apartment Danny can remember, before the DeSoto and before prosperity, the man on the top floor kept a flock. Danny would go up to the roof and watch him fly his birds. He circled a long bamboo pole first to route them, then to funnel them home. When he got a new bird he and Danny would clip it and let it walk the roof feeding on corn. You'd hope when it finally flew it would want to come home.

The green DeSoto goes under the river, comes up in Manhattan, submerges again and rises in Jersey. In the tunnels the family is quiet, to allow Mr. Meadoff to concentrate. Lights pop by, yellow in the gassy air. On the long catwalk a uniformed guard walks from station to station.

Mr. Meadoff drives with his hands firmly on the wheel. He drives so rarely that any outing is an adventure. Crossing rivers and state lines is an expedition. He is uncertain of the engineering principles of bridges, tunnels, overpasses. The spans and trusses compute, he is sure, they seem stable, but those people are human too. Just so the architect of the Pulaski Highway didn't have bills. Or factors. Just so he wasn't worrying about paying for his mother, about how long she would live. Sweat forms in the small of his back as he takes his family through the chutes and banks of the turnpikes. No wonder people these days are less religious, what the *Trib* was saying yesterday. The churches and synagogues are losing their congregations. No wonder. People use up their faith just living. What is left over for the Sabbath?

The sedan comes out into the countryside and he relaxes. He chances lowering his hands on the wheel. The countryside pleases him: driving his family through stretches of road that are not city, are in fact between towns. Expanses of grass, the sight of horses in a pasture.

It is late into summer, and yet wildflowers bloom by the side of the road. Tall yellow ones, blue flowers batched on stalks. He wonders about their names. There is no one to teach him, and if he does not know, there will be no one to teach his children. His own father, fleeing the pogroms that followed the death of the czar, the old Nicholas, equated country life with peasantry. Pete came not to find land, but to find cities. Factories were jobs, a job was life.

"Look at those maples," Mr. Meadoff says. They are driving through suburban Englewood. "See the way those trunks are spotted. Like a disease. But I think they are healthy. I don't think that's a disease."

The maple trunks have elaborate patterns of khaki, yellow, brown. Giraffe patterns. New and old bark, of different shades and thicknesses mottle the trunks. In some places the bark has dropped away.

Danny worries about the time. He doesn't own a watch and the dashboard clock has never worked. He and his pals have tickets tonight to Ebbets Field. No mean trick. Tonight is Pee Wee Reese Night. It's been sold out for weeks. Mr. Rappaport came up with the seats through his stockbroker. Upper deck, down the left field line. The paper says festivities start at six and the game at eight.

[135

The visit with Bubbeh goes slowly. Danny sees the seconds as clearly as if they were bubbles blown from a toy pipe. Each is a globe. There is nothing to do. The old woman seems unhappy that they've come, and keeps resolutely to her television shows. They sit in a row of chairs in back of her. If they were a U.N. delegation she would be the ambassador. They sit in large rattan chairs in the rec room. Bubbeh is waiting for a particular character on the soap opera. The nurse has told them she has a favorite. When the woman finally appears, Bubbeh breaks her silence and says something dark and unintelligible to the screen.

Joyce gets Danny to play ping pong. Before they can start a game, an old man in a cardigan sweater several sizes too large for him comes over and takes Joyce's paddle.

"This isn't for you," he says. The sweater is blue with two red stripes on the left arm. In front there is sewn on a large red "L", with a cloth patch of a diver.

After a respectful period, the Meadoffs decide to go. One by one, the children put their cheeks to their grandmother's. Hers is leathery and veal-colored, and Danny dreads the moment. Afterwards, Mrs. Meadoff stands in front of Bubbeh, blocking the screen, holding her hands. Speaks to her. Mr. Meadoff kisses her on the top of the head. Her hair is thin and brittle. Danny's father's eyes glisten as if he might have a fever.

On the trip home there is little talk. They pass by a fenced park with two ballfields. The basepaths are covered with water from yesterday's rain, and sea gulls walk amid the puddles. Danny visualizes the giant green tarpaulin they use to cover the infield at Ebbets. It is probably being rolled up now. The game will go on. They won't cancel Pee Wee Reese Night. A corps of men squeegees off the excess water then peels back the tarp onto large aluminum rollers. Danny has seen them do it.

His father stares ahead, his hands again holding the ivory wheel taut at two and ten. His mother says, "She seems happy," and his father makes a sound.

It is an odd word, his father thinks. Happy would not be a word I would have chosen. If there were a painless, shameless way to end it, wouldn't that be better? Drowning, maybe. The worst part of swallowing water is spitting it up. If you could be satisfied with breathing water, only for the moment, there would be no coughing. Drowning would be a quiet end.

There is the shame. The stigma. How about if you found a substance that fish eat? What if fish ate rawhide, for instance? You could bind yourself with rawhide to a heavy pipe and ease yourself into the ocean. It would look accidental. Of course you would have to know about fish. You would have to rely that the fish eat the rawhide, that they would be there in the first place. Maybe that is too complicated. Maybe instead a substance that dissolved in salt water. There is so much to know.

It is also a ball park, but it is an arcade, an arena, and when the crowd melts into open roar, a cathedral. Hard to know if you're better off in left with the Dodger Symphony or out towards the right field line. There are no bleachers in right, but you can sit by the foul line and watch Furillo play the three-story manual scoreboard, see the frown on his face, see him watch the winds, play it Red Barber used to say like an organ.

Tonight is Pee Wee Reese's thirty-seventh birthday, and the fans are giving him a night. The three boys come out of the subway and in the streets it could be V-J Day. They cram in with the crowd, thirty-five thousand, that's all the field holds. But once you're in Ebbets, you're there. The field is inches away, the players can reach over and shake your hand and maybe they will. Under the floodlights, the ground is impossibly green, translucent. The Phillies are dressed in grey road uniforms with their girlish red lettering. The Dodgers wear white, Arthurian white, trimmed in royal blue.

As he enters, every fan is handed a candle and a book of matches. The ceremony begins. Some nameless person from the administration introduces Reese. They give him golf clubs and a bedroom set and a pass to some resort in the mountains where Rick had tried to get a job. An announcer tells everyone to watch left center. They open the bullpen gates and five new cars drive out. The crowd cheers. Each has a banner across the hood, announcing the dealer. A Lincoln, a Buick, a Chrysler, a Caddy and a Chevy wagon. They announce that Pee Wee is going to pick one. The crowd is outraged. They jeer. They begin to chant, *All five, All five.* They introduce Pee Wee's daughter. She is going to pick one key from a fishbowl, blindfolded. The crowd cheers. They introduce the dealers, they get booed, especially the Chevy dealer. The Caddy dealer gets cheers. The crowd is backing the Caddy. The people on the field are embarrassed. The kid picks the Chevy. The crowd is angry. All the other cars are worth more, and the crowd wants Pee Wee to get the most on his big night. Now they're yelling *Fix* and the announcer can't get them to quiet down and the kid looks scared. But Pee Wee is the Dodger captain. He holds his hands over his head and smiles. He picks up his daughter in a white dress and hugs her and people who were booing see that and see he's pleased so they cheer, and Pee Wee gets in the driver's side and his girl gets in the other side and they drive off to left center.

"Turns out O.K.," Rick says to his friends as they settle in for the game. "But I'd rather have the Caddy."

"Me," Angie says, "I'll take the Imperial. More leg room."

138]

"More leg room? Are you crazy? Cadillac is the top of the line. What do you say if you want the best bowling ball? You say, the Cadillac of bowling balls. Not the Imperial. You ever heard that Meadoff? The Imperial of bowling balls?''

"I'll take the Imperial,'' Angie says again and they think, maybe he has a shot at it. "More leg room.''

Danny fills in the scorecard as the opening line-ups are announced. Richie Ashburn is digging a hole deep in the box to plant his back foot. He leads off for the Phillies and the game is underway.

At the end of the fifth inning, the man comes over the P.A. and says they're going to turn off the lights and light candles. Everyone holds his candle and sings Happy Birthday. Reese comes out of the dugout and waves his cap. Thousands of candles wink in the round stadium. The candles get blown out and the lights stay off. Angie has brought a sparkler and he lights it. In the darkness he writes his name. The faster he does it the better you can see it but the first letters vanish from the eye before the last is written. He writes Angie, Rick, then Danny and Danny watches, hoping the lights won't come on but they do. Reese has gone oh for three so far. The Dodgers are ahead and need his bat. Danny says that to make allowances, but Rick says, he's almost through. Thirty-seven. Danny looks at the moon-faced shortstop, from some farm town in Kentucky. His grandmother, too, is almost through, but he can find no connection. When Reese is through will he have an attendant stand on a chair to change stations on his television set? Will he decline to recognize his children? Without Reese, will they be the Dodgers? He knows they will be the Meadoffs without Bubbeh. They already are. If the body replaces cells at the rate of a million every day, as the *Times* said Sunday, and all cells have virtually been replaced every three months, where is the person? Perhaps the team could leave Brooklyn and remain the Dodgers. His friends stand with everyone else to see a close force at second and he misses the play.

The game ends in an easy victory and the crowd pours out, walking down Bedford Avenue and beyond. Rick is talking of the Series, of how the Yankees will be there again and how fate awaits the Dodgers the way the bridge awaited Roberto. The bell will toll in October, he says.

"Could this happen in Yankee Stadium?" Angie asks and they assure him it could not. "You know who goes to Yankee games?" Angie asks. "Tourists."

Danny rides the train home. His friends have gone different ways. Most of the passengers on the train were at the game and they exchange inside, satisfied glances. One man holds his rolled scorecard and shakes it in triumph at Danny, and Danny waves back. He gets off at Flatbush, walks down the platform to use the men's room. It is dark and foul smelling, but he prefers it to the crowds at the stadium. Only a few bare bulbs burn by the sinks. As he turns to walk out, he sees Hoot sitting in one of the stalls. Hoot sits on the closed lid, smiling at him.

"Hey, Hoot. How ya doing?"

"Very fine," Hoot says distinctly. Then he says it again and grins. Danny stands and watches him for a moment, then leaves, ascends the stairs and walks home in the familiar air. He is contented. Not merely with the win over Philadelphia and the speckled sight of the lit candles. He takes a measure of pride in Hoot's overcoming his handicap. A diabetic. Danny can tell because he knew one at camp. Why else would a man sit in a toilet stall, rubber tubing wrapped around an arm at the elbow, giving himself an injection?

Wonderful that Hoot would refuse to be slowed by a disease, would go on with his music. It was like a testimonial dinner or one of those Bill Stern stories of people who conquer adversity. A gratified surge sweeps over Danny: he is beginning to understand the world after all.

- **16** -

Danny's numbers brighten the eyes of John Everett Raycroft.

"You should consider this as a career, kid," he tells him. "Your future lies before you. You have a knack, a certain *je ne sais quoi*. You speak French?"

"Spanish," Danny says. "I take Spanish."

"That means you have a certain talent. You have a certain talent for selling." Raycroft is a small man. He eats a breakfast of cheese blintzes with sour cream, and he rests his hands by the plate as he chews. His hands are activated by his voice: when he speaks they flutter and lunge in the air. When he chews, they crouch by the plate.

"I had my doubts when you first come on. You're a little bashful, you know that? Hiding your lice under a bushel. But," and he brushes crumbs of rye toast off the sheets Danny has handed him, "these tell me I'm wrong." Raycroft washes down the last bite with coffee, signals the waitress in an urgent scooping motion.

"Now what I'm gonna do, 'cause I like you, wanna see you make it, I'm gonna get you into the new Fuller line. Cosmetics. Look at this."

He pulls a case from beneath his feet, opens it, begins to pull out its bounty. Pancake make-up, lipstick, rouge, cold cream. Nail polish, one jar for the hands a second for the toes.

"Is this something? Is this the cat's ass?"

Danny agrees.

"And it'll hardly cost you to get into this. Look," He unfolds a pamphlet. "The complete line. I sell you a full demonstration line and five hundred of these pamphlets for thirty-nine fifty. You never see it. It comes out of your commish. You make it back in the first week."

"No," Danny says.

"What's that mean?"

"No. I'm an independent businessman, an entrepreneur, right? And I don't want to buy. You want to give it to me, fine. Otherwise I sell brushes and households."

"Meadoff, kid, be reasonable. This will make you back three, four times." Danny shakes his head. He inflates with a new gas of importance. This is how Rick would handle it.

"Don't need it," says Danny. "Not at that price. I'm doing fine."

Raycroft blinks. Slowly to show exasperation, to remind Danny of his origins in the business. He waits. He waits for Danny to falter. Finally he says, "Tell you what. At my cost. That's as good as I can do. Twenty-four fifty even. Think of what you'll make at twenty percent."

"That's another thing," Danny says. "The commish. I don't think I'm on full commish. Maybe I ought to talk to Hartford."

"Look, kid," Raycroft folds up the brochure, shakes it off. "Don't push this. I mean, you're good yes, but you're not John Everett Raycroft. Here it is. You handle the cosmetics. You pay a penny apiece for the brochures. The demo line I throw in."

"And the commish?"

"The commish goes to twenty-five percent of all brushes and household over a hundred a week."

"On everything," Danny says. "Cosmetics too."

"Cosmetics too," Raycroft says reluctantly.

Danny is late for the second breakfast at Bernstein's. He walks in amid Bernstein's complaints. Bernstein's radio has disappeared. The voice of the Dodgers at Flatbush and Nostrand. For years customers have stopped in to pick up the score, and now he's dark.

"Can you believe someone would steal a radio outa a candy store? While I'm in the back?"

"You got to spend more time on your business," Rick tells him. "You can't be in the back. There are elements on the streets."

Danny distributes the brochures, announces the new plan in triumph. His friends punch his arms in celebration.

"More money for the ponies," Angie says. They are planning for the track that afternoon. Rick is quiet. He eats around the filling of a Danish, until he holds only a varnish-colored crust in the shape of a cross emblazoned against a field of moist poppy seed. Danny asks him what the matter is.

"I wonder how much we left on the table," Rick says.

Danny does not seek an explanation. He changes the subject. He pulls a *Telegraph* from Bernstein's rack and opens it to the day's card at Aqueduct. He makes three or four selections, and they head to the streets for a morning's work.

The limits of Danny's territory begin with Bay Ridge and Frances Gunnerson at one end. He goes the other way. He gets off the train at Grand Army Plaza, a miniature of the Arc de Triomphe, dedicated to the fallen soldiers of the Union, and walks past the entrance to the park, past the deco facade of the library. Up Eastern Parkway, luxury apartments stand. He chooses one at random, the Key West, watches until he sees an elderly lady pulling a two-wheeled grocery cart behind her and falling in step follows her through the lobby. In the elevator she eyes him suspiciously.

"You're not a salesman, are you? Salesmen aren't allowed in this building."

"Do I look like a salesman?" he asks.

She has pushed seven, he the top floor, nine.

"So Mr. No sales? What are you."

"An area representative. I give out free lipstick."

"Really?" she says. "So why are you going to nine and not to seven ell, Herskowitz?"

"Mrs. Herskowitz, I'll be around. I promise you that. And I'll save you a lipstick."

"Better make it three," says Mrs. Herskowitz. "I have two married sons. You give to one daughter-in-law you got to give to the other. You can't let it should get out of balance."

"I'll be there," he says. "Seven-ell."

At the track they no longer need to be accompanied. They are known. Sid has lost a client. The boys see him every now and then. He runs bets for the swells in the clubhouse, consoles losers, congratulates winners. Steady work, pay's not so hot but it's a job. On a good day, when the wind is at his back, he does a little touting. Greenhorns and kids, mostly.

They don't need him because they've been working a guard, a ticket taker in orange and blue. A schmeer of samples: cologne and hair cream. Once in a while a pre-paid disappears, moves or just disappears, and they have a bottle brush or a bag of clothes pins. He collects their tickets and the bottle brush and decides they are of age.

This afternoon they determined their horses. Scientific determination, not picking. Picking, says Joey Ceravolo, you save for your nose. Joey Ceravolo's wisdom weeds out the losers. Pass the horse giving the best return and the worst return. Study the claiming price. Look where the horse has been running. They arrive early and visit the paddock—watching for what they do not know. It is only that summer that any of them has seen a horse without a policeman attached. Their diligence pays off. They collect on the first three races. But they put it back and more in the next four and by the eighth they are looking through the glass bottom of their capital.

Trouble is, the eighth presents an inductive leap. The night before the Giants beat Brooklyn at the Polo Grounds in the final inning. With two out and the game but over, men on second and third, a pinch hitter tops a slow roller across the home infield. Gilliam steps in to harvest the ball when it strikes a Bronx pebble and bounds over his shoulder. The Giants win by one. In the eighth race today runs a gelding with no record going off at twenty-five to one, a gelding named Lucky Bounce.

"You can't ignore the signs," Rick argues. "This is too good to be true."

Angie protests. "Hey, listen. On science we're even. On signs we been taking a bath."

Rick has a vision. "My father says every time you take a bath is a chance to get clean. We get whole on one race. The Dodgers lose last night for no apparent reason, today the reason crosses the wire by two lengths."

Carfare aside, they have six dollars. Angie and Danny agree to risk it. Rick wants that and more. Danny protests. That is all there is.

Rappaport looks at them and smiles. "We got more," he says. "We got the downs."

It is true: all three are carrying downpayments collected on routes that morning. Over Danny's remonstrance, they produce the entrusted funds from separate pockets.

"You can't use that money." The moral issue troubles Angie. "What if we lose it?"

"We won't lose it. Have you ever seen a better sign? Every so often one falls in your lap." A compromise is reached. Danny's downs can be traced, since Raycroft knows about him. The others give receipts to their customers but the company has never heard of them. If the customer complains, Fuller Brush has no way to find them. Angie and Rick's downs go into two twenty-dollar tickets to win on Lucky Bounce.

Lucky Bounce runs eleventh in a field of twelve.

"They should have taken off the blinkers," says Rick, "and put on headlights." They skip the last race and board the train for home. Tomorrow, they agree, they will spend a day working for those lucky housewives indemnified by their honesty. The train travels the surface in Queens, parallel to the Long Island Expressway. From their seats, they see thousands of automobiles pointing east and at the wheel of each the morose face of its driver, docile, caught.

"What do you think?" says Rick. "How many cars on the Expressway? What if everyone decided to walk. Park his car and walk. What happens? New York closes down. They could make history."

"Do you think," Angie asks, "there are more cars on the Expressway than stars?"

Rick turns to him in disbelief. "Stars in the sky?"

"Yeah."

"C'mon."

Angie holds ground. "I'm serious, what do you think?"

"Is this a bet?" Rick asks. "You want to bet there are more cars? I'll cover that. I'm fading the universe."

"How do you prove it?" says Angie.

"It can't be proved."

"Valerio, Valeriani," Rick says. "What do you think? How many people live in New York?"

Angie shrugs. "Eight million."

"Give or take," Rick agrees. "And how many work in Manhattan?"

"I don't know, say half."

"Half. Half are women, goombah."

"So. Maybe a quarter."

"O.K., let's say a quarter. And how many of those commute to Long Island? Taking in mind Westchester, Brooklyn, Bronx, Jersey, where else?" he asks Danny.

"Connecticut."

"Connecticut."

Angie is getting angry. "How do I know? Do I look like Rand-McNally?"

"I'll give you a quarter. Where are you now?"

"Five hundred thousand" says Danny.

"Five hundred thousand. So, how many of those left early or got sick or went to Jones Beach? Maybe fifty thou. And some of the rest work late or eat Chinese, or go to see a girlfriend. Now, we are down to maybe three hundred, four hundred thou. How many drive a car?"

Angie shrugs. He is defeated.

"Half. At most. So maybe there's a part of one hundred fifty thousand cars on the Expressway now. So, how many stars are there?"

"Do I know?" Angie says. "Am I clocking the stars? Let's just skip it."

"More than a hundred fifty thousand," Rick says. "I can tell you that. Go stand on the roof and look tonight. It'll give you a sense of the infinite."

"I don't need it," says Angie. He has decided on smug. He turns his back on the subject, but Rick will not have it.

"Don't need it? Why don't you need it?"

Angie is watching telephone poles go by. He counts ten, fifteen poles before he answers. And he is holding the solid gold, jacks-and-kings answer.

"I already got a sense of the infinite, Rappaport. I got it from looking at the cars on the Expressway."

Danny slips into the house carrying his secret under his shirt like a lifted carton of smokes. The use of somebody else's money—even though he believes the money will be replaced—has a fixed moral position. In his life, landscapes of choice and decision have been graded in broad lines, much in the way the American West he studied last year was graded and surveyed during the opening of the continent, so that even the unexplored areas can be defined, cross-hatched, and their dimensions identified. He does not mention the outing.

He remains silent as well about the appearances of his father's shadow under the tree. A tour from a New York garden club comes to visit the copper beech. Early one morning as Danny is preparing for work a knot of them appear at its trunk, clucking approval. Danny wonders whether the apparition will appear to them. He can find no way of speaking to his father about these scenes. He has no flash-card vocabulary for whatever he has begun to feel. Physical symptoms, yes—the Meadoff children are encouraged to announce their symptoms, since physical health, like good grades, is a family endeavor, a dinner table topic.

Possible it was not his father that he saw. Entirely possible. If it was not his father, it was not anything.

And how could it have been he—this man who returns from work every evening at the proper time, the crossword of the *World Telegram* done, the papers rumpled where he has peered into their every concern? Danny begins to decide that he was dreaming, that branches cast odd shadows and on special nights shadows walled in the white bricks of moonlight have shadows of their own. If it had been his father, Danny knows his duty. He is to look the other way. The Bible has a passage about someone coming across his father's nakedness, and the punishment he receives for it. It makes no sense. No one had meant any wrong, and nakedness should not be the same as evil. It is hard to take the Bible seriously. Brothers cheat each other, kill each other, steal each other's wives. God tricks one man into preparing his son as a sacrifice then rewards him with the leadership of a tribe made to suffer. And another man gets punished because his father was embarrassed. God seems to pick up on petty concerns.

Danny works Bay Ridge. It is predictable, more affluent than his other neighborhoods. Days he can, he drops in to see Frances. In the morning she brews a fresh pot of coffee for them, and in the afternoon while Danny nibbles from a cellophane bag of cookies she pours a long glass of wine. She is interested in the cosmetics line and has Danny try out the presentation. She licks the blue nib of an eye pencil and draws a Nefertiti line over stretched skin, samples the face powder, dabs tint to her bleached cheeks. She holds a compact to her face and looks in its mirror. Danny holds his breath. She inspects her art. The result is the look of someone in a play, someone made up to look dead.

Rick asks Danny how he is doing with Mrs. Gunnerson, and Danny chooses not to reply. The innuendo troubles him doubly, once as it comes from Rick's ever-leering tongue and worse, more sharply, as he wonders whether Rick is not right. Is this an opportunity? Some day he will make his move.

Only if the situation presents itself—although he cannot establish what that means. Whenever he visits, Frances is partly dressed, flouncey, like a bundle thrown from a truck. Eventually the chance occurs: her apartment has a balcony overlooking Prospect Park, and she invites him out to drink milk and eat graham crackers. She shows him the view and says how lovely it is, and that is the chance: he is thinking to say, as are you. But looking down at the red canvas marquee and the speck of doorman under his nautical hat makes Danny vertiginous and he withdraws. Back seated in the kitchen the cracker he has dunked in the milk saturates, comes loose, falls to the bottom of the glass. The mood has gone.

The cosmetics line moves well. Danny sells, Rick and Angie sell better. If they were to place all orders through the company, Raycroft would be astounded. They have not quite caught up their deficit from the track. Like the horses who race against their picks, their debt seems to gallop ever just a little faster. As it is, Raycroft raises Danny's commission to twenty-eight percent and showers him in giveaways. But Aqueduct has taken hold of them and they are $400 in the hole, a hole dug with cash advances from expectant housewives. Danny doesn't worry so much about being caught—his name is nowhere in the chain—as about upsetting some adult order. Some clockwork that accommodates commerce, subway trains, lives as plentiful as taxis. All these seem to click around, one gear driven by the spring of time, the gear's teeth ratcheted into the teeth of another and another turning in a universal market. He is puzzled by the complexity, how it all seems to fit. It is order where you would expect, given the diversity, the bubble gum and sewer lines and bridges and the need of every living thing for fresh water, you would expect chaos. When you think of the possibilities, of how they exceed the actual world the way stars exceed cars on the freeway, you would expect chaos.

The possibilities make him dizzy. They cannot be kept in mind. The man who has a million choices shares a cell with the man who has none. A function with infinite paths is not a function at all. Best would be two—the right way and the wrong. The choice must be a choice, not chaos.

He tells all this to Frances one morning. It doesn't take, he must not have thought it through, so he leaves it. He tries instead to tell her of his father.

"I don't know what's going on with him," he says. Danny sits by an air conditioner the super has that day installed in the window of the breakfast nook. It hums like a spacecraft on afternoon television and drips condensed water into a cake pan Frances has set beneath it by the molding.

"He hardly sees anybody. He doesn't seem worried at all. My mom does. That's how they divide it. He gets the DeSoto serviced. I know that she worries because she tells him all the time he has to make other arrangements, things will not fix themselves, he's sitting on a land mine."

Frances looks at him and blinks. Maybe no one connects in this world. This morning on his first call he got a woman in a hair net who listened to his entire pitch. Must have been a quarter-hour. She took free packets of face cream and a bottle stopper. And when he asked did she want to buy anything, she said, "I'm at wits' end. My child won't stop eating lemons. Have you any idea what a strain that is?"

"What do you suppose she means, Frances? A land mine."

Frances tidies up the glass table. She rearranges the chocolate-covered wafer sticks on the plate and refills Danny's glass with milk. Then she pours a half cup of coffee for herself and tops it off with the pink wine she likes but drinks straight only in the afternoon.

"And he doesn't know what's going on with me. Anything at all. I mean, I can't tell him about you, he would never understand. And the track? He would hit the roof if he knew about the track."

Frances takes a long sip from her cup.

"Why do you think people get married, Frances?" he asks. She shakes her head and touches her finger to the surface of the coffee.

"I don't know," she says.

"Is it love?" Danny asks. "Do you think it is love?"

Frances pulls the shawl collar of her robe at the neck, covering the blue-white patch where her throat joins the chest. There is something in her skin that does not look healthy.

"Love?" Danny can tell from the way she says it she doesn't think much of that answer.

"What good is love? There is nothing you can do with love."

Danny stares across, but Frances's eyes are lowered at the liquid in her cup. Are there dozens of people like me? People who bring this women her needs, munch her sugar cookies and Fig Newtons and vanilla wafer sticks and go back into the streets? Everything in this apartment has been carried here, delivered. Perhaps this woman has never been outside. Perhaps she would melt in the sun. Danny gets up hastily and leaves.

For two hours he prospects. Move them down the slide, John Everett Raycroft urges. Move them from suspect to prospect.

He drops off catalogues, leaving his name and number and a note telling them to read over the materials and promising that he will come back to pick up an order tomorrow. Then he cold-calls: doorbells of strangers, no history or brochure. At each he stays only minutes and pleads for the smallest order.

He works diligently. He keeps the schedule the next day, skipping lunch with Angie and Rick, skipping their trip to the track. He pursues a theory of the world that has appeared to him in fleeting, wooded sightings. His father often says that to find one truth you first embrace many falsehoods. So he approaches his new idea. His theory—that money has more to do with things than anyone lets on—astonishes only because it contradicts the impression his father has imparted.

It occurs to Danny that if he works hard and accumulates money, an explanation now cryptic, perhaps the very secret he has wind of, will be revealed to him. That night at the table he watches for clues but none appears. His mother discusses screens for the porch and how several have warped so they have sprung their frames. The old frames were painted so long ago that if you re-do any you'll never match the faded color. They dine on cold chicken, pumpernickel bread, coleslaw. Gervaise boiled the chicken the day before and for her part his mother has doused it in paprika.

Rochelle tells about some appliance she needs. Something that straightens your hair, like an iron, but it's not an iron. This is built especially for hair. Her mother tells her to borrow one from a friend, that they are not going to spend nine ninety-five so she can straighten her hair.

"I thought you wanted curly hair," Danny says. "I thought that's why you bought that home permanent crap from Arthur Godfrey."

"Watch your language, young man," says his mother.

[153

"Ma, 'crap' is not cursing. You use it all the time."

Mrs. Meadoff denies this and Danny recants. Danny inspects the pebbled skin of the chicken thigh in front of him. Rochelle returns to the iron. All her friends have straight hair. Danny's father is silent, apart, neither sullen nor angry, simply not engaged. While Mr. Meadoff attends silently, Danny studies his father's face. Deep lines run from his nostrils curving out to the corner of his upper lip, lines of renunciation, lines that might appear in a wood carving that had not been oiled. When his mother talks of the veneer of the period lamp tables in the living room, announces that they are drying up, she says they are alligatoring. Would the skin of his father's face alligator with age?

After dinner he calls Angie and tells his friend he is coming over. Angie's house is a short bus ride or a long walk. Danny walks with his thoughts. When he reaches the Valerianis' place, his mood has left him. Angie's family sits in the parlor of the red sandstone house, gathered around the television set. An immigrant Italian shoemaker is answering obscure questions about opera. Angie wants to watch and by the time of the big jackpot, Danny has become involved. Angie's father pounds Danny on the back when the contestant wins the jackpot.

" 'At could be you, Danny. Danny," Mr. Valeriani announces to everybody, "is 'at smart. 'At could be him." Danny feels like a celebrity. He sits on the stoop with Angie for an hour. They discuss Jayne Mansfield, citings of unidentified flying objects in Nevada, the underhand foul shot. Danny says it's a thing of the past.

"Why would they want to land in Nevada?" Angie asks. "Nobody's there."

"Maybe that's why," Danny says. "Maybe they want to land and assimilate with us. So they can mix among us and not be recognized."

154]

"Maybe they eat sand," Angie says. After a moment Danny turns to him.

"Doesn't that make you sad?"

"That the Martians are coming?"

"No. I mean the foul shot. You play basketball. Doesn't it make you sad that the underhand foul shot is a thing of the past?"

Angie shrugs. "No. I mean, I can shoot one-handed. I hit as many that way."

Danny says good night to the Valerianis. Angie's mother presses cookies on him to take home for his sisters. He walks over to MacDonald Avenue and gets a train.

For reasons he cannot name, Danny wakens. Is it a dream or is it a dream's final curtain call? Do dreams end? Do they have exposition and denouement, follow a chalk peak like *Lear* on the blackboard? He understands it is late into the night, for a piece of moon that had not risen when he walked home from the subway now shines through the slatted wood of the venetian blinds. He goes to the window behind his desk and looks out. Moonlight has chased off the yellow of the street lamps, and the Meadoffs' lawn is frozen in this untimely bath, this blue-dot bulb of daylight that neither bursts nor fades but balances between explosion and darkness, balances steadily. He looks at the white night and the shadows cast by the mottled maples and the glistening beech.

And again under the beech is the shape. A shadow of his father's shadow. It is still, its head is held up but not watching. It stands in the palpable dark of night, amid the broken rays as if trying to hide itself from heaven. Somehow Danny notes, knows its eyes are closed. Its face is lifted and its mouth is open.

[155

And now the slightest sound, the sound the wind makes across the throat of an empty bottle, a whistling, piping sound. But it is a clear Brooklyn night in July. There are no clouds and there is no wind.

- 17 -

"So you're crumping out? No more ponies?" Rick asks him. They are at Bernstein's, perched on the chrome and leatherette counter seats. Angie stirs his coffee and squeals his stool by pivoting off one foot to the other.

"I got to make some bread," Danny says. "You guys screw off if you want."

"We don't need bread?" Rick says. "Angelo, tell him of yesterday's outing when the bulls ran in the street and life was good."

"It's true, Danny. We came out forty-one bucks ahead."

"When you lose it's the downs, when you win it's yours. You see anything wrong with that?"

"Only if you get caught," says Rick. "Only if you get caught."

Danny has the *Tribune* open to the stock quotes.

"Rick, let me ask you something. I got two hundred eighty-five, maybe ninety bucks saved. When I'm ready, how do I put it on Boeing?"

"No, no," says Rick. "Not Boeing. That's yesterday's news. My father's heavy into Polaroid. They make a camera, you don't have to get the film developed."

"No way," says Danny. "How do they do that?"

"It all happens inside the camera. It's chemical."

"So how do I put it on Polaroid? Is it only win, or is there a place and show?"

"I'll handle it for you. My father and I will handle it for you."

Danny is pulled by tugs of envy and irritation. "How is it, Rappaport, that when you don't know something you can't say so?"

"What's with you?"

"I mean, if you don't know how I buy Polaroid, just say so."

"My father knows. What's the big deal? You don't want his help, fine. Go ask *your* father."

Danny flushes.

Bernstein emerges from the back room with a Pyrex pot of coffee. He places it on the hot plate, checks the level of malt in the white opaque container marked Carnation.

"So what do you think? I need to buy a new radio?" His question is for any of them.

"How long it's been gone?" Rick asks.

"Week, maybe ten days."

"What are you waiting for?"

"Maybe it'll come back."

"Bernstein," Rick says. "When the Israelites left Egypt did they come back?"

"You think my radio was set free? Emancipated?"

"Moses has it in the desert."

Bernstein nods his head. "The joke is on him then. The batteries are dead."

"They're at it again," says Angie over the *News* centerfold.

"Who is?"

"The UFOs. From another planet. Look."

The *News* has published an amateur photograph. Someplace in Utah. Above what look like bed sheets hanging on a line are two fuzzy almond shapes, identified with black arrows.

"There are no such things," Danny says.

"Look, Danny." Angie holds the paper up to him.

"They could be fighter planes or kites. They could be finger-prints. Jesus, Valeriani, don't be so gullible."

"No, I think he's onto something. Look," Rick says, holding the paper closer to his face. "What if they are twenty feet tall with four arms?"

Angie lets go a low, descending whistle, a V-2 of respect. "Christ," he says. "Think of the Knicks."

"The *Daily News* is not scientific," says Danny. "You need proof."

"Everything's not provable," says Angie. "Look at the Bible."

"The Bible doesn't say squat about UFOs." says Rick.

"It says God made man in His own image," says Danny.

"But that's man. What about non-man?" Rick says, persevering. "Did God make non-man in non-God's image? Or maybe there is a different God for Venus and Mars? Like a general manager."

"That's blasphemy," says Angie. "Only one God, no other gods before Him."

"Before, not after. They don't mention after," Rick says, alive to the possibility. "That's just the way that shit in the Bible works. Trick answers." They ponder this.

"Look," says Danny. "Maybe this is the skinny. Maybe there's one God but different Bibles. The guys hovering over Nevada in the saucer from Pluto are reading their Bible. It says God made Plutonians in God's image. In our edition, God tells us the same thing. If we never get together, who's to know?"

"It's a con," says Rick.

"That's not a con," Angie says. "That's legit."

"So what happens when they all meet?" Rick asks. "Everyone thinking God looks like him and then everyone looking around at guys with eyes on their fingers. Guys who have cauliflower where their dong is supposed to be. Whose side is God on?"

Angie was recently confirmed. Veterans of fast days, Rick and Danny saw him through the twenty-four hours before his confirmation communion, when not even water was to pass his lips. He is looked to for theological revelations.

"Rappaport," Angie says. "You got it all wrong. God doesn't back one team. He moves around. Look what happened in Fifty-one." They are silent, considering the argument. In 1951, God inexplicably and all but corporally moved into the Giants' dugout.

"He gave us the toss," Rick says in His defense and they nod in sympathy. In 1951 in a three-game playoff the Dodgers won the toss. They could have chosen to play the first game away and the last two at home. At Ebbets Field, the ball that Bobby Thompson hit into the seats would have been caught in left center for the last out.

They leave money on the formica for their Danish and coffee. Bernstein is in the back room, stacking policy slips to deliver to the collector. Rick walks around the counter, slides a glass door quietly and removes a small box of White Owl cigars. Danny and Angie fold the papers, put them back on the stack. Danny is left with wonder: the momentous times of history have such altitude, they must have been produced by great forces. Branca was fated to let that second fastball slip away from him, much the way the old man had a rendezvous in all the seven seas with that fish. But where does it stop? Does it come down to him and his sample case? The sale that he will and will not make, whether the leaves from the beech fall to the ground or brush the shoulders of the lurking figure? He cannot decide.

The crisis occurs when no one watches for it, when everyone's eyes are on the television set or the headlines or looking to see that the latch has been turned. These are dangers that are not locked out by latches: they seep through tears in the screen, through keyholes, through spaces in the attic sash where the wood has cracked. They are dangers spawned of coincidence, and the happenings that coincide can lurk in the draperies Mrs. Meadoff had cut to size by the Rumanian woman on Pitkin Avenue who is so reasonable, linger in the maid's room that Gervaise no longer uses now that she's only twice a week, lurk in the corners with the dustballs that we would not have had if only we had put in wall-to-wall carpeting when we moved in.

Rochelle has borrowed an iron. The parents of a curly-haired friend, the lender, bought it for their daughter. They do not suffer from the economies declared by the Meadoffs. Rochelle and her friend have determined that tight curls belong to old people and immigrants, that straight or at the very least wavy hair belongs to Grace Kelly, and they have determined to side with Grace Kelly. Rochelle has been instructed by her friend on the use of the device, and employs Joyce in attendance. Rochelle shampoos her hair to tame it to its most flaccid state. Then she sits on the end of the bathtub to iron. But when she plugs in the straightener, a cheap appliance that looks like an electric divining rod, a cracking spark frightens her. She drops the iron to the floor, to the puddle on the floor in which sit her feet. A nauseating jolt runs through them and through Rochelle's body.

In an instant that only electricity can measure, a spasm dances Rochelle's limbs, blue and white light spits from the socket, a fuse blows and Joyce screams. Rochelle hits the floor in the darkened bathroom. She hits the floor with a deadness that is cinematic. The tiles on the floor are orange and on the wallpaper, in silver and green, bubbling fish swim through diagonal patterns of waves. Joyce's scream brings the family in seconds: Danny from his room, Mrs. Meadoff from the kitchen, her husband from his desk on the first floor landing. Mrs. Meadoff runs so quickly she passes her son and husband. Mr. Meadoff has only turned as she goes by, and still holds in his hand the three checks he cannot get to balance.

By the time Mrs. Meadoff has dragged her daughter into the hall, where she can look at her under the light bulb, has examined her potato white face in the light of the hall chandelier, Rochelle is coming around.

"Call Dr. Eberhart," Mrs. Meadoff tells Danny and he runs and dials the number written on the white semigloss panel by the phone. Mr. Meadoff is now over-looking the scene, late, impotent, unnecessary. He holds the three checks in one hand, a silver ballpoint pen in the other.

"What happened?" he says.

"It's all right," says Mrs. Meadoff. She has counted her daughter's pulse and pushing back the girl's eyelids has examined her pupils. Where she learned to do this she cannot say. "It's all right. Rochelle must have gotten a shock. From that hair thing. But she's going to be all right."

Joyce is crying. The blue flash, the crackling pop, the smell of burning paint. She could not have said the acrid smell was not the snuffing of a life.

Rochelle moans in a low voice, and moves a hand to her face.

"She'll be all right. She got a shock."

"I can't get him," Danny shouts up the stairwell. "Only his answering nurse. Do we want the doctor on duty?"

Mrs. Meadoff looks her daughter over again. The crisis has passed. She tells Danny never mind. "Never mind," she says again but more softly, as part of the cure. Finally Joyce catches her breath and swallows her sobs.

"Are you sick to your stomach, honey?" Mrs. Meadoff asks Rochelle. Her daughter shakes her head no. Pink comes back to her cheeks that, without blood in them, were no color at all. What do we look like dead? Danny wonders. Does everyone in heaven need to get some sun? Who is selling Debutante blush door to door? Now Rochelle is coming to.

Just as they reach consensus that it was a lucky accident Mrs. Meadoff and her children agree, even—especially—the victim agrees that it was a fortunate accident compared to what it could have been, just as that warm decision is made that allows them to congratulate each other, Mr. Meadoff begins to yell.

The sound alone is startling. He never yells. No one has ever heard him lose his temper, certainly not at home. Now he is shouting at Rochelle, who lies umbrellaed from harm, her head cozy in her mother's lap. He is seized with shouting, seized with an energy none of his family has ever seen. He trembles and the checks in his hand riffle.

"How could you do that? What if you'd killed yourself? Don't you know better? Not to handle electricity in the tub?"

He is shouting at her, and she is lying with her head in her mother's aproned lap. The scene makes no sense. Rochelle does know better, Danny begins to explain to his father, but Mr. Meadoff cannot be distracted. His trembling becomes broader, a palsy. Now all the children are alarmed. Rochelle, fresh to consciousness, begins to weep softly. Never long quelled, Joyce sobs again, fresh sobs. It is a frozen moment, without precedent or antidote. Without time.

162]

Mrs. Meadoff responds from where she sits. Coldly in a voice thin and straight as a wire.

"Stop what you're doing." He stops.

"How dare you attack this child? Have you no love for any of us? Don't you care about any of us? What is the matter with you? She might have died and now you terrify her."

They hold their ground on the second floor hall of the Dutch colonial clapboard house in the Doctor's Section. Mr. Meadoff stands on the balancing point. It is as if they are in a small boat and only he has arisen. He must either disembark or reseat himself if the craft is to stay upright. He hesitates. He considers the deployment of his family. His wife and one daughter sit on the floor before him, his second daughter clings to the wall. Danny is on the landing nearby, but whether it is his distance or his discomfort, his presence offers no moment to the balance. Mr. Meadoff opens his mouth to say something, closes it again, turns and walks down the stairs.

The incident is over. Rochelle is helped to her room and put to bed. Mrs. Meadoff's considerable nursing skills are brought to bear on her. She is bathed, fed tea and toast, her pulse and temperature checked that evening and again the next day. Mrs. Meadoff secures the craft that floats her family, lowers its center of gravity.

That night their father reappears at the dinner table. He inquires of Rochelle, about her health. No other mention is made. After dinner, as Danny replaces the large roasting pan on the shelf his mother cannot reach and helps stack and store the dishes, she raises the event with him. She raises it to lay it to rest.

"Daniel, I want you to forget about this hair straightener."

"All right, Ma."

"I want you to put it out of your mind. Your father's not himself lately. He is very worried about the office."

Geologic shifts open fault planes to the eye. Cracks in the mantle rock may run together to form a cleavage deep to the next fold, to some fundament, to some buried heart of the rock. They are unseen. Or the fault plane may run shallow, may crease the layer of marl on the surface. His mother has never observed to Danny that his father worries.

"What should I do?" Danny asks.

His mother looks at him carefully.

"About the office, I mean."

The corners of her mouth pinch as she sucks on her lip in thought, but if she is considering his offer she does not respond to it. After a moment her face springs back to its shape. She speaks as she moves about to secure cabinet doors already closed.

"It's not your concern, Daniel. The office is not your concern. There is nothing to be done."

The incident passes.

On the following day, Danny discovers a change in the household. Above the passageway between the house and garage is a small bedroom. They used it for Gervaise when she was full-time. It has no bath. She would use the facilities, as Mrs. Meadoff calls them, in the basement. The room has a single window and because it is built over an outdoor corridor, its floor is cold in the winter. Rochelle had wanted to have a friend live in it for a week over Christmas vacation, but Mrs. Meadoff said she would catch pneumonia from the bare wood.

The following day, Danny realizes, his father moves into that room.

-**18**-

How could he not have noticed the ring before? It is the size of a knuckle. Lindenauer wears a ring on the last finger of his right hand. When he folds his hands, as he is doing now, his fifth finger tucks under and that ring chocks his hand, secures his body against the desk top. It is a square of gold, large as a molar, with a faceted red stone in its center. Its size would make you hesitate before antagonizing this man, even with his small and tended hands. If ever he hit you with that ring, you would bear the mark.

"They can't be lost," Lindenauer is saying again. Mr. Meadoff says nothing. They are lost, he has told Lindenauer, and Paradise Fashions is not insured.

"I wish I made it up."

"Tell me again why they're not insured," Lindenauer says.

"Because our purchasing agent screwed up. Because if you don't buy the insurance before you ship they won't sell it to you after you ship and particularly when the goods are lost."

Lindenauer rises from his swivel chair, faces the corner of the window where the panes come together, tucks his hands in the back of his pants to smooth down the shirt. That Mr. Meadoff has never liked him has not seemed important until now. It has not seemed to matter. Mr. Meadoff does not engage the people he works with in his thoughts. There are pleasant people and, especially now that he thinks on it, unpleasant people. It should not signify. He wonders what Lindenauer will do. He has seen Lindenauer enraged, hate in the lines around his eyes. Scream into the telephone with curses that God Almighty wouldn't use, slam down the receiver and go cool again.

Lindenauer's secretary comes in. She is carrying a stack of documents for him to sign. He takes them from her with both hands, one over and one under, and lowers them to his desk. He begins to go through them. Meadoff rises and walks around the office. On the desk is the glass paperweight, the one with the frozen flower. Meadoff decides not to pick it up. He remembers its smoothness, its density.

The view to the west is of office buildings. Mr. Meadoff lets his eyes lose focus. He relaxes the squint that he needs to see distances, and the hard edges of window, cornice, post and beam melt away. What is left is color. Color softens line, even shape. It is a lovely sensation. Behind him, Lindenauer has found something in the documents and asks the secretary. She doesn't know, she says. They came that way. Lindenauer reaches for the telephone, dials a number.

The older buildings to the west have tarred roofs. They are built of brick, the shorter buildings are invariably brick. Those that have been painted are emerging from their decoration, decades old. No one paints a building anymore. The unions. There is an occasional dark patch in what Mr. Meadoff sees, a glass building. The new architecture, the architecture of Park and Madison and Fifth, is glass but you don't often see it on the West Side.

Lindenauer is yelling into the mouthpiece. "That's not the way it's supposed to be," he says. It doesn't have anything to do with what he called Mr. Meadoff in to talk about. It has to do with radio tubes, their cost or when they will be delivered. Mr. Meadoff cannot tell if Lindenauer bought them or sold them. Lindenauer is very angry. Perhaps if I listen more carefully.

But the view pulls him back. He gets up and walks to the window. Maybe there is another stage of unfocus, an even softer stage, if he can only find it. The shapes and colors make an abstract picture and if he again can dissolve his vision he will be able to see it. Like seeing a painting up close, then stepping back and seeing it whole, then farther back and seeing it through glass brick. Or from under water.

Once when he was a young man he went to the museum with a woman. She called all the paintings canvasses, and she was devoted to them. She told him at each stop what the artist had in mind. He was very much in love with her and he was not troubled by how she went on. Together they saw a painting of women dancing naked in a circle. It was a modern picture and there was no embarrassment in their nakedness. He never forgot the painting. The dancing women were clay pink against the sky, stretching and free. He had never gone back to that museum. He cannot remember where it is. Somewhere on the upper East Side, with the new offices of glass skin, where thousands of strangers work, somewhere as he stands looking west and Lindenauer curses into the phone, curses vilely and gets his way, somewhere behind him.

"He's in on it," Lindenauer says. "He's got to be."

Mr. Meadoff thinks he is still talking on the phone. Lindenauer's tone is different but it is not pleasant, and Meadoff thinks it is still the conversation about vacuum tubes until Lindenauer calls his name.

"What did you say?"

"He's in on it. That agent."

Meadoff walks back to the guest chairs in front of the oversized desk and sits down. When he was looking out the window he had wandered behind Lindenauer and noticed the desk top. It was odd. All of the appointments—a pen-and-pencil set given Lindenauer for some charity, a brass carriage clock, the crystal paperweight with the flower—have been stationed an equal radius from where Lindenauer sits. Just beyond his grasp. You don't notice that when you're sitting across from him.

"What makes you say that?"

"He's in on it. All the other shipments he insures, but this one, the big one, he forgets. If it had been insured the carrier would pay us and then investigate. On the scene. They'd find the jerseys, believe me." Lindenauer leans across, reaches out to the perimeter of toys and appliances and from a walnut humidor fetches a fresh cigar.

He slips the cigar end into his mouth and wets it. "But we, we are stuck here. What do we do to find the goods? We call our fucking agent."

Meadoff considers this. That is what he did when the cartons failed to appear. He trusts the shipping agent. He has for years. Morales and Sons. Morales has two sons in the business. Would a man with two sons in the business do such a thing? It sounds improbable. The sons would have to know, would have to find out. Then what would he say?

"I don't think Morales is involved in this," Mr. Meadoff says. Lindenauer sticks the end of the cigar in his mouth and twirls it back and forth. He touches his toes to the carpet and swings his chair around to show the back of his head.

"That's great," he says. When he speaks he holds the cigar in his front teeth. His words come out *at's gray*, but Mr. Meadoff knows what he means.

"At's gray. At'll hep us get the goods back." Lindenauer swings back.

"I could go over. I could find Morales and we could investigate." He is not eager to make the trip. He has been to the Philippines only twice, once when they started doing business and a second time when they changed banks. It is a long flight, over an endless expanse of water, and he is sure he will die by drowning. He has known that for a long time. Lincoln was shot, but of course he was a president. No one shoots an importer of knitwear. It is a needless use of bullets. Mr. Meadoff doesn't even know anyone who owns a gun. Where has he seen them? Parades, Armed Forces Day, on the hip of policemen.

Lindenauer studies him. He holds the cigar and looks at the darkened tip. He could be imitating a comedian, the way he studies the cigar. He flicks a toggle switch on the panel on his desk, and Mr. Meadoff hears the intercom buzz at the secretary's desk outside the door. They wait together for a moment. The secretary comes in carrying a steno pad and waits silently at the doorway. She is ignored.

"See," he says. "The thing is, the goods are gone. You're not going to find them. Morales, he hid them, he's not going to find them either. Thing is, Meadoff," he pulls an ash tray from the semi-circle and rests the cold cigar in it. "Thing is, I don't think you could find Morales. I don't think you could find your *tuchus.*"

Lindenauer nods at him. Mr. Meadoff cannot see the secretary but he knows she is there. He feels uncomfortable for her. She shouldn't have to watch this.

"I think you're wrong about the shipping agent," he says.

"You think?" Lindenauer explodes. "Who gives a flying fart what you think? You can start to think when the factors squeeze. 'Cause when they squeeze, it ain't gonna be my nuts in the vise. I didn't put *my* house up. I won't lose *my* house."

Lindenauer grabs the cigar and reaches for a table lighter behind him. It is an enormous piece, silver plated with the moldings of a Greek funeral vase.

"I won't lose my house either," Mr. Meadoff says quietly. He has considered his position. He has computed the numbers. "There's still equity in the business. Before I lose my house we can liquidate the business. There'll be enough to pay off the creditors."

Lindenauer is sucking in the flame. It pops from the nub of wick set in silver. As the cigar lights he lets go mouthfuls of smoke each with a gasp, a satisfied gasp.

"You're a *schmuck*, Meadoff. You know that? What makes you think I let you off the hook? We're fifty-fifty partners. You can't liquidate without my vote. And you think you're getting it? You ain't. You sign a bank guaranty for the business, fine. The factors squeeze, you just pay them. You can't pay them, too bad. You lose the house. I keep the business. No complaints."

Lindenauer slows his speech, softens his tone. He breathes around the cigar. The fragrance of smoke fills the air. Mr. Meadoff's father used to smoke cigars and the fragrance is the same. Perhaps it is the same brand. He doesn't remember his father's brand.

Mr. Meadoff rises and walks to the door conscious of his limp. "I'm sorry you had to hear all this," he says to the woman standing in the doorway with the pad.

"You know your trouble?" Lindenauer calls to him in a friendly voice. "You're always looking in the wrong direction. You should have seen this when you ordered the jerseys. That your agent might screw you. You got to look ahead." Lindenauer signals his secretary with his cigar, waves her in. She sits in the chair that Mr. Meadoff has left. Mr. Meadoff turns and walks out the door.

I do not think it is fair to judge a man for his meanness. Meadoff awaits the elevator. It is a modern elevator, with numbers that change in a window. In his building there is an ancient pointer that rotates to tell you where the car is. Lindenauer says to me what he says because he sees it that way. He sees life from his appetites. He has not thought to himself, I want to be like Gandhi, like Lincoln, but the hell with it. Instead I will act like Lindenauer. He acts from his needs. What was it that makes

Lincoln write to the mother? She had lost five sons in the war. And Lincoln sat at a desk, his knees probably hitting the underside, and wrote his letter. "How weak and fruitless must be any word of mine which should attempt to beguile you from the grief of a loss so overwhelming." He wrote from his pain. He must write to endure the pain, and only he could have written those words. That is what makes him Lincoln as surely as this day, that paperweight, those uninsured cartons make Lindenauer.

That is pain. Not what I suffer. What I feel is dust in the air, the static you get on the radio. The universe is full of it. If Lincoln could deal with his, if Lincoln didn't make himself into Job, who is Meadoff to be different?

He suddenly remembers the name of the man who painted the dancers. Henri Matisse. He was famous for this picture. Others too. Perhaps one day he would go back and ask at the museum. They would surely be able to find the painting. He has not forgotten the name of the woman. He recalls her name easily, although he has not seen her for a very long time.

- **19** -

Every apartment in Brooklyn has a smell of too much living. Even an odor they intend, Danny decides, and even when they spray for it. The lilac freshener lies on top of the onions, white pine forest hazes over the plastic slip covers, the marinara, the rug shampoo.

He finishes a floor of the Samedna. It is the Winter Palace of apartment houses, filling a square block, and sits around the corner from the Rappaports. First floor pays the lowest rents. All the windows are barred, and street level is suitable only for sound sleepers who can ignore the dawn garbage collections. He makes no sales, is finally chased by a super who threatens in dark accents to call the police.

Minutes before five, too late to start a floor of promise. He will drop in on Rick. If Rick isn't home yet he can shoot the breeze with Lou. He has not seen Rick's father in months. Mr. Rappaport has all the kids call him Lou. When Danny tells his mother that, she says, not in my house.

Lou is a pal. Lou tells Rick and his friends jokes, funny ones, dirty ones. Danny has never heard his father curse. Lou is a gambler, has been to the casinos in Vegas and Havana. Lou brought home playing cards from a Cuban vacation with pictures of men and women. Can you believe it, Danny said, but Rick saw nothing odd. Lou has always been his father.

Rick lives in the Neville Arms. It's higher class than the Samedna, you can tell from the way its name scrolls in Gothic script on the awning. If we lived in an apartment, I wouldn't have to mow the lawn. And the super is always there for the sash cord or the leaking radiator. You don't have to wait for Handy Andy Brown the colored man or screw it up yourself. Apartment living is urbane. Rick's house in particular. The Neville Arms has heraldic shields of concrete over the front hall doors, and its elevator is covered in gilt mirrors, even on the ceiling.

This evening the place looks a little worn. Danny's eye, now exposed to a hundred apartment houses, sees the attempts at grandeur. The lobby smells of cabbage. Cooking cabbage is the most popular smell on his route. Who eats it all? And in the elevator someone has carved initials in the thin gold spray of the mirror, initials and what started to be a heart but all the arcs strayed off in straight tangents so the letters are enclosed in a jagged box, a crude diagonal sun.

Rick is not home, only Mrs. Rappaport. That uncomfortable possibility occurs to Danny not until he sees a speck of opalescence move behind the lens in the peephole under 7H. A dot of liquid darts by the glass, and he is seen. The chains rattle off and Mrs. Rappaport is hugging him, she hugs with arms, pelvis and kneecaps touching, and is smacking wet lips on his cheeks.

"Daniel, darling. You've come to see me. How wonderful!"

Danny moves through the apartment. He concentrates on its glass animals, hammered brass bric-a-brac. Mrs. Rappaport talks on—he has lost the subject. He hears the word "ormolu" several times. She seats him in the living room, on puffy cushions of dark red velvet. He moves four throw pillows aside to make a place on the couch. She calls it a davenport. The room, so unlike those in his parents' house, could be foreign. He could be in East Africa or the Ottoman Empire. The fabrics are stiff and elaborate. They are noticed. Mrs. Rappaport redecorated last year. Danny remembers, because of the carpet. The room feels new, just out of the box as if no one has used it, has sat on the brocades and velvets. A gleaming oval coffee table with turned legs and a delicate hutch rim sits in front of Danny, perches on a small prayer rug which itself lies on top of the wall-to-wall carpeting. The carpet was the first project in the refurbishing. For weeks after it was installed, Rick and he had to take off their shoes and leave them on the corrugated plastic runner in the front hall. Danny remembers the carpeting man. He wore kneepads and he pointed around the room with a device that fit to his thigh to stretch the material. He showed Rick and Danny the depth of the pile and how the pad added feel. That's what he called it, feel. He bent the cutting of carpet back and insisted they rub their hand over the bend. It was a brand new color, he told them. Pacific Mist.

Now Danny sits looking at his shoes, at the National Geographic on the table, anywhere but at Mrs. Rappaport who is talking without stop.

Danny stands up. "Can I use the bathroom, Mrs. Rappaport?"

"Sylvia," she says and he nods. "You got to go, you got to go."

He wanders down the hall. Its walls are hung with antique maps, heavily matted in browns and mauves. Rick's room is at the end. To get there he passes the Rappaports' bedroom, averts his eyes. Still he sees, or knows, what is inside. A giant bed— it is, Mrs. Rappaport has told him, king-size, a new concept— covered in a sateen spread of burgundy. It is a mesa, a landmark, a prominence. He goes to the little bathroom off Rick's room. Even the Rappaports' toilets are different. They are color coordinated, the bowl and sink and tub match the tiny initialled towels hung from the rack. Danny pees into the burgundy bowl, flushes the toilet and watches the noiseless swirl. He rinses his hands, wipes them on his jeans. The towels cannot be meant for him, cannot possibly absorb water. They are monogrammed in gold.

He dawdles, wanders into Rick's room. Its bed is covered in a spread that matches the king's. In miniature. Everything is in its place. Not like his walls, where pictures and clippings stick with randomly colored thumbtacks. He envies Rick the black wood frame of the '52 and '53 Dodger team photos. National League Champions. Both teams lost to the Yankees. In '51 and again last year, the Giants went to the Series. It is fate: last year when the Giants went, they got to play a round-heeled Cleveland team and beat them in four straight. The Dodgers never have the breaks. God may not roll dice with the universe, but I'll bet he's made a fortune betting against Brooklyn.

Astonishing. In the last six years the Yankees have won five Series, the Giants one. Brooklyn has lost three. In the entire galaxy, teams from New York—if you count Brooklyn as New York for just this purpose—had over eighty percent of the slots in the Series. The odds against that are enormous. In any single year, thirty-two to one. Two years, thirty-two times thirty-two. Nine hundred and eighty four. For six years, thirty-two to the sixth power. The numbers touch the cosmic. A manifestation of divinity, as if He is trying to reveal something through the National League standings. The U.S. is the world's anointed nation: perhaps this borough is the very spot on the forehead where the oil is daubed. What does that do for us? It's like being the chosen people. It makes us the marks.

Sylvia is rattling pans about in the kitchen. She calls to him to go into Rick's room and amuse himself. He opens Rick's closet. The Meadoffs have nothing comparable. A closet organized like a miniature men's store, an elegant store, with its own light switch and two fixtures, with seamless Pacific Mist on the floor. Rick's clothes are displayed, arranged by season. Winter jackets, two-season shirts, summer. The hangers for each season are separated by a carving that Sylvia bought in Vermont, a cedar squirrel suspended from a ribbon. And all of Rick's shirts are ironed and draped from hangers. The effect is comforting. It is reassuring somehow, as if Danny were not there alone. It gives him a sense of order and satisfaction, a sense of a family with a defined purpose. You can tell from the closet that this is a family with plans. The closet has custom-built shelves for Rick's baseball mitt, his collection of zinc pennies—he plans to sell them when he is thirty and buy a Chris-Craft—his shoe polish kit.

And Rick's shoes. The floor of the closet has a rack so that all the shoes line up. Their heels notch over a furring strip and their toes point straight ahead. What fascinates Danny he cannot say. The shoes all bear a glistening shine, one Danny is unable to produce on his shoes with the thin liquid he uses. It is all military, marvelous.

And there in the corner of the closet, a wire wrapped around its midriff, is Bernstein's radio. What else could it be? A white Philco with gold lettering. Danny picks it up. His pulse races. There is the chip in the frame where Bernstein hit it with the salt cellar in 1951 when Thompson tagged the pitch that space suspended.

"That old thing," Sylvia says. He spins, as the crime programs would say, an accessory.

"That old thing. Your friend bought it for five dollars. Though why I don't know. He has a new clock radio. See?" Sylvia points: by Rick's bed, the latest General Electric technology, a radio that wakes you up, silences when you have fallen asleep. The world of tomorrow here on Kings Highway and Avenue L.

"And it doesn't go with anything," Sylvia says. "You ask him why he brings that in the house, it matches nothing. He just buzzed." This last leaves Danny mystified—what has Rick done now?—until he hears the front door open.

"He buzzes to tell me he's home," Sylvia explains.

Danny replaces the stolen radio. He cannot stay his heart's drum. He arranges the plug to sit on top as he found it, and walks quickly to the living room.

"Ricky-Ticky," Sylvia is saying. "Look who's here. Look who never comes around anymore now that he's got all the horny housewives in Greenpoint waiting for him."

Rick is carrying his sample case and order book. He pegs his friend with a startled look.

"This some sort of surprise?"

"I was down the block." Danny moves his hand in loose circles.

"He'll stay for dinner," Sylvia says. "We're having veal parmigiana, just like you like, Ricky. I have plenty."

The boys break the stare. Rick brings Danny back to his room, puts away his things, changes into high-topped black sneakers. Lights up a Chesterfield, offers the open pack to Danny who waves it off. Danny lies on the bed and they talk of the day's sales. Danny doesn't mention the radio, and when Rick opens the closet to put away his shoes, he looks away.

A dinner bell rings. When they walk into the dining room, bayberry candles burning in the two hurricane lamps, Sylvia is still holding the bell by the tip of its handle. She is smiling.

"Ding, ding," she says and again she rings the porcelain bell.

Danny pulls up to the table, slides the cloth napkin from under the heavy silver fork, and spreads it on his lap. Three plates sit on batik place mats, and on each plate a thin slice of veal, spaghetti under a red mushroom sauce, fresh asparagus. There is ice water in the bottle-green goblets, and the glass catches the candlelight and the dimmed bulbs in the chandelier over the table. The bulbs in the chandelier are fluted, to suggest candle flame. Sylvia's house is like a hotel, Danny realizes, and the table could be at a fine restaurant.

It occurs to him what is missing.

"Where's Lou?" he asks. "Aren't we going to wait dinner for Lou?"

Sylvia looks at Rick, who studies a stalk of asparagus on his fork. He rotates it to view both sides.

"Lou doesn't live here, darling," she says at last. Danny flushes. How could he have asked?

"Lou lives in Manhattan. On East Seventy-sixth, no less. Can you imagine that?" Her voice is thick and warm, and though the question she asks doesn't sound as if it needs an answer, Danny tries to think of one. The sincerity of her words hang over the table.

But the fact is, he cannot imagine. In Manhattan he knows only the movie houses, a few Chinese restaurants, the Garden. For Sylvia's sake he tries to imagine East Seventy-sixth but cannot.

"On East Seventy-sixth off Lexington. A nice block. With the receptionist from his firm. Who," she says evenly, "I should add he is *shtupping.*"

The air is cool from the air conditioner whirring in the kitchen window. The murmur is the sound of a constant surf, interrupted only by the pebble-plopping drips of water into a pan below.

"You know *shtupping*, Daniel? You know what I'm saying?"

Danny turns his water goblet on the place mat. It has sweated and plants a ring of moisture exactly the footprint of its round base. He turns the goblet in that ring.

"Sylvia," Rick says. "Leave it."

"Leave? I didn't leave. Your father left. I'm still here." She is smiling now, a kindly smile.

"You're embarrassing Danny."

Sylvia reaches over and pats Danny's hand, the hand on the glass.

"No, no. No need for him to be embarrassed. Daniel didn't do anything wrong. Daniel didn't leave. Your father left. He needs something younger, juicier. Tighter. You understand what I'm saying, Daniel?"

"Sylvia, for God's sake." Rick balls his napkin up and throws it by the plate.

"That's how he treats me," Sylvia says. "He throws me on the junk pile. He just throws me out." Sylvia has tears in her voice but somehow Danny does not think they are genuine.

Rick turns to Danny. " 'I wish the boy were here,' " he recites. His face is set. " 'I wish the boy were here and that I had some salt.' "

" 'The fish is my friend too,' " Danny replies, grinning. " 'I have never seen or heard of such a fish but I must kill him.' "

The boys finish their meal. The meat is very good, and it also goes well with the spiced sauce. Danny would like seconds on the spaghetti but when Rick offers, even when Rick goes to the kitchen to fetch some, he declines.

"This is terrific, Sylvia," he says while they are sitting alone at the table.

Sylvia has stopped eating. She holds her chin in her left hand, and with two fingers touches her lower lip. She looks very sad. Danny cannot remember enjoying a meal as much.

"Look at this," Rick says. He has finished dinner. He grasps the crumpled napkin by two corners and raises it as a bunting.

"*Mira*. This is the flag of permanent defeat."

The boys clear the table and leave Sylvia sitting holding on to her face. There is nothing to say. Two tracks run from the corners of her eyes, dusty with lavender eye shade, and every so often a large tear leaks down the track.

"There's lemon crisp in the refrigerator," she tells them.

They take the plates in and load the dishwasher. The Rappaports have re-done the kitchen, and the dishwasher is also new. Aztec Tan. Danny sells a polish to protect the surface and enhance the color. He wonders if Sylvia has some. Danny removes a flat Pyrex baking dish from the refrigerator and takes off the wax paper. He cuts two large squares of lemon crisp and they sit on the counters across from each other, eating.

[179

"Your mother's a great cook," Danny says. Rick doesn't answer. "She really is."

Danny tells Rick about the odds of an all-New York World Series.

"I think God is in mathematics," he says.

Rick looks at him. "What do you mean? You saying God is fading the Phillies?"

"No. Just that God probably doesn't speak in language. I think if He speaks at all it's in mathematics. Or music."

"What about the Bible? He speaks all the time there, in English."

"Not English, dummy." Danny slides down, cuts another slice of lemon crisp. "Hebrew. He speaks in Hebrew there."

Rick is impressed. "Is that right? Smart guy."

"An ace."

"But He doesn't speak algebra."

Danny pokes his friend on the arm. "But He's stopped talking. In the Bible He speaks Hebrew, Aramaic, Greek. But no longer. He's stopped talking to anyone."

"Like Garbo."

"So, I figure maybe He's just changed languages."

"To mathematics?"

"You got it. Or music."

"Music?"

"They're related. He could speak in mathematics or in music."

Rick shows by a slow nod he is prepared to consider this.

"Tell you what. Saturday I'll tune in to WNEW, the Make-Believe Ballroom. He does a guest slot, I'll let you know."

Danny walks down Flatbush towards his home. It is dusk, with its early and melancholy message of how quickly the summer moves. If Flatbush Avenue were a desert island, could you live with nothing but what you could scrounge from the stores? On a single block? He passes Morris Cleaning/Pressing/Alterations, Harvest Moon Chinese, Awalt Grocery, Green Cross Medical Supply and Prosthesis, Ebinger's Bakery. This is a good island. A good block to be washed upon in a lifeboat. If Green Cross couldn't fix you up with a prosthesis, perhaps Morris would be able to alter you.

The next block is spiritual. Holy Family occupies half of it, both the rec center and the church. Danny knows the rec center well. He and Rick met Angie at the rec center, where the three of them played for the Holy Family Tigers. The Holy Family basketball court is the best in the neighborhood. The temple's has rafters that obstruct the long set shot. Jewish architects had not considered the outside shot. The Tigers finished runner-up in the borough that year. Danny has the trophy on his bookshelf, victory rampant between a Messerschmitt and Howard Fast's *The Tattooed Man*. Victory is a woman with considerable knockers; she wears a nightgown, stands on a white plastic pedestal and holds a laurel wreath over her head.

After Holy Family the Jeffers Funeral Home, then a little *shul*. Nothing more than a storefront. *Rodolph Shalom*. Danny has seen it on Saturdays, filled to overflowing with piety. Since the building has no balcony, the women must sit in the back or not come at all. The orthodox are an odd set. Ten men required to start prayer. Nine men and ten thousand women won't do. Do they really think God cares? If God can pretend that this is a synagogue and not an empty store with soaped windows and SHIT chalked on the door, does He really count ten men?

A vast Coupe de Ville going up Flatbush on the far side crosses two opposing lanes and parks by the curb at Danny's side. It is an astounding stunt even without traffic and Danny comes alive to the boldness, the danger. When he sees Joe Cera-volo behind the wheel, the collector he knows from Bernstein's back room, he relaxes.

"You the Meadoff kid?" Joe asks.

Danny is pleased. He didn't think Joe knew his name. Joe is smoking a Raleigh cigarette—you can tell from the cork-colored filter—and he has it stuck in a short yellow holder. He clenches his teeth as he speaks, and the cigarette bobs up and down.

"Listen, I want you should run a message for me."

"Can't, Joe. I got to get home."

Joe nods. "That's right. I want you should take this message home to your father. C'mere."

Danny is startled. Those two people would not know each other. His father doesn't play the numbers, doesn't hang out at Bernstein's. Danny does as he's told, walks over to the open car window.

"C'mere," Joe says again, motioning him down as if he wants to whisper something to him. Danny leans over, puts one hand on the open driver's window, leans in.

Joe takes the cigarette holder out of his mouth and holds it in his fingers the way you'd hold a pencil. For a moment he watches the smoke rise.

"Just tell your father I got his message. I got the message and it's no go. No extensions. No delays. The twenty-first is the twenty-first."

Danny listens carefully.

"You got that?" Joe asks him.

"Yeah. I got it."

Joe looks up at him to make sure. "Good," he says in a soft voice. "You're a good kid."

Then Joe takes the cigarette like a pencil and lowers it to the back of Danny's hand, gently lets its red end rest there until Danny pulls away with a shout.

182]

"Hurts, don't it?"

Danny steps back. He has dropped his sample case and is rubbing the back of his hand, looking at Joe with wonder. He feels nausea well up in the fleshy back of his throat. Joe looks to see that the ash is still in place, sticks the holder back between his teeth, and drives off. Again he crosses two lanes going against him and again not a single horn sounds. The huge Caddy wobbles as it steers across the yellow line and down Flatbush.

Danny has a moment when he is sure he will double over and vomit into the gutter. It passes. His mouth tastes of pennies, and he breathes in through his nose. The little grey smudge on the back of his hand is throbbing. When he rubs the grey comes off and it is faint pink underneath. He hates fear, lives his life to avoid it, crosses night streets when knots of strange kids walk towards him so he doesn't have to confront them. Cowardice he hates also, but most of all he hates pain. Now the spot is red and perfectly round. A dime of pain. It is beating. It is a signal on the radio of the test that will broadcast only in the event of an emergency.

What should he have said to Joe Ceravolo? What should he say to his father? If only he had spoken at first, when he first saw the figure beneath the tree, if only he had spoken to him, inquired about him, brought him inside. How has Ham offended when he looks upon his father's nakedness? What is sinful? The nakedness? The humanness of our father? Is it better to look on him or to look away?

Danny cannot pull the thread to its end. He can think only one thought. The red emergency button has been pushed. But his feelings are several. When you are served carrots and peas, the taste of the two do not change, but when you have new feelings and they are strong, the result is a feeling completely different. So when your parents suddenly appear as people in front of you it is frightening. You want them to be parents, because people, even by then you have learned, change. They age, they change, they die.

- 20 -

When the alarm sounds, Danny is dreaming of Joe Ceravolo. Or he is awake and imagining him. Danny has spread a murky yellow unguent on the spot on his hand but he can bring back the pain with a glance. He carries a message that might be important, along with the apprehension of delivering it. But when he tells his father over bowls of Quaker Puffed Rice, his father simply nods. Danny doesn't mention the cigarette.

Mr. Meadoff goes off to work considering whether the day will again be warm. He slept only in patches last night, and the lack of sleep from that night and several like it during the week leaves him light-headed and dizzy. A pleasant dizzy, the four cups of wine to celebrate the exodus.

Seated in the dark subway car, he loses the faint buzz. He cannot find an answer to his predicament. He cannot find the setting for contemplation. The times he has to himself are spare, shaving and dressing in the impersonal morning, standing in his yard in the middle of the night. He tries to find a solution and knows that there is none and that his solitude is limited. How much more difficult to think of the answer on the quiz show while the studio orchestra is playing music to measure time's passing.

Mr. Meadoff boards his train, finds a seat, tents the newspaper in front of him. Others do the same. It is a hospital ward, in which each patient may cultivate a little dignity behind his paper curtain, each there able to examine himself, scratch at his nose or the wax in his ears.

When Danny arrives at Bernstein's his friends are finishing coffee. Bernstein is in the back, on the telephone.

"I saw Joey Ceravolo cruising the Avenue last night," Danny starts. "What do you suppose he does?"

"He's a collector," Angie says.

"I know that. But I mean, what else?"

Rick is looking over the counter. "Hey, Bernstein. I'm giving myself five singles for a fin." Rick rings the oversized No Sale button, takes dollars out of the drawer, waves a five-dollar bill at the open door to the darkened storeroom and puts the money in.

"What are you doing, Rick?" Angie asks him.

"S'all right. He trusts us. Besides, he never even heard me."

Rick pulls the cash drawer toward him to close it and settles back on his stool. But he hasn't pulled hard enough, and the drawer springs back open. This time when he leans across, he looks into the compartments, pulls out a fifty and waves it. Angie hits him on the arm. He mugs his Harpo mug, opens his mouth wide, waggles his tongue. Angie hits him again, harder, and Rick leans back, replaces the bill, and shuts the drawer with a chunk.

"I mean," Danny continues, "does he lend people money?"

"Who?" Angie asks.

"Joey Ceravolo."

Rick arranges the five singles into a large roll he carries, bound by two wide rubber bands. The bills are in order by denomination, singles on the outside. Once he has ordered the wad, he snaps the bands around it. Then he hefts the roll, tosses it into the air and one-hands it, sticks it in his pants pocket.

"Meadoff, where you been?" Rick says.

"What do you mean?"

"Where you been? You grow up in Arizona or someplace? Ceravolo works for the shys. He collects for the numbers, he rents cigarette machines, he collects for the shys. The shys lend money. But I tell you, pal o' mine, you don't want to borrow."

Rick has always made it hard to ask. He knows, but he makes it hard to come to him.

"Why is that?"

Rick snorts a wise snort. "You don't want to borrow from the shys, *Inglés*. Believe me."

Angie closes the *News*. "He's right, Danny. You want to steer clear of them. They charge an awful lot to borrow money and then it's tough to get rid of them."

"Who?"

"Joey and his friends. They wanted to lend my father money. For his painting business. He had to get his brother to tell them no. They lend you money, they just move in and take over. Rick is right. You want to stay away."

Angie pays for his coffee and Danish, leaves the money on the counter. Rick says he's staying for another cup. They leave him behind.

"Something going on?" Angie asks him.

Danny nods. Maybe it would help to tell Angie, he thinks. "Things I don't understand," Danny says.

"I'm telling you," Angie says. "Ain't that the truth? Why wouldn't they build O'Malley a larger stadium if that's what he needs to keep the Dodgers? Explain that one to me."

"I don't know, Angie. Maybe he's just bluffing."

Mr. Meadoff is not surprised by the policeman's call because he has lost track of sequence. He does not doubt that the policeman fits into his troubles, but he cannot say where. He has so many adversaries he has lost track of how they fit together. He is trying to place the precinct number when the officer repeats himself.

"I said, Detective Larson with the Eighty-second Precinct. Are you still there?"

"Yes, officer. I'm just wondering where that is."

"Newkirk and Bedford. Newkirk stop on the BMT. Reason I'm calling, Mr. Meadoff, is we have your son here. And two of his friends. It's a serious matter. Wondered if you'd like to come down and talk to them."

"Serious how? Are they hurt?"

"No sir. No one's hurt. It's a till tap, Mr. Meadoff. Newkirk and Bedford. I'll tell you then."

Mr. Meadoff feels uncomfortable in the train to Brooklyn. He is leaving the island too early. He used to do it more often, give himself an early day. One of the kids' birthdays or just because it felt good. But with the kids grown and business bad he feels like a thief. He is unsure about a till tap. He should know but cannot think what it is, nor why Danny should be at the Eighty-second Precinct. Law enforcement carries a sinister tone. He is thankful for the police, but their intrusion in his life gives him no comfort. They are insiders, cossacks.

At the precinct house he moves through the procedures without difficulty. Officer Larson treats him courteously. It is fortunate he is carrying fifty dollars. That is the amount in the complaint from the man with the candy store. The man tells him how he is certain it is the boys because they were there at the counter and he doesn't have so many fifty dollar bills that he would forget. Mr. Meadoff is sympathetic. Everyone has hills to climb and they all look steep. Fifty dollars more will not help, fifty less will not hurt, but this man is earnest and his son has been locked up. Mr. Meadoff pays fifty dollars and the complaint is dropped.

The boys sit in a holding pen off the squad room, a little cubicle with a glass panel in the door. He looks in and sees them, glum and silent. They are sitting around a yellow oak table in straight, fan-backed chairs. The squad room doesn't much resemble what Mr. Meadoff expected in a police station except that at the back is a wall of bars. He has never been inside a police station before. On a coat rack in the corner, a square wooden pole with brass hooks, a fat leather holster hangs, its housed pistol pointing down menacing, obscene.

It is while he is listening to Detective Larson that he decides not to instruct the boys. There is too much instruction in life. If instruction worked no one who went to church or synagogue would be evil, no one who studied the law would do wrong. Do you instruct a young horse that he must run fast if he is to clear a fence? Instruction is for the civilized and the old, the urban and the imprisoned. It prolongs the sentence.

Outside, the boys thank him and shake his hand. The Italian one says he's glad it was Mr. Meadoff because his father would kill him, and he really appreciates it. He offers to pay Mr. Meadoff sixteen dollars and change, his share, but Mr. Meadoff says no. The other one, the smart aleck, doesn't say much except that it was a bum rap after all the business they do at Bernstein's, he won't be caught dead there again. Daniel is silent. The boys begin to move off and Mr. Meadoff says to his son, quietly, Come, we'll walk together.

"So where do you go now?"

"Back to Ocean Parkway. That's where I was making calls when the patrol car picked us up."

"They picked you up in a police car?" Mr. Meadoff has not thought about the history, how his son came to be there. The police car part disturbs him. Patrol cars, flashing lights, link Danny to adulthood, criminality, even more than the holster hanging like a pod of fruit.

The day is pewter grey and the light so diffused it produces no shadows. They pass a chocolates store. Mr. Meadoff points to the window.

"It's your mother's anniversary tomorrow. Wait. I want to stop and get her a box of those candies. The ones she likes."

"Loft parlays," Danny says.

"With the nuts." They go in. Mr. Meadoff has the box wrapped, a gilt wrapping of pink and silver with a large red bow. When his father pays, Danny notices him looking into his billfold as if to count what's left.

"Here," he says to Danny, and he hands him the wrapped box. "Carry this in your case so the bow stays nice. Then you give it to me tonight."

He can hear his son sigh, hear a cup of air escape from him to acknowledge that they can once again talk about something else. Mr. Meadoff did not intend forgiveness; he merely wanted the bow preserved.

"Poppa," Danny says as they walk back out to the street. "I think I know what happened to that fifty dollars. I didn't have anything to do with it, but I think I know what happened."

"Daniel," his father says. They walk back out into the street and although there is no direct sunlight, Mr. Meadoff squints from the glare. "Daniel, let me tell you something. Nothing stays forever. Not these candies, not the police department, not Mr. Bernstein's fifty dollars. Nothing. You are gonna live alone. You are your only company. You better like it, because you don't get another pick."

Danny listens. His father stops at a street corner. Stairs descend to the BMT line, back to Manhattan. His father will leave him here. "That's it," his father says.

"Yes, Poppa." His father reaches out and touches him on the cheek. His fingers are warm, warmer even than the heavy air, and soft. Then he turns and goes down the stairs. Danny watches him go, bobbing from his limp and from the descent, one hand on the bannister. Not the hand that touched him on the cheek. Danny stands a moment and his father disappears around the corner and down the second stairwell.

He catches up with Angie on Ocean Parkway, and they finish the afternoon together. Angie sells courtesy and cheer and when women say they don't want anything he is so pleased, so understanding several change their minds and buy. They alternate doors. During Danny's turns he spins outrageous stories trying to make Angie laugh. He tells one woman Angie is his probation officer and another that Angie is deaf and dumb and that this is a new training program for the severely handicapped. Mr. Fuller thought of it because his son is in an iron lung.

"How is he supposed to sell?" the woman asks.

"The young Fuller boy?"

"No," the woman says, pointing with mild horror at Angie. "Him."

"They sign. Make hand signs. And they have a sixth sense for demonstrations." The woman buys the Queen's Boudoir comb and brush set and six plastic napkin rings painted silver.

Rick is nowhere to be seen. Danny asks about him, but Angie hasn't seen him since the police station. They do not talk about the fifty dollars.

"Did you ever notice how, once things begin to change, it's hard to stop them?" Danny asks.

"Like what?"

"Like your parents. Once you start to see them as people, it's hard to think of them as your parents any more."

"Not for me," Angie says. "Not my parents. What are my alternatives?"

"It's just that they seem so tiny in the world when you see them as people. I mean, think of everything going on at that station house. And that's one precinct. Think of the whole borough, the city. Guatemala, Asia, San Francisco. Once you see them that way it's hard to change them back."

Angie is unconvinced. "They'll always be your parents. That doesn't change. Guatemala doesn't change that."

On the way home Danny passes by the newsstand. Sarge sits in the shed, listening to the radio.

"Hey, Sarge," says Danny.

"Hey."

Danny asks him how's business, and Sarge tells him not so good. There's television, Sarge says, and Danny acts as if that comes as news. People watch television at night and don't buy the afternoon paper. They read the morning paper on the train both ways.

"You seen Hoot around?" Danny asks. "I haven't seen him for a week."

"Hoot's gone. Hoot's long gone."

"Where'd he go?"

"I don't know, kid. He don't tell me."

"But you're his cousin, aren't you?"

The black man looks at Danny with scolding eyes. "I ain't his cousin. He ain't no family to me. What makes you say that?"

Danny is embarrassed. He cannot remember where he heard that, but he's known it for years.

"He ain't my cousin. I tell you something else. My name ain't Sarge. My name is Clifford. You folks like to call me

Sarge, that's O.K. by me. But it's Clifford. I never even been in the Army. Wouldn't take a one-armed man, would they?''

The Meadoff house admits no change. It dresses for the seasons: screens, storm windows come down and go up, slipcovers go on—their purpose is mysterious to Danny. Is there some summer blight that attacks the rough surfaces of the sofa and chairs, some parasite that comes with Daylight Savings?—but the pattern is recursive, periodic. Danny thinks of the house as one of the tall-masted ships in a favorite book, the one he got with the measles. Different times demand different sail settings, and it is his mother who inspects, orders the rigging, oversees that the excess canvas is properly stowed. When he walks up the path he sees that the narrow flower beds bordering the housefront have been edged and turned.

This evening a surprise awaits Danny. He knows the man sitting on the front porch, rocking on the swing chair, but the man is in the wrong place. He belongs somewhere else.

''I need to talk to you, Meadoff.''

''Sure thing, Mr. Raycroft.''

The man hops down from the swing and stands on the porch looking at Danny at the base of the stairs.

''There's something funny going on.'' He is holding several slips of paper in his hand. ''I got receipts from five women in your area who are still waiting for their deliveries from Fuller. They paid a down, but they're still waiting.''

''Let me see.'' Raycroft hands the papers down and Danny recognizes Rick's writing on each. He is relieved that there are none of his. He has kept ahead of his track debts, but Belmont has opened, eighteen chances a day to get rich, and Rick is at the horses more than he's selling.

"These aren't mine."

"Yeah, that's the funny thing. They had a Fuller catalogue and ordered Fuller stuff. And they're in your area."

"Did they tell you what the salesman looked like?"

"It ain't you, I know that much."

Danny walks up the steps. Standing level with Raycroft, he is several inches taller. He looks at the papers with stage concern.

"Let me hold onto these," he says. "I'll hold onto these and look into it."

Raycroft watches him. Finally he nods.

"O.K. You're doing a good job, Meadoff. I gave you a good territory and you're doing a good job with it. Only, don't look a gilt horse in the mouth. Know what I mean?"

"Absolutely," Danny says.

To Danny's relief, his parents know nothing of the purpose of his boss's visit and do not ask. They are deciding who should take the car into the city to pick up Rochelle and Joyce at Grand Central. The girls return tonight from summer camp, tonight at 9:05. They decide to go together. His mother has dressed up for dinner and has put on lipstick. When she goes around to pick up her husband's dinner plate, she touches his shoulder with the fingers of her hand. His father says nothing about the precinct house. At dinner the talk is about the flower beds, the possibility of recognizing Red China, Governor Stevenson's speech in Los Angeles. Because his parents had not both planned to drive in to the City, they are rushed to get ready. Danny tells them to go ahead, that he'll clean up.

He has finished the easy stuff, the plates and glasses, when his mother enters the kitchen. He is trying to decide whether to start a new Brillo pad. His desire to dispatch the frying pan quickly, new soap, new scrubbing, competes with the family's economies. His mother's entrance tips the balance, and he reaches for the mash of discolored wire in the soap dish.

"Daniel," she says to him.

"Yes, Ma."

"If you go out, lock the doors. Back door too."

"Yes, Ma."

He turns from the frying pan to find her looking hard at him. Are there other instructions? Does she know about Raycroft? About the fifty? She is wearing a blue dress with small white dots and a lace collar, and she looks pretty. He means to tell her.

He turns back to the sink. She walks up behind him and tugs the hair that is creeping over his collar.

"You know what would be nice?"

"What, Ma?"

"It would be nice if I didn't have to tell you to get a haircut. If someday you just got it."

He nods. She says his name.

"Daniel. I want you to be nice to your father."

"What do you mean, Ma? What did I do?"

"Nothing. You didn't do anything. I'm just saying."

"Sure, Ma. I will."

He is eager for them to leave, to be alone with the pans to be washed. His father comes down the stairs jingling the car keys. He calls "Miriam" as if he cannot find her, though he must come through the kitchen to get to the garage.

"Daniel," his mother says. "You're a good boy."

They go out together. They disembark the flagship. When his mother takes the car alone, Danny rolls back the heavy wooden door of the garage for her. Tonight Danny leaves this task for his father, although it is easier for him. He can tell that, at sixteen, he has the easier time with the dead weight of the door. Danny stays at the sink, scrubbing with the shred of fibre that is left of the pad. That is the second time in a short while someone has used those words to him, and he is trying to remember when it happened before.

They stay up late after his sisters come home. Rochelle shows her nature study certificates and Joyce has made a present in shop for everyone in the family. She gives their mother a chopping board cut in the shape of South America, their father a pouch for pipe tobacco, Danny a box with portholes in the side and a rope latch. "It's a bosun's knot," she tells him. "You can use it for your baseball cards."

"He threw them out," Rochelle says.

Joyce looks alarmed. "No I didn't," Danny says. "I kept a few. I can use it for the ones I kept. The valuable ones, the collector cards." He can get a couple off Angie.

It is almost midnight when they go upstairs. Danny is in bed, has twisted to reach the lamp switch when Joyce knocks and comes in.

She walks around the room. Her box sits on his dresser and she straightens it. She tells him she just wanted to see if everything looks the same.

"Does it?"

"Kind of," she says. "But kind of different too. It's hard to say."

"Like what?"

"Oh," she sits on the end of his bed, "like the new doormat. Did you notice the new doormat?"

"Doormats wear out, Joyce. Mom got this one before you went away."

"You sure?" She writes in script on the bedspread with her finger.

"Danny," she says after a moment. "What's with Dad?"

"What do you mean?"

She keeps writing in large, looping letters.

"Well, we were coming back from the City and Rochelle was telling about the overnight hike and then about the last campfire and what we sang. I was sitting in the front seat with him, and Mom and Rochelle were in the back seat and you couldn't see anything 'cause it was dark. But when we got into the tunnel? You know how it's lit? Well, I could see there. And there were these tears on his face."

Danny listens. He cannot think of what to say.

"You sure?"

"Yes. At least, I think so. I mean, I almost asked him but then I had this feeling he didn't want me to, and when we got home they were gone."

"Maybe you imagined it. Maybe it was streaks on the windshield."

Joyce writes more, considers this. "Maybe," she says reluctantly. "But that wasn't all. We get home and we're kinda standing around and RoRo is unlocking the trunk?" She says it like a question. It is a way of speaking she has picked up at camp. "So what does he do? He gives me this hug. Really hard."

"Well?"

"Well, he already hugged me. When we got off the train? I mean, he'd already hugged me and said hello and everything."

"Well, I wouldn't worry, Joyce. You were probably wrong about the tears. Sometimes in the tunnel you get a funny reflection."

Joyce looks up from her penmanship. "Think so?"

"Absolutely. The tunnel does funny things. When I was real little and we drove through the tunnel we got a drop of water on the windshield and I was sure the tunnel was leaking. I didn't say anything until we got out and Mom noticed I'd been holding my breath and asked what the matter was. But I was sure the tunnel was about to cave in.''

Joyce laughs. It is a story that has been told at the dinner table countless times and on most trips through tunnels. She pinches his toe through the bedspread and walks out. Danny turns and switches off the light.

- 21 -

This morning he selects the express train. He abhors the crowds it carries, how the crowds prop against each other, fuse together by the speed and the sway in common, twice-breathed air. He selects it in spite of his discomfort, because of his discomfort. The heat will anneal his resolve, solder it so that his plans stick.

He takes the Brighton line and changes at Atlantic for the express. When the train comes he is pleased to find a cylinder of space by a center pole. A civilized space where a body can lodge itself upright. Behind him board a small, Persian-looking man who darts hostile looks at him and a pretty girl in a flowered dress. Her eyes meet his and send him, he thinks, a sympathetic glance. She seems to know how difficult this is for him. He responds by folding his *Tribune* lengthwise, to two-column width, and focusing on a story about Taiwan. Still, her hand is on the pole above his, the Persian's at the bottom. Like the way Danny's friends pick teams. Mr. Meadoff has seen them. They toss a bat in the air, one grabs it and then they alternate grips to the top until there is no room left. Who invented such pure justice, the perfect system? The top grip wins, chooses first. If the winner is challenged on his grip at the nub, he must swing the bat around his head three times.

Without looking up, Mr. Meadoff takes his hand and places it above the young woman's. Sure enough, she moves her hand higher. He looks up and she is smiling at him. He does not want to think that he is flirting with her. He smiles back.

"Shall we choose up sides?" he asks her.

She says, "I don't think either side will win."

The train stops at Borough Hall. Here the beaded lines on the map that are subway routes converge. The West End Line, the New Lots and Livonia trains dump passengers to change for the Broadway express. Sure enough, the girl gets off. The Persian stays, but he is soon camouflaged in the undergrowth of bodies that board Mr. Meadoff's car. Everyone's space disappears. The pole fills with hands, hands overlap hands, their fleshy heels sit on top of strange thumbs. It is hot, and the fan in the car pushes waves of heated air. It will be better when the train starts. Hot air from the tunnel will blow through the open windows.

The train gives two jerks, two false starts. The contents settle into the package, and the train pulls its cargo into motion. As it does, Mr. Meadoff is thrown against the chest of the man next to him. He apologizes, the man turns away. Through his light summer suit he could feel the man's flesh, can still sense his warmth, his aliveness. There must be some way to avoid this. It is an indignity to both of us, that we are offended and allow it to happen to us. Allow ourselves to be thrown together, like combatants or lovers.

Why have I taken the express? Lindenauer doesn't expect me, so it is not possible to be late. I could have saved myself this indignity and have arrived just as easily. Lindenauer will not know whether or not I came by local.

Mr. Meadoff gets off at Times Square and walks east to Sixth. If they wanted people to use an Avenue of the Americas, they should have picked a street that had a name, not a number. Like Park or Lexington. Fat chance, their giving Park Avenue to celebrate all the Americas. The people on Park wouldn't stand for it. Still. If they wanted us to use the name, they shouldn't have just changed Sixth. People count. Fifth, sixth, seventh. You can't change that.

There is Lindenauer's building. I could stand here and pick out his office. From the sidewalk. People would think I was a greenhorn, somebody from Cleveland, standing looking up at the buildings. But I could pick him out. Forty-first floor, southwest corner. I could count up. What if I stood here counting and he looked down and saw me? How would that be? There's some poor *putz*, he would say, doesn't know where to go. I pity him. I squash him. I take my crystal paperweight with the flower that reminds me and I crush him. Why would I be sorry? The end of just some poor *putz* standing counting floors.

Mr. Meadoff is asked to wait. "That's quite all right," he says to the receptionist. "Even providential." She looks to the low couches used for waiting and he goes to one and sits down.

He needs time to go over his notes. He has two sets, written in his precise hand on long paper, a rough pad he bought just for this purpose. It is white paper, lined in blue, like the Yankee pinstripe, and he has been over and over the numbers. One set shows the mess he has gotten himself in. He didn't think he would show that to Lindenauer. Not his business. Two promissory notes to the factors, the bank loan against the house, then the loan from Ceravolo's people to cover the interest to the factors. That was dumb, he knows. But he had to do something. At the time it seemed if he could get by until the large accounts paid, there'd be some room. Paradise Knitwear could pull out.

[199

No reason to show those to Lindenauer. Lindenauer knows I'm in trouble.

It is the other numbers he wants to show. He'll show Lindenauer this can work out fine. Lindenauer will see he won't be cheated. He said he wouldn't liquidate, but when he sees these numbers, how he gets cashed out, how all the creditors, even the factors, get whole, Lindenauer won't complain. Why would a man insist that his partner lose everything, just to keep alive a business he could start up tomorrow? What does he want? I'll agree to whatever Lindenauer wants. Lindenauer can have the furniture and the name. Paradise Knitwear. It didn't work out, let's be gentlemen and shake hands and if you can't get along without Paradise Knitwear, you start it up tomorrow. Without Meadoff. You get your money and go home. I get my money and pay off my debts. I save the house. You don't have to be Gandhi. It's just common sense.

The lady at the desk is very pleasant. Asks if he'd like another coffee. She took his name in when he first came, but nothing has happened. Every so often through the door he hears a murmur that must be Lindenauer. Odd how you can tell a person by his sound. Not even his voice. When the kids were small and one of them would cough, he would awaken, the skin on his forearms tingling, and listen. That was Rochelle—what is she coming down with? What is going around? Did Danny swim in the public pool? Isn't a cough the first symptom of polio? Then fever. You could be in a thunderstorm, a war, you would hear that cough. Last week he was crossing Fifth, by Best's, when someone dropped a dime. Cars, taxis, horns everywhere. You should have seen the heads turn. Everyone heard it hit, everyone knew it was a dime. Two dimes and they might have tied up traffic, shut down the intersection. The sound of a meadowlark, the bugling of rutting elk you couldn't hear over the horns, but the sound of a dime yes.

What is the sound of a meadowlark?

A buzzer goes off, and the secretary enters. She carries a ball point pen and one of those steno pads with the rings at the top. Why do they make them that way? What's the matter with a notebook? She is wearing a grey suit and she is handsome, you would say. Mr. Meadoff doesn't apply that word to women, but it is appropriate here. Handsome. As he is thinking on the world, she comes back out, smiles as if to apologize, returns to her work.

Inside he hears a thump. Did Lindenauer lift that paperweight and drop it? Did he mean to? Did he slam it to the desk in fury? The thump was more of an inadvertence, a fall not a slam. Perhaps he had a stroke. Perhaps he couldn't get his vacuum tubes delivered for all the cursing, and gritted his teeth in anger, gritted so hard that he stopped the flow of blood to his brain. The way a balloon stops the flow of air at its neck if it doesn't want to be blown up. It refuses air. And Lindenauer, his neck reddening with rage as he denounced the errant vacuum tubes, stopped the flow and fell dead to the oiled wood surface of his desk. That is why he has cleared a space among his toys, for his stroke, so he could show that fucker who didn't deliver the vacuum tubes just how important they are, the vacuum tubes, not the no-good fucker, and true to plan, the head of the collapsed Lindenauer hits midpoint among the lighter, the clock with the nautical design, the crystal paperweight.

No, Mr. Meadoff realizes. No stroke. He hears another noise, maybe the chair moving, and Lindenauer's laugh. And the words "cardboard" and "only to you and me." He looks over at the secretary. His presence is making her uncomfortable. She is busy typing but he wonders if she isn't merely making work

[201

while he's there. He looks at his watch. He has been waiting fifty-five minutes. Surely he will get in soon. This man is my partner. He will be courteous. He will listen to common sense.

I would agree not to compete, if we liquidate. I wouldn't mind. Perhaps if we liquidate I will stop wearing a watch. I will find something to do, teach children something, the names of trees, where I will have no need for a watch. And live in the country. We should be able to drop those things we no longer need, like watches and keys and ties, as we age. The perfected human body will drop away body parts after they have no use. A man in later years will shed his prostate, a woman who has borne children her tubes. We will become deciduous. Trees are ahead of us. They shed their leaves, go dormant, awaken with a new vigor each spring.

That is the way the human should evolve, so that its parts simply fall away. Fact is, the evolution has started. After breeding is over, we lose what we needed to trap the other sex: men their hair, women their figures, everyone our looks. The skin dries and loses its sensitivity. Time is preparing us.

"Mr. Meadoff," she says again, and he realizes she is talking to him. She has her hair turned under with a net and it emphasizes her efficiency; still, as he looks into her grey eyes, she is a handsome woman.

"Yes?"

"I really don't think he's going to have a moment to see you. He's got an appointment downtown and then he's due for lunch."

"Yes."

"Why don't you make an appointment? I'll be happy to make an appointment when you're both free."

He doesn't want to trouble this lady. His presence is an inconvenience. It will doubtless make Lindenauer unhappy that he is still here. Better to make an appointment. He approaches her desk and she retrieves a large, soft-covered diary from her center drawer.

The thing about the sky is, it's not a factor. Danny walks down DeKalb Avenue tracking Rick. No footprints or scat, he follows the Fuller Brush Fall Special catalogues rolled to a baton and stuck in the screen door handles. Rick is canvassing, dropping off materials that he'll pick up later.

How can you live in a place where the sky is not a factor? Danny feels the breeze warm on his neck and looks up to see a high ceiling the color of smoke. If you don't look for it, you don't know it's there.

Turning the corner at St. Felix Danny spots his friend. He moves with energy between the row houses, swinging his sample case. Rick sees him.

"Salud, compadre. Que pasa?"

Danny has made this trip for a purpose but now at his friend's side he is happy to walk and speak of the things they always talk of.

"How you doing? You doing well?"

"Que va, am I doing well. We are having much luck, *Inglés.* This is a fine day. This is a fine day to blow up the bridge and to die."

Rick jams his hand in his pants pocket and retrieves a fat roll of bills. He gives Danny a broad wink.

They walk up steps to the door of a dilapidated brownstone. The cramped entry hall has several mailboxes and doorbells. Rick selects the first floor front and pushes its bell twice. A large woman sticks her head out of the front window a foot from where Danny stands, still on the outside landing.

"Yeah?" she says. She must have seen them climb the stoop to have responded so quickly. She is a large, flabby woman. The flesh on her arms dimples with weight and on her chin sits a grey mole the size of a marble. Danny tugs on Rick's shirt, pulls him out on the landing.

"Good morning, madam," Rick says with exaggerated cheer. "I'm breaking in a new salesboy for the Fuller Brush Company and we're looking for someone to receive a complimentary package of our new cosmetics."

"Complimentary," the woman says.

"Free."

Rick is emptying his pockets like a suspect in a lock-up, loading little packets of ointment and color through the window. This one is made from jasmine gathered in Ceylon and that from Tibetan juniper. Rick's enthusiasm, his expansive descriptions continue without a breath. The woman keeps taking, her eyes brightening to the encounter. Goods fall to her—she pulls them in, a gambler pulling, concealing her hand, stashing them in the hole. When Rick finishes he moves easily into items that cost a little but give a lot. Soon he is writing an order for twenty-three forty, she is handing him a twenty and a five, and he is making change.

What does it mean? His friend outdoes Raycroft in imagination, gall. Maybe in results.

"Fassscination," says Rick. "A winner every time." He pulls his lump of cash from his pocket.

"Here you go, little fin in front. Hamilton in the back, back to back, belly to belly. And I say to thee go forth, multiply, and be fruitful." Rick adds to his bills, takes the wide rubber band and snaps it around the wad. He spirals it four feet into the air, one-hands the catch, stows it in the deep pocket of his trousers.

Rick's facility brings Danny back to his mission. There is something so slick about his moves, so assured, Danny is troubled. He brings himself to the question with a deep breath.

"Rick, I gotta ask you. That fifty bucks. . . ."

"What fifty bucks?"

Danny is falling, he is off the high board.

"The money Bernstein was missing."

"Yeah?"

"Did you take it?"

Rick carries his satchel so it swings high. "*Inglés*, I am surprised by thy stupidity. Thou must use thy head. Why would I take Bernstein's money?"

"Well, I don't know. I just thought, you were kidding around about it. And before, those cigars. . . ."

Rick points up the steps of another brownstone, climbs up while Danny waits below.

"Earning bread this way, why would I need Bernstein's?" He rings the bell, checks his pockets for samples. His back is to his friend.

He waits and no one comes to the door. He waits, Danny thinks, too long.

"I took the cigars for a joke," Rick says bouncing down the stairs. The sample case swings high, as high as Danny's face. "Just the cigars, nothing more. *Nada mas*."

Danny nods and they turn down the block for the next call.

"I don't need his dough when I can make it like this. You kidding? Better than stealing. Next you'll be telling me I took his radio."

Danny stops. He can go back to the Avenue and catch a bus to his territory. He tells that to Rick.

"I just saw you doing this block and thought I'd come by."

"Sure thing," Rick says.

On the bus he thinks about what to do. He has no appetite to ring doorbells. The way Rick buzzed through enervated him, embarrassed him. If Frances is in, maybe she would know what he is feeling. Rick's denial sits in his mouth like soured milk.

The grey smudge has cleared—was it clouds or smoke?—and a light blue sky flashes in the transom windows of the bus. Danny perches in the back row and watches the storefronts pass. He transfers to a bus headed for Frances' neighborhood.

What do you think of that? All of what Rick said made sense. It just wasn't true. So much for sense. Live and learn, they say. What if they're wrong? What if you live and forget?

The bus rumbles past several blocks of produce stands open to the air. Bushel baskets of onions cover the walks, of yams, wax beans, sweet corn, and shoppers stroll by, examining, criticizing, buying. The bus stops for a red light and Danny watches the watchers. And there, by the flower stall, is Frances.

He is sure it is she, leaning over to sniff a bunch of red blossoms, long stems in green tissue paper. He has never seen her outside the apartment, never seen her in lipstick and a real dress, but he is sure it is she.

He leaps up and pulls the bell cord. At the next corner, the bus veers to the curb, opens its rear folding door and lets him out. He runs the block, keeping his eye on the spot where he saw her and the blur of peach and white that was her dress.

When he catches her, he is out of breath.

"Frances," he says.

She is holding the bunch of flowers in her arm, the way a beauty queen would hold her trophy. Each bloom is red, the size of an apricot, and has a yellow pupil at its center. The flowers rest there and Frances looks happy. The word hits Danny between the eyes, the word that he could not have put with her and

206]

did not know was missing until he saw her here, in a peach dress with a stiff white collar bracketing the bumps of her conspicuous collar bone. The lipstick she wears is a shade he has sold her, with purple in it she had said after they studied the color chart, and when she smiles at him her gums show oversized and pale underneath.

"Danny." Her voice hits a sharp note on his name. He has surprised her. She stares at him smiling and he, feeling moronic, smiles back harder. He cannot think of a thing to say.

A man he has not noticed until then leans between them.

"Yes," he says to Danny.

"Yes?"

"Yes. Can I help you." The words are not an offer. Danny is about to mistake him for the shopkeeper, the florist, despite his tan checked suit and silk tie. The man has a small moustache, a blot of brown where his lip was rubbed with a dirty eraser. Not established like Raycroft's. Though in Danny's experience, no mustachioed man is to be trusted.

"Danny," Frances says. "This my friend Mr. Kelliher. This is Danny. He delivers to our building."

"Pleased to meetcha," Mr. Kelliher says and sticks a hand straight at Danny's gut.

Danny looks at her for a moment, then at the pasteboard stiff hand, straight fingers thumb cocked. Will it go off? Danny reaches for it and it closes around his hand with force.

"Pleased to meetcha," Mr. Kelliher says again.

"Likewise," says Danny and immediately wants the word back.

"So," Frances says and looks around vaguely. "What brings you down here? Are you selling here?" She begins to wave her bouquet, then, seeming to think better of it, nests the bundle of flowers again in the crook of her arm. There is something in the colors, the red button of the cut blossoms, the dark smear of lipstick, the blanched pink of her gums, that overcomes Danny with sadness.

"No," he says. "Not selling. Just passing by. I thought it was you and I was just passing by."

"Well," she says. "It *was* me."

They have reached a pause. Danny bows, not a gesture he can remember ever using, but he finds himself bowing and taking a step or two backwards, a shuffle step.

"We should be running on, Honey," Mr. Kelliher says. She reaches over and touches the sleeve of his jacket.

"Yes," Danny says. "Me too. I should be running on." He bows again and steps back. He waits to see which way they will go and when they turn in his direction he walks the other way.

- **22** -

The spine of the Meadoff house is a wide, center-hall stairway. The front door opens to it, the rooms of the house hang off it. The single landing of the stairway is oversized, large as a cozy parlor. It is centered in the gangways and indeed centered in the dimensions of the house, and at midpoint in the landing sits a square maple desk. Mr. Meadoff walked by the desk at Holy Family's rummage sale, and paid Handy Andy Brown ten dollars to fetch it in his truck and, with two helpers, to hoist it to its site. His mother had offered the men beer and they sat on the steps of the front porch each with a can of Piel's in his hand and Danny sat with them. One of the movers offered up the can and Danny, this four years ago, took a taste. He assumed that the good stuff, the Trommer's White Label stowed under the cellar stairs, must taste better—else why would anyone drink beer?—

and he wondered whether the workmen knew they were getting the beer his mother bought for tips.

During the daytime, his mother would use the desk to pay bills and to compute, and Mr. Meadoff would often sit there at night, sometimes writing notes from the Lincoln biography, sometimes just sitting. When he read he tore strips of newspaper to mark pages in the blood red books, and later he leafed through the books removing his markers and transcribed his thoughts onto lined sheets of paper stacked in the middle drawer of the desk.

If the house was a ship then the desk was its wheelhouse. Square-rigged ships were Danny's specialty: the frontispiece of one of his Hornblower books showed a cross-section of a clipper ship, every sail labelled, and he knew their names from flying jib to spanker. Midships stood a deck where the captain could assist the helmsman or, as Hornblower had been forced to do several times, could take over the wheel. From there the officer in command could see all that was happening above decks. Most of the time the trouble in the stories was not above decks. It was below.

This evening Danny comes home early to find that his father has arrived before him. His father has already taken his station at the desk. He is figuring, he mutters arithmetic aloud, mutters about what gets carried and what goes into what. It is a trait Danny associates with dumb kids, kids who read moving their lips. His father's habit he does not judge. It is a private matter.

Something in his father's posture alerts the son. Mr. Meadoff leans close to the desk, gripping the yellow pencil down by the cone of its point, pushes hard on the paper. Danny walks by on his way upstairs.

"Anything I can do, Poppa?"

His father says a sound without vowels. Danny goes upstairs, writes out his sales report. One more week before school starts. Raycroft gets back the samples, the case, the literature. One more week his father faces Joey Ceravolo's deadline. He is sure he could help if he knew what was afoot. Danny gets A's in math, and he sees his father struggling with columns of figures, the pages strewn over the desk with anxious and dark lines discrediting their conclusions. If Danny knew what the facts were, he could help calculate.

He will ask at dinner.

But his father does not come to dinner. Works through a kitchen supper of cold cuts and cheese, pitchers of lemonade. Works through and, more curious, his absence draws no mention. The major forces in life, Danny realizes, are excised from conversation at his family's table. The permissible range goes from whipped cream cheese at the new deli to misgivings about John Foster Dulles. A broad spectrum. But a compact has been struck—by whom? has he participated?—to exclude the forces that move his life. Death, sex, change, money, and troubles find no host at family dinner. They do not belong to the family. They are to be borne, enjoyed, contemplated in solitude, private matters. It is not coincidental: the treaty specific as if the Meadoff family had conferred at Bretton Woods, but the agreement is tacit.

After dinner Danny passes his father again, asks the same question, receives the same sound. His father is no longer computing. He sits in front of a dozen sheets covered with numbers. They might be equations for telemetry, for resolving the relationship of the planets. Danny is letting go of cause and effect. Once you get out on the street, once you come upon Frances out of her apartment or Rick with his winnings, cause and effect do not seem sufficient. Do not explain things, do not apply. He wants to tell his father what he suspects: that the answer cannot be on these sheets of paper, that the answer lies elsewhere, but no one has told him the question.

Danny cannot sleep that night. He rises often, goes to the window. He has decided that if his father's shadow appears, he will go and talk to it. But the shadow never shows itself, and the only light on the black, newly mown lawn is cast by street lamp. And the only watch that is set for the night is Danny's.

In the morning he finds his father has gone.

"Don't you think I'm entitled to know what's going on, Ma?"

His mother puts a bowl of cold cereal in front of him. It was the wrong way to word the question.

"You're entitled? Why are you entitled?"

"I'd like to know, Ma. I'd just like to know, is all."

She sits across from him at the metal kitchen table. She holds her chin in her palm, pinches her lips between forefinger and thumb. All the while she is looking at him to find what he does not know. Can she see years on a face, the rings of age a cut tree shows? Odd that you have to kill a tree to determine its age. Maybe age doesn't matter for trees.

"Your father's in trouble, Daniel." She regards him with her black eyes. Danny cannot remember that he ever noticed his mother's eyes. They are sure, they lock in unafraid. It strikes him that he knows nothing about this woman. What has she thought life would bring her, what did she find? She begins to say a lot of things he doesn't understand. A jackpot of words, of secrets. They pour out so fast he cannot hold them, they spill to the gutter.

Some of what she tells he has heard before and many of the names he knows. Factors, compound interest, Lindenauer, collateral. She does not mention Joe Ceravolo and neither does he. She tells him about creditors and assets and liquidation. He doesn't understand liquidation, but he is made to realize that if Lindenauer would do what his father asks, what his father believes to be reasonable, they could save the house. His father would not be ruined. If Lindenauer persists, his father will go through bankruptcy. That much is clear.

He asks his mother no questions. She might realize how little he gets and stop. Is bankruptcy a place that you went through? Is it far? In one of the Dickens books the whole family goes to Marshalsea Prison to visit the father, goes to live with him. Do you come out different?

"So today's the day. Soon he's got to cover a consolidation loan he made from the sharks. If Lindenauer won't do something to help, he's lost. Everything goes."

That takes care of Ceravolo. His mother does not have the name but she knows that her husband has been borrowing expensive money.

"So what is he doing today?"

His mother studies him. Whatever she is searching for Danny tries to show on his face. He meets her eyes straight on. He looks into the round opening in his mother's eyes.

"The same thing. Only it's our last chance. He's meeting with Lindenauer. Trying to get him to go along with what he's already said no to. More than once."

His mother breathes out in a soft, rustling sound and Danny feels the air on his neck, cool. You would think breath would be warm, but his mother's sigh is cool on his hands.

"When? When are they meeting?"

Mrs. Meadoff turns her head in her cupped hand to see the red teapot clock.

"Now," she says turning back and pursing her lips again. "Now, if Lindenauer will see him. The bastard.".

Danny says nothing. He carries his juice glass and cereal bowl to the sink and rinses them out. Then he walks upstairs. He slips into jeans and a dress shirt pressed from the laundry. The City requires a dress shirt.

He has no fixed idea even as the train crosses under the river and hurtles towards Times Square. He has never met Lindenauer. He isn't sure what liquidation is or how it could help, but he believes his mother that it will. And he has never heard her swear before. Not a damn, not a hell. If she called Lindenauer a bastard, she had cause.

The telephone book lists Lindenauer's address, and he finds the building easily. Brass revolving doors with polished glass panels sweep him, paddle him into the lobby. He enters from Forty-third Street and the present, and he is spit out in the future. Occupying one half of the lobby is a bank. Its vault door is massive, steel cylinders and wheels. Danny stops to behold it. A bead chain of workers pops through the revolving doors behind him, for it is only nine o'clock and many people are only now arriving at work. The other half of the lobby rises two stories high, marble on the floor and black marble columns. And acres of plate glass expose it all, the workers, the pillars, to the street.

Danny peers around. If he stands gawking he will become conspicuous. At the far end of the lobby—a half-block away for the building sits the entire breadth of a city block—is a directory board. Danny approaches, stops when the tiny tin letters come into focus, inches closer. In front of the directory sits a rough-stone desk manned by three guards. They wear military-style hats and coatless grey uniforms with white script on the front of their blouses. Danny stands where he thinks is outside the range of notice and squints.

"Can I help you, Kid?"

Danny takes two steps. "That's O.K. I'm just looking . . ." but he cannot find the name ". . . for Lindenauer Investments." As he says it he spots what he is searching for. The guard consults a Rolodex on his desk, and Danny lets him finish. The script on the man's shirt spells out the building address. It seems an odd thing to inscribe.

"Forty-one oh three. Second elevator bank."

He passes the first corridor of elevators. They serve floors one through fifteen. He no longer imagines he has come upon the future, but the past. It is a scene from *The Boy's Book of Knighthood and Chivalry*. A son from a humble village, a vassal's son who could not imagine life in court, arrives to see the chatelaine. Are these our courts, our liege lords?

As he pushes on the brass bar to the offices of Lindenauer Investments he has no more thought of what to do than when he left the enamel table in the kitchen that morning. He might simply wait for his father, wait and ask him something to cheer him up. It always heartens his father to ask him something. Perhaps he will have a chance to sit among the magazines and think. There are magazines all over the room, on every glass table, on the leather hassocks, on the burl wood end tables by the several sofas.

A woman looking just like Donna Reed comes out from one of the hallways. He was hoping to be able to sit alone and think for a moment, but she says, not helpfully, "Yes?"

"I'm here to see my father."

This surprises her, she must have thought he was to pick up or deliver, and her eyes open on him.

"I'm Danny Meadoff. My father is with Mr. Lindenauer."

At this she nods, accepts that. Her recognition is a great relief.

"Yes, he is. They're busy, though." She nods towards a double door, panelled wood of concentric squares, off the reception room. "Why don't you have a seat?"

Danny chooses a sofa immediately by the double doors. As he sits he hears a booming laugh coming from the room. An amplified, high-fi laugh. That's a good sign. It must be going well.

He picks up some magazines, *Holiday* and *Golf Digest* and *House and Garden*. He reads five ways to lower your score by controlling your temper and about the Renaissance gardens in the Northern Italian town of Lucca. Was Frances there? She loved her trip to Italy so, I wonder if she got to Lucca. From behind the door more laughter, only the one voice. He looks up, the pleasure of recognition on his face, and finds the receptionist looking at him with, if expressions have opposites, the opposite.

"I'll give Mr. Lindenauer a note," she says. "Let him know."

Danny never cared for Donna Reed until she was especially nice to Montgomery Clift in that war movie. That's the Donna Reed this woman looks like. He needed a friend. He had a buddy in Sinatra, but he needed somebody else. You just knew Sinatra wasn't going to be enough because Sinatra had his own troubles, Ernest Borgnine was out to get him, and a buddy doesn't serve the same purpose. Of course in the end, not even Donna Reed helped. They ran Sinatra through a meat grinder, Lancaster lost Deborah Kerr, and a Jap zero gunned down Montgomery Clift on the parade grounds of Pearl Harbor. It's like Frances says, what can you do with love?

The receptionist has walked past Danny through the panelled doors, closes them behind her, but when she comes out he hears a voice saying, "Leave it open," and he takes that to mean the door. Now he sits next to the open doorway and knows his father is around the corner, but does his father know he's there? Danny is no closer to knowing why he has come.

"I got to tell you that's typical," the voice is saying. "Typical. I tell you your nuts are in a wringer and you tell me Abraham Lincoln. Like this is some debate. This ain't a debate. This is the way the world works. You come in here and I give you an hour of my time listening to your shit and then you bring your kid."

Next Danny hears his father's voice. He cannot make out the words except for a few, *mistaken,* and *Wednesday,* and *all I said.* He knows it is his father's voice from the timing and the timbre, but it sounds distant, as if his father were far away or packed under newspaper in a large carton. It troubles Danny to hear Lindenauer's language, to hear Lindenauer curse in his father's presence.

The voice goes on. Even the receptionist listens. Danny can tell because she no longer looks over in his direction.

"What am I supposed to do, feel sorry for you? That's why you bring out your family? I feel sorry for them. That such a *pisher* is the head of the family. Who is to provide, with this *pisher* who quotes Lincoln and gets himself overextended?"

Again a murmuring, a low voice.

"You want to liquidate, take me to court. Be my guest. You know what they'll tell you? They'll tell you, Meadoff, you don't stand a chance. They'll say, sorry *pisher*. You think of everything too late. You want to make Lindenauer liquidate, get the agreement at first. Not now, *pisher*. Now it's too late. Now he's got you by the short hairs."

Lindenauer's voice fills the reception room. It blows anxiety, blows everywhere it can be heard. Danny stares at pages in a magazine that show a high tower of red brick against the Apennines.

"That's it," the voice yells. "That's it. You don't like it, call my lawyers."

There is silence. Danny expects to hear the pushing of a chair, the shuffling of feet. Perhaps his father needs help getting up. Perhaps he shouldn't have come.

Danny rises. He turns the corner and is in the room. It happens without effort, as if he hasn't taken the steps. Behind a grand table an angry Buddha sits glaring at him. The guest chairs have high backs so Danny cannot tell which holds his father. As soon as he enters he forgets about his father. He moves toward the man, into the line of sight of the man who is watching him. He moves up to the desk and presses his thighs against its edge, but it does not budge. He has nothing to say, but rage has locked his eyes on the man's. He stands silent, presents himself. A thought is coming to the man's throat, Danny senses the thought rising, and wants to prevent it from coming out. If the man speaks, Danny will have no reply. He must keep it from coming out. He picks up something in front of him, something from the desk. It is hard and smooth, weighty as a stone. He looks at the object in his hand: it is a flower encased in glass. Again he sees words rising in the throat of this man. In a sudden and fluid motion, a discus motion, he hefts the glass in his hand and flings it. He intends to throw it into space, but he has not considered the intervening world and it sails past the man's head. It may even graze the few thin strands of hair that spring from the man's pate. The glass is made for throwing, throws easily and full of its own density, a wonderful kinetic linkage from shoulder to arm to glass, sails past the man's head and cracks into the corner window.

With the sound, an odd peace pulls its hood over Danny. Snugs down and ties under the chin. He looks over and observes a hundred spidery lines that have appeared on the adjoining plates of glass. The crystal weight caught the windows at their crotch, and the patterns made by the fissure are quite different. The object ricocheted off and has tumbled unbroken to the thick carpet behind Lindenauer's chair.

"Do what my father asks," Danny says.

He turns. His father sits upright in the chair to his left. He goes to him, lifts him by the meat of the arm and together they walk out.

"Thank you," Danny says to the receptionist who looks like Donna Reed and she smiles warmly at him and says, "You're welcome."

He and his father do not speak in the elevator or in the lobby of grey marble floors and black marble pillars or indeed on the street. They do not speak until they reach the subway stop on Sixth. The day is lovely, cool with a blue sky that Danny first noticed through the fractured windows, a sky stretching to Jersey on the one side and down the harbor, down the Narrows out to the Atlantic on the other. They say that spring is the season of rebirth but fall slips Danny that note too, the new year, the new school year, blood running faster to meet the cold weather.

When they get to the subway stairs Danny says he has to get back, he has to return all the Fuller Brush stuff and then he wants to get out to see Angie because it's the first day of practice with pads.

- 23 -

He does not wait for Angie. He leaves the practice during wind sprints and starts the walk home.

At Cortelyou and Flatbush, he meets his globed reflection in the chrome ball atop the barber pole, and thinks to get a haircut. Only one of the three chairs is filled. He opts for the owner. Fathead Marrone is, the adults say, the best barber. If you're a kid, though, he bores the joint of his middle finger into your skull, once to start and again to tell you you're through.

"Hey, Mr. Marrone."

"Hey, Kid."

Perfect hexagons stripe the floor, white tile and black, and the pattern stretches forever in the mirrored walls. The shop smells of vinegar and Vitalis, a clean smell.

"Make you a deal," Danny says as Marrone begins, tucks the pencil-striped sheet under his chin and collars his neck in tissue.

"You skip the knucks, I don't call you Fathead."

Marrone stares at him in the mirror. "How you want you hair?"

"The usual."

Marrone holds the chair, regarding him. Then pedals the lever and Danny falls back, unknuckled.

"Yes sir, Mr. Meadoff. The usual."

The snips are arrhythmic. Marrone starts with scissors, clicks on the electric clipper for sides and back, scissors again, finally the razor around the ears and neck.

"It's true," says the man in the next chair. His black and white wingtips sprout from the grille footrest on a line with Danny's head.

"It's true. The dead grow hair. Ask any undertaker. Why do you think an open coffin costs more?"

[219

"The price of a shave?"

"You got it," says the man. His feet jiggle with pleasure.

"Never heard that," says his barber. "Hey boss, you ever hear that?"

Marrone raises Danny upright, measures his work in the reflection.

"Not respectful to speak of the dead," Marrone says to Danny's eye in the glass.

The straight razor burns its arcs on Danny's neck. After the trim, Marrone pours green witchhazel from a stock bottle on his shelf and douses the slick skin. Then talc. Finally an amber oil smelling crisp and antiseptic that mortars and glistens his hair. Marrone spins the chair a half turn and frees him with a matador's flourish.

Danny inspects the mirror and hands Marrone two bucks. "Change is for you." Four bits is an extravagance.

No need to tip the boss, his father has told him. Still it never hurts.

"See you, Danny."

"Next time."

Mr. Meadoff is uncharacteristically late for dinner. He has been on the telephone, arranging payment schedules. All of his creditors accept his proposal, even the sharks. The documents for Lindenauer will be ready in the morning.

He does not change but presides in his suit and tie. At the table there is only passing mention of the day's events. He announces over white angel food cake that he and Danny have decided to liquidate Paradise Fashions. That is the way he says it, proudly, and Rochelle and Joyce take it as news unrelated to their lives.

"I've had it with Lindenauer," says his father. "No more Lindenauer for me. The man is a low-life." He looks down the table at his son, over the round half-gallon of Breyer's strawberry ice cream that centers the table like the stump of a tree. Mrs. Meadoff cuts and serves the cake, and Rochelle spoons the ice cream. Rochelle pokes the ice cream free with the finger of her left hand, licks her fingertip between servings and goes uncorrected. Their father looks over the cardboard tub of pink and smiles. Danny smiles back.

Angel food cake is special, like a celebration, though it is no one's birthday.

"What's more," Mr. Meadoff says, "I'm going in with Mortie Kaye."

"Who is he, Poppa?" Rochelle asks.

"Mortrose Fashions. Very good firm. From across the airshaft."

"So you have a new partner, Poppa?"

"Not exactly a partner. Not yet. In a little while maybe. This is a courtship. I'll teach him how to buy belts made in the Philippines. Then we'll see partners."

After dinner, Danny organizes his things for school. This afternoon he watched Angie catch two passes in the scrimmage. It looks to be a good year for the Buff and the Blue. Rick came out, too, although they won't see much of him. Rick finally has his job on Wall Street. A runner, but that's how some of the biggest people on the Street started, Rick says. It will mean he has to drop out of the college prep courses, but half of the biggest people on the Street never went to college anyway. Rick's father knows them, and half of them went right to work after high school.

[221